TURNING POINT

A SPY STORY

By S C Brown

Cover Photo by Dimon Blr on Unsplash

For Sarah, Mum, Dad and Andy

.

Also by S C Brown:

Initiation: A Spy Story

Prologue

Paris, 1944

'Is the *Führer* alive?'

SS-Brigadeführer Sauer, Chief of SS Counterintelligence in Paris, shouted into his office phone, trying to make out the faint voice at the other end.

Nervous faces veered from watching Sauer to watching the door handle. Judging by the violent way the handle was being rattled from the outside, whoever it was on the other side was very determined to get in. It was only a matter of time before the door was going to be kicked in.

Sauer, never good in a crisis, knew he was only just keeping his composure. He held up a hand for quiet as a new voice appeared on the other end of the phone.

'*Sauer? Sauer, can you hear me?*' said the voice.

'I, I can. Who is this?'

'The *Führer* is on his way, please stand by.'

The door continued to shake as German voices outside demanded to be let in.

Sauer then made out another voice on the end of the phone, an unmistakable one. Keeping an eye on the door, Sauer automatically stiffened to attention.

'*Mein Führer.*'

'*Sauer, Sauer, you recognise my voice?*'

'Of course, you are alive!'

'*Indeed I am. Traitors in the Army - the German Army, Sauer - attempted to kill me today but failed. They will attempt to take power but they are weak and will be destroyed, Sauer. Destroyed. You understand?*'

'Destroyed. Yes.' Sauer looked at the door again. '*Führer*, they are here knocking on my door now,' he continued.

Glancing out the window, he went on: 'My headquarters is surrounded. I'm watching my men being rounded up on the street as I speak.' Sauer jumped as the door nearly came off its hinges with a sudden bang.

'*Sauer, is that the Army at your door now?*'

'It must be.'

'*Then let them in. Tell them I want to speak to their officer.*'

'You want me to let them in?' Sauer said slowly, receiving shocked looks from the others in the office with him. Every head facing him was shaking with a vehement 'no'.

'*This instant.*'

'But…'

'*Open the door,*' came the voice again, insistent.

'Open the door,' said Sauer with sudden but unconvincing determination.

Everyone in Sauer's office right now was SS and fanatical in their loyalty to Hitler, but the situation presented a serious test of their mettle. Slowly, an arm reached out, moved the chair away from the door and let it open.

An Army officer fell through the now open door, only just keeping upright.

'I'm here to arrest you and all your staff on

General Von Kettler's orders! You are to come with me. Now.'

Sauer held the phone up, so the man on the other end could hear. 'For what purpose?'

'The *Führer* has been assassinated. General Von Kettler has assumed command of the city. The SS is implicated in the *Führer's* death and you are all under arrest.'

'The *Führer* is dead?' asked Sauer smugly.

'Yes,' said the Army officer, uncertain at Sauer's tone.

Sauer handed the Army officer the phone 'Here,' he said.

'What?'

'You need to talk to the person on the other end of this phone. Now.'

The officer took the phone as if it were smeared in poison. Sauer pushed it a bit closer to the officer's ear.

'*What is your name?*' asked the voice.

'*Hauptman Huber*, who is this?'

'*Hauptman Huber, this is Adolf Hitler speaking.*'

'And I'm Marlene Dietrich.'

'*Listen to my voice, Hauptman. This is your Führer speaking. Don't you recognise me?*'

The Army officer winced. He did and didn't want to believe it was true. 'What proof do I have? Verify yourself?'

'*A fair question; please wait.*' Silence ensued.

Those who could hear shuffled closer to the earpiece. Army and SS alike switched between eyeing each other nervously and staring at Huber. The smell of sweat hung in the room.

'Hallo, yes?' asked Huber. He raised his eyes to look straight at Sauer as he listened. He put a hand over the mouthpiece. 'It's *Feldmarschall* Kietel, I recognise his voice at least.'

'Well?' encouraged Sauer.

Huber refocused, listened, and repeated back his instructions. 'Yes, of course. The *Führer* is alive, and he is about to address me again.'

Huber said to everyone, 'It's going to be the *Führer* again.' The room became noticeably less comfortable. Huber listened intently, nodding to the instructions he was being given.

'Of course, my *Führer*, we will obey. *Heil Hitler!*'

He handed the phone back to Sauer, who placed it reverently on the receiver.

Huber hesitated for a moment, carefully choosing his next words, accepting that if he got this wrong, they were likely to be his last.

'*Brigadeführer* Sauer, clearly there has been a mistake. I'm to free you and your men and I await your instructions.'

'About time,' blurted Sauer. There was an audible letting out of air from everyone crowded into the office; shoulders across the room drooped in relief.

'You're working for me now, Huber, don't you forget it - and we've got traitors to arrest. Proper ones this time. Get your men together; we are off to the Hotel Majestic, you understand? I want Von Kettler taken alive. He's not getting away with it this time.'

PART ONE

Thursday

Despite the rain, Paris was heating up. The hope and, for some, the dread of liberation permeated the muted and hesitant city.

Walter Berner, German counterintelligence officer and double agent for the British, turned purposefully up Avenue Foch towards the Metro station. Like every day since he chose to spy on the Nazis for MI6, he was taking extra special care to stay alive.

Berner had only been working and living in Paris since December, and yet the streets already felt different. As the Allies approached from the landing beaches of Normandy, the citizens had grown a little more confident, a little more bloody-minded, a little more ready to turn against their occupiers. And as for the occupiers, Berner was witness to a growing sense of paranoia, nostalgia and resignation seeping through every barrack door.

Berner watched a few Opel *Blitz* trucks full of sombre-looking German soldiers rumble past before he descended into the Metro. Taking a deliberately circuitous route to Mirabeau to be certain he was not being tailed, he stepped back out in the open, blinking against the Parisian sunshine. With one hand in a pocket, Berner sauntered between the puddles, taking in the view of the Seine, smiling into the relative calm. There was little traffic these days; fuel, like time, was running out.

Berner turned a corner and stopped to look into a shop window. He let those walking ahead of him move on and everyone behind him pass so they were now in front of him. He walked on a bit longer and slowed again, pretending to study another shop window. No one disappeared into a doorway, no one had suddenly climbed out of a car for a walk. Happy he was on his own, he approached the outdoor café. Berner spotted Eve, his MI6 link to London, approaching from the other direction, bang on time.

Ignoring her to start with, he casually took a seat at the last remaining table and gestured to a harassed waitress. To signal he was ready to meet, Berner placed his newspaper on the table and then settled in to take in the view and wait. People's voices were quieter now. Spies no longer had the monopoly on conspiracy and apprehension around here.

What Berner had not noticed was a podgy, anxious-looking man hissing to his neighbour. 'There he is, he's just sat down.'

The man being whispered to twisted around slowly to see and sure enough, there sat Berner, in his usual, slightly baggy suit. He reached into his jacket for his revolver as the other man fussed like a nervous old lady, bobbing his head around to keep a wary eye on his prey.

'He's waiting for someone. We'd better be quick.'

'We?' asked the man, mockingly. 'No time like the present then,' he said, sounding nonchalant, trying to cover his nerves. 'OK now?' he asked.

'Now!' came the order, the man barely containing the urge to shout.

Franck, a member of the French Resistance in the city since '40, rose ponderously to his feet, locking his gaze on Berner.

'Hello, Franck,' said a female voice unexpectedly.

A tall woman had shifted quickly to grab his pistol arm, blocking Franck's view of Berner.

Franck tried to recoil but the grip on his arm only grew tighter, fingernails stabbing into his bare arm. Trying hard to make it look like they had collided by accident, Eve used the little height advantage she had over Franck to push him back down onto his chair, staring straight into Franck's uncomprehending eyes.

Wincing from the pain in his arm, Franck relented and sat down. Maintaining eye contact, Eve reached out and swung around a chair to sit on.

'You're not killing anyone today, especially him,' she said, quietly but determinedly.

The other man raised himself up, halfway between sitting and standing.

'Get down, you,' hissed Eve, shifting her glare from one man to the next for a split second.

'Not now, you silly girl!' spat the man. Eve recognised him instantly as Agent Oberon, a Frenchman working for London, Franck's boss. Right now, he was puce with anger.

'*Sit down*,' Eve ordered slowly, uncompromising. 'I can see what you two are up to and for a good reason, I'm not going to allow that.'

Franck struggled a little but nowhere near enough to get Eve to release her grip.

'Enjoying this, are we?' she asked.

Franck's answer was cut short as a grey BMW screeched to a halt behind Eve. Eve and Franck both glanced over. A black Mercedes mounted the kerb and three German military policemen, got out and walked straight to Berner. Eve felt the muscles in Franck's arm tighten once again. She intensified her grip and glared back into Franck's eyes with a firm message: *don't you move a muscle*.

One of the soldiers clicked his heels. '*Obersturmbannführer* Berner?'

Berner nodded.

The policeman continued in German. 'You're under arrest and you are to come with us, please. Now.'

Eve watched Berner's head ease back in surprise. He stood slowly, turning his newspaper through 90 degrees to signal danger. Keeping his hands where everyone could see them, he buttoned his jacket and turned his head for the briefest of moments towards Eve. After the tiniest of shrugs, he turned towards the car and got in. The doors banged shut and the car sped off.

After a short silence, conversation at the café resumed: this had been an everyday occurrence in Paris since 1940.

'They nearly got us all there!' Oberon was back to his hissing self, mopping his brow with a handkerchief. 'Anyway, what do you think you're doing, we were about to get him!'

'Well, if you'd have shot him, you would have done it right in front of the *Feldgendarmerie*. Not such a clever move, eh? I think I just did you a favour there but I know you won't thank me for it.' Eve shrugged. 'Anyway, orders are orders and you are to leave that man well alone. You understand?'

Angry, Oberon got to his feet. 'Come on, Franck, let's go and leave this silly little girl to it.'

Eve remembered how Oberon had always called her that when she had the upper hand over them, literally in this case. Eve slowly released her grip and Franck replied with a leer. Rubbing his arm as he stood up, Franck looked Eve up and down approvingly. Eve felt her skin creep.

'Oh, she's a darling when she's angry, isn't she?' joked Franck, walking away.

Glad to see them go, Eve's thoughts returned immediately back to Berner. If Walter Berner, the double agent she worked for since January was under arrest and on his way to interrogation, Eve was almost certainly next.

A waitress huffed in frustration. For the second time that day, a customer had taken a table but left without ordering.

Rammed in between two policemen, Walter Berner felt an empty pit of dread growing in his stomach. He looked out of the car window as they sped down Avenue Foch, catching what he knew could be his last glimpses of the world outside a prison cell and a site of execution.

Walter Berner, a professional counterintelligence officer, knew better than most the many ways to catch a spy and interrogate them. In a manner of speaking, he had written the textbook. Berner's head had been full since the winter of all the lines he would use if being questioned to throw any pursuer off his track. As he watched the trees speed by, Berne rehearsed his lines. Every time he played one back in his head, he spotted an error, a tiny chink in his armour. *Play for time,* he told himself, *play for time.* But it was of little use, replied a growing voice in his head. Where you're going, they use torture - and everyone talks in the end.

Berner felt empty, scared, alone and not ready for what was to come.

But something was wrong. Lost in his sinking thoughts, Berner noticed how the wide road was empty of traffic, even more empty than had become the norm.

Berner's mind began to race when, instead of turning into SS Headquarters, where Berner would expect his interrogation to take place, the car sped on.

Berner dipped his head to the right so he could see and caught the briefest of glimpses of Sauer on the phone, looking out of the window from a packed office. The two men made eye contact for the tiniest of moments but Berner was certain Sauer had not recognised him. Still the car continued on; Berner glanced over his shoulder to watch SS men and women, with their hands on their heads, being herded out of SS HQ by soldiers of the German Army.

All the roads leading off Avenue Foch were barricaded by the Army and patrolled by nervous-looking soldiers. The car turned left and made straight for the Hotel Majestic, the headquarters of the Military Governor of France, General Von Kettler. In the winter, before Berner had been transferred into the SS, Berner had worked here as Von Kettler's security adviser.

The car sped through the hotel's archway and Berner creased forwards as the car came to a halt. Sullen military policemen lifted Berner out of the car and shoved him through the main doorway, down the stairs and along a maze of dark, familiar, subterranean corridors. When they halted at the door to the cell that he had used for months to interrogate prisoners, Berner smiled ironically. Life could have a cruel sense of humour, he thought.

The cell door was opened and Berner shoved in. He had to sidestep quickly to avoid tripping over someone sitting on the ground close to the door. Looking down and then across, Berner saw how the room was packed with prisoners. All were officers of the Paris SS, and Berner could see all too clearly the fear in their eyes.

The door slammed and Berner found a small space on the floor to sit. He received nods of acknowledgement from the other prisoners, but no words were exchanged.

Out of the frying pan and into the fire, Berner thought to himself. If he was going to face a firing squad today, it appeared he wouldn't be doing it alone.

* * *

Lieutenant Colonel Smithens had thought, with some justification, that his days of bringing bad news to 'C', Head of the Secret Intelligence Service, MI6, were over. How wrong he had been. He looked glumly at the decrypted flash message sent on the emergency frequency from Paris.

'You're sure it was her, Billy?'

The Foreman of Signals was adamant. 'It's her all right, Colonel. She was in a rush, but I know how Eve taps a Morse key. No doubt about it.'

Billy had been receiving messages about arrested agents since the war began. Reading and passing on the news of someone arrested and due to be tortured and probably killed had not got any easier.

Smithens sighed and stood up, rubbing at the pain that shot through his back from an old wound. 'Well, I had better go and ruin the old man's evening then, hadn't I?'

'Rather you than me,' said Billy, watching Smithens hobble down the corridor.

After a few hours, the air in the cell became filthy and hung in Berner's throat. All eyes turned as the locks on the door began to turn with a nasty, foreboding, metallic scrape. The door swung open; a soldier put his head through without stepping in and called out two officer's names. The called officers stood up, eyed each other nervously, and walked out to be handcuffed.

Berner glanced at his watch. The stench in this room must have suppressed his appetite: he would normally be ravenous by now.

Berner stopped to think of when he interrogated

Eve in this room, only a few months ago. He wondered where Eve was now. Far away, he hoped. Far away, safe and untraceable. She was an excellent agent and Berner knew that, having seen him be arrested, she would be in hiding by now, all her usual haunts long gone.

The fact that Eve had never told Berner her escape plan gave him even greater faith in her. Berner knew that it would not matter what anyone did to him now - he would never be able to betray her whereabouts. As long as she kept to the rules and tradecraft, she stood a very good chance of getting out of this alive. Berner thought of Eve making her way from the city and smiled.

'Berner's arrested?' asked C, not wanting to believe the news. He clenched his pipe tightly between his teeth. 'Where's Eve?'

Smithens shared a glance with the Chief of Staff before replying honestly: 'We don't know, but she wants more instructions sent to her at 2000 hours local time tonight. Not sending her escape plan to us tells me she's very wary of telling anyone anything right now.'

C went silent as he digested the information. 'That stuff she's been sending us about the location of the V1 sites; was it accurate?'

'Too early to say for definite, Sir,' said the Chief of Staff, 'but all the signs are good. It's potential gold-dust.'

C fell quiet again and, ignoring the knock at the

door, locked eye contact with Smithens. 'Berner is one of our most valuable agents and Eve is his key. What if Berner's arrest doesn't lead to anything? All we'd need to do is put him in quarantine for a bit to make sure he hasn't swapped sides again and then get him back to work with Eve. Get Eve to a safe house for now but don't let her out of France. Not yet. Ideally, keep her in or near Paris. Let's give it a couple of days and see what happens. Work out an escape route for her in case we need it.'

Someone knocked on the door again and opened it C could barely contain his irritation. Uninvited, the silver-haired head of C's personal secretary appeared.

'Mrs Wilkinson, I said no interruptions.'

Despite C's instructions, Mrs Wilkinson walked forward with a knowing smile, clutching a message form. Smithens saw in her bright blue, intelligent eyes that Mrs Wilkinson was in no mood to compromise.

'I'm very sorry, but you really do need to read this,' she insisted.

By the look of it, even C knew that at moments like this, it was best to let Mrs Wilkinson have her way. She placed the message on C's desk, positioning it so only C could read it before clasping her hands tightly under her bosom, about to burst with excitement.

C glared at Mrs Wilkinson before submitting and staring at the yellow paper on his desk. Smithens watched the old man's eyes skim over the text. Then he watched C read it again before standing up slowly, blowing out and walking across the window.

C wiped his hand over the remaining hair he had left.

'You'd better read that,' said Mrs Wilkinson.

C span round, clearly not liking it when someone else was giving the orders in his own office - but he nodded to his Chief of Staff. 'Go on, read it then.'

Falteringly, the Chief of Staff read the message and then it was his turn to blow out hard. 'Well I never…'

'Never what?' asked Smithens, feeling suddenly very left out.

'The message says radio intercepts in Berlin and Paris report Hitler as dead. Someone's blown him up and there's a coup underway. If this is true,' he went on, looking at C, 'this could mean the end of the war.'

C said something quite unrepeatable. Clearly he didn't quite share his Chief of Staff's optimism. Not yet anyway.

* * *

The cell door opened again and in walked *SS-Brigadeführer* Sauer, in a murderously good mood.

'Good evening, gentlemen,' said Sauer. He coughed and looked suddenly sickly, presumably as the smell of the room got to him. Sauer turned to a soldier behind him. 'Get some air in here for God's sake, will you?'

The soldier nodded and disappeared instantly. Sauer turned back to a room packed with weary and wary faces. Sauer's eyes glistened like a child with a new toy.

'This has been an … interesting day,' Sauer let the words fall out his mouth musically. Berner could see he was savouring this moment and hoped the wait for an explanation would be mercifully short.

'Earlier today, the Army attempted to kill the *Führer.*'

There was a loud and collective intake of breath. Berner's cellmates shared looks of disbelief. Berner, however, kept his eyes fixed on Sauer.

The room hushed as the prisoners waited for more news. Sauer continued, puffing his chest out: 'The Army failed to kill the *Führer.* The *Führer* telephoned me personally, in my office, to reassure me he was alive, well, and determined to avenge this treachery.'

'The Army also attempted – and failed – to win power here in Paris.' There was another sharp intake of breath. 'That is why you, the Parisian SS, were arrested: it was the Army trying to take control. After my chat with the *Führer*, we agreed that I should confront General Von Kettler and demand he suppress this uprising. Once he had the *Führer's* message delivered from me, he complied immediately.'

This statement interested Berner on two counts: firstly, Sauer, never short of a boast or two, was portraying himself as one of Hitler's inner circle of advisers and Berner knew that to be a lie. Secondly, Berner had lost count of how many times Sauer said it had been *the Army* behind all the events of today. Not only that, Von Kettler, head of the German Army in France and Berner's old boss, had needed someone to tell him to stop the coup in Paris, implying he had not thought to do that himself.

Then another thought hit Berner. If what Sauer was saying was true, then Berner wasn't in this cell for being a suspected double agent. No. He was here simply because he was in the SS like everyone else in the room. Berner felt himself physically slump with relief. Fortunately, all those around him took Berner's outward show of relief to echo their own – that the *Führer* and the Fatherland were safely in the hands of the SS once more.

Sauer kept going: 'The Army is full of traitors, *full of them*. It's our job to find them, arrest them and kill them.'

Berner's sense of relief was short-lived. Looking around, he could feel the mood in the room change from shock, through relief, to gleeful realisation: they had just been handed a licence for murderous retribution.

Berner seemed to be the only man in the room not grinning eagerly.

'Colonel Berner,' said Sauer, looking down, 'you will play a particularly important role in the investigation. You will come with me. As for the rest of you, your instructions will come in time. Right, you lot need something to eat. And a wash. I will get someone to see to it immediately. And then, my loyal ones, the retribution will begin!'

Sauer, his blotchy skin shiny with a film of sweat, sped out the room with Berner walking stiffly behind, trying to keep up.

* * *

'Take a seat, Berner, you look dreadful.'

Berner did as he was told and sat down in an office not far from where his own had been only a few months back. Sauer sat heavily into a new and bigger chair. 'Now we are alone, Walter, we can speak more … privately.'

Berner tried not to show it but he could feel his pulse jump. With Sauer, speaking privately meant speaking conspiratorially. The question was whose conspiracy they were going to be talking about.

There was a knock at the door and in walked a neatly dressed, very tall, slender man with dark hair, a slight stoop, and ears that stuck out a bit too far. Berner recognised him instantly: SS spy-hunter Horst Lemke.

'Walter,' said Sauer, 'I want to introduce you to Horst Lemke. He was on his way to Paris as my new deputy and his arrival is, well, timely, I think you'll agree.'

Lemke and Sauer shared a small laugh together, Berner smiled to play along; these two go way back, he thought to himself. And so much for speaking *privately*.

'Hello, Lemke,' said Berner, standing to shake hands. 'What a day to arrive in Paris!'

'Yes, isn't it? There's me thinking I could enjoy a summer in the city of love. And now this.' Lemke looked dark and brooding but Berner knew of Lemke: a man of considerable charm and intelligence and with a ferocious temper. A conversational bully. Sauer had never managed to be much of a threat to Berner, but Lemke was in a different league altogether. Berner knew he would have to be on his guard. Who knows, thought Berner to himself - maybe he was the reason Lemke was in Paris right now.

Sauer shuffled uncomfortably in his chair and forced his next sentence out to regain control. 'Horst, I want you to listen in on this little chat. As you know, Berner was an Army officer until only recently but now the *Abwehr* is defunct, he works for us, the SS.' Sauer couldn't resist any opportunity to rub that little fact in.

'I don't think Walter will mind me saying,' Sauer continued, 'he's had some good successes in bringing in terrorists from across the city. He's also running a disinformation campaign into London for us, aren't you?'

Berner was about to respond when Sauer kicked in quickly. 'Sending London all the wrong information dressed up as the truth. The British are just lapping it all up, aren't they, Walter? What with Berner being ex-Army, he looks every bit the classic traitor in the eyes of MI6. Oh, he sends them truthful stuff as well, Lemke, just to, how do you say it Walter, *to whet their appetite?* But being ex-Army and after this hideous attempt on the *Führer's* life, he looks even more like a double-agent and traitor to London than ever before. Berner might have just become even more useful to us.' Sauer beamed like the owner of a prize-winning dog.

Sauer carried on boastfully: 'What you probably don't know, Lemke, is Berner here was once Admiral Schneider's favourite in the *Abwehr*. Schneider got Berner a nice job working for Von

Kettler as his own personal security adviser, no less. But none of us believe any of that. We think it was just a nice place to hide someone like Berner so people like us didn't get any look in on the *Abwehr's* work.'

Berner said nothing but what Sauer had said was true. Berner looked across at Lemke who was, like him, a well-regarded spy-hunter; diligent and thorough. Berner had read and studied Lemke's successes over the years. Berner wracked his brains as to why Lemke was in Paris so suddenly. Yes, the coup attempt needed investigating but there was no way Lemke could have travelled from Berlin to get here that quickly, could he? Perhaps Lemke's arrival was proof Berlin suspected there was a spy in Paris, which, of course, was also true.

Sauer looked like he was getting more than a little piqued with Berner's silence, not supporting his self-indulgences. 'And this is where it gets interesting, isn't it? I mean Schneider's been under house arrest for months and Von Kettler put the SS in jail yesterday. They don't look too loyal, do they, Berner?'

Sauer's voice was gaining an edge to it; did Sauer suspect Berner as well? Berner knew he was getting paranoid, but it was difficult not to at times like this.

The truth was that Berner was not the only spy in Paris; the city was teeming with them. French, British, German and even the Soviets were here, nudging the Communist Resistance groups towards creating a socialist France once the Germans were gone. In other words, there were a number of spies Lemke could be here to hunt. Berner just had to make sure he was not going to be one of them.

Walter knew Sauer well enough to know any rounding up of real traitors, suspected traitors and even the innocent he didn't particularly like, gave Sauer, like most Nazis at times like this, an opportunity for self-advancement. The snout was sniffing the trough and if Lemke or Sauer got a whiff of what Berner was really up to, Berner was a dead man.

Yet even in this moment of potential danger, Berner smiled as an opportunity came to mind. Sauer's appetite for promotion and status was one of his many weaknesses: yes, Berner was sending messages to London but with the express and vocal support of the SS's main man in Paris. In other words, if Berner was a dead man, it wouldn't take much to ensure Sauer was next.

Berner returned to the situation playing out in front of him as Sauer started to talk again. 'The problem is, Walter, all your old friends are being rounded up, either because they are proven traitors or so close to the plot that they *must* have known something.'

Just where is this going, thought Berner to himself.

'So, Colonel Berner, what's been going on?'

Berner's stomach wrenched. 'What do you mean?'

Sauer leaned forward, gripping his hands together into one big fist. '*You know exactly what I mean*,' he said, coldly.

'Sorry, I don't. I infiltrate resistance and intelligence networks. I send mostly false information to London. All my activities are on record. That's what I know has been going on. As for this coup attempt today, well, I'm as clueless as you seem to be.'

Sauer did not like that last bit and stubbed what was left of a roll-up viciously into an ashtray to give himself time to think. Reaching into a pocket and lighting another cigarette, Sauer leaned back, suddenly all smiles, 'Come on, Walter, we all record our *official* activity. It's everything else you've been up to that we're interested in.'

Volts of nervous energy pulsed through Berner's body, but he stopped himself from speaking, knowing Sauer would say something else eventually - something that would give Berner a clue as to what was actually going on.

Sauer soon obliged. Stabbing the air with his new cigarette, he went on: 'We've seen you at all the usual haunts, rubbing shoulders with all your old mates. Out to dinner on an all too regular occurrence with a British agent.'

'Really?' asked Lemke, sitting up, looking from Sauer to Berner and back again.

As calmly as he could, Berner replied: 'She's my link to London. I arrested her here in Paris in January and she turned very quickly.'

'And what a girl she is, Lemke. Beautiful.' Sauer traced the shape of an hourglass in the air with his hands, leaving a waft of smoke through the air. 'But I think there's more you should be telling us.'

Fat chance, thought Berner to himself. As casually as he could, he replied: 'No, there isn't. Lemke will know', implying Sauer wouldn't, 'this is standard stuff: creating a false network of agents and radio operators in Paris that London thinks is working for them, when it's actually working for me. Us,' said Berner, gesturing at the other two. 'I've done it before, and it seems to be working well for me again here.'

'Are all your transcripts to and from London verified?' asked Lemke.

'Why wouldn't they be? Someone should be listening in to every broadcast my agents make, as well as any response we get from London.' Berner looked across to Sauer. 'That is our standard procedure, isn't it?'

Sauer broke eye contact quickly, not having a clue if Berner's messages were being monitored or not.

Berner knew his messages *should* be monitored but this was 1944, after Stalingrad, after the Normandy landings, after almost any realistic chance of winning this war had gone. The sharp edge of the German Army and the SS had dulled. Berner knew it and assumed everyone else knew it too, but to admit it was the short cut to getting a 7.65mm round to the back of the head.

Lemke looked more animated. 'Has London said anything that could have been a clue to what happened today? Anything to give away any intention of a coup attempt?'

'Nothing,' said Berner.

That was an easy answer because it was the truth.

'So today came as a genuine surprise to you?' asked Lemke.

'Of course! I was getting ready to meet with my go-between to set up my next message to London and before I knew it, I was being arrested by some

Feldgendarmerie heavies. As I said before,' said Berner looking straight at Sauer, 'in this regard, I'm as clueless as you.'

Lemke gave the tiniest of smiles as Berner's insult landed on Sauer.

Sauer's eyes blazed with anger. 'Berner,' he said, 'we have very little time to investigate this *Putsch*. Berlin is demanding – *demanding* - arrests and action now. Today. I can arrest who I want, interrogate who I want and who knows, maybe even shoot who I want with no need to ask anyone's permission. This … coup is unprecedented and calls for unprecedented measures.'

'True.'

Lemke brushed the thigh of a trouser leg thoughtfully. 'But we have more subtle measures available to us as well. Perhaps, Sauer, this is what you had in mind?'

Sauer looked lost, pretending to go along. He smiled and said, 'Go on.'

Lemke looked to be playing along to spare his boss the blushes. 'Berner, don't you agree people tend to open up more to their friends than their adversaries? You're famous for not using violence.'

'I agree. People get talking in the end and when you don't beat them, they tend to be more truthful. Yes, that's usually the way.'

'Precisely,' said Lemke, leaning gently towards Sauer. 'Sauer was saying earlier how we want to know everything about who tried to kill the *Führer* and who was behind any plotting in Paris. From there we may be able to trace people, actions back to Berlin and the very centre of it all.

'It strikes me how you know some of the potential ringleaders: they're old friends and colleagues of yours. So how's about I— sorry, we,' he said, nodding charitably towards Sauer, 'enlist your help in interrogating them? We could divide the work up. I'm the new boy here in Paris so I could be looking for clues as the outsider looking in, whereas you, Berner, will be listening from the inside. In other words, Berner, go and chat to all your old mates.'

'All right.' Berner could feel the tension in the room begin to ease.

'Oh, with your permission, of course, *SS-Brigadeführer,*' said Lemke, suddenly realising he was giving the orders.

'Permission granted. I was about to suggest the same myself,' lied Sauer.

Berner could not miss the contempt in Lemke's eyes. Sauer could probably see it too.

'So where do you want me to start?' asked Berner.

'How's about General Von Kettler?'

Berner stood up. 'I had a funny feeling you were going to say that.'

Berner left the office with a new mission and so far, not under immediate suspicion of being the double agent he was.

Berner started the walk back to his office on Avenue Foch. Betraying his enemies was easy, he thought to himself. Betraying his friends would be much more difficult.

Eve had mentally rehearsed her escape many times. Unaware Berner was no longer under arrest, Eve could only assume she was a hunted woman. She was certain Berner could hold out long enough in interrogation to buy her the time needed to get far away from Paris and disappear for a bit. She looked at her watch. As well as escaping, she also needed to be ready to receive instructions over the radio at 8pm.

On the train to Orléans, she could feel the same cold sweat of fear clinging to her back as when she first took a train through Nazi-occupied France after landing in December. She had become very accustomed to working as a secret agent in Paris, being close to the enemy on a daily basis. But things were different now as far as Eve was concerned, she may be the subject of a national 'man-hunt'. Every glance she received, every lingering look from a man, every quizzical look from a child, every man in a hat and overcoat, could betray her and bring about her arrest. Eve tried her best to remain outwardly calm and normal, resting her arm on the suitcase that carried her radio. She could see the fear in her own eyes reflected back from the carriage window.

On time, the train pulled up. Eve lifted her heavy suitcase as elegantly as she could and descended the steps onto the platform and straight out onto the street. Around a corner stood the pre-arranged bicycle. All was going to plan.

Eve strapped the heavy suitcase to the back of the bike. Faltering at first, she rode off towards the countryside. Every kilometre she pedalled from the city took her further from discovery and further into obscurity and safety.

She knew the area well as she had holidayed here many times when growing up. The familiarity of the lanes, the fields, the millions of sunflowers, gave her comfort. Gradually, as the likelihood of meeting a German patrol subsided – they were all up North fighting the Allies according to Berner - the fear of capture eased, and she began to steer long curves down lanes she had not been down in years.

Stopping at a crossroads, she glanced at her watch again. A few moments later she came to a halt and pushed her bike across a field and into a wood.

It was well gone 8pm when Eve, with her radio stashed back into its suitcase, stopped de-coding and read the message Smithens, her case officer back in London, had sent, which said:

HAVE HEARD THE NEWS. CALL BACK IN TWO DAYS. YOUR RURAL ACCOMMODATION UNTIL THEN IS ARRANGED. ENJOY A SHORT HOLADAY. S.

Eve smiled. She was to go to the urban safe house she had arranged, not the urban one in Chartres. Also, the deliberate spelling mistake in the message was where it should be. She knew this message had come from Smithens personally and it could be trusted. It told her everything she needed by using deliberately vague language. Smithens was being doubly careful not to put Eve in any more danger than she was already in. Eve appreciated the gesture.

Never one to pass off on an opportunity, Smithens' message was giving Eve two days off in the countryside in the company of the wonderfully hospitable and cheery Duval family. Eve had to admit it, she welcomed the prospect of a break – she had not been out of Paris for months and being away for just a few days was going to be a blissful distraction. And as safe houses went, the Duval's was one of the safest: it was so remote German troops had not come to check up on them for over a year. Eve said a silent thank you to Smithens before putting a match to the sheet of paper with the message on it and then pedalling off to the farm.

Before long, Eve turned onto the windy track leading to the Duval's farmhouse, alone amongst gently rolling, open fields. The wind whispered through the wheat.

The Duvals poured out the warmest of welcomes, just like old times. Eve had not holidayed here for years and yet Mrs Duval hadn't changed a bit with her plump figure and messy hair. Chantale, the daughter, was a young woman now and Jules, the son, had really filled out: a lot more handsome and muscular than before.

It was good to be back.

Friday

Von Kettler looked tired and nervous, rising to his feet to welcome Berner. 'Good morning, Walter. You're well?'

'I am. You?'

'In a word, no. My God, Berner, if this hasn't been one of the worst nights of my life. I feel like a man teetering on a gallows stool. You?'

'Well, unlike you, General, I was arrested for treason yesterday. I wouldn't recommend it. Stuck in that cell I had a good mental picture of what that stool would look like, I can tell you.'

'Ah, yes, of course. ' Von Kettler smiled weakly. 'I'm sorry about that.'

Berner waited for Von Kettler to take a seat before himself relaxing into one of the armchairs, smiling. 'No offence taken. Apology accepted.'

Von Kettler smiled, forgiven.

'But still, Berner, what a sorry day yesterday turned out to be. I wonder if other people in your line of work will be as forgiving as you.'

In the space of 24 hours, Von Kettler appeared to Berner to have shrunk a little. He decided to keep the conversation purposeful but light. 'I'm as surprised by all this as you probably are.'

Von Kettler gave Berner a questioning look. 'What do you mean, "probably"?' He seemed to stiffen. 'Walter, what is this exactly, a social chat or something a little more … professional for you? In other words, am I talking to Colonel or *Obersturmbannführer* Berner today?'

'You mean, am I representing the German Army or the SS?' Berner said cheerily, getting up to walk over towards the General's desk. 'The honest answer is both, I suppose. I … carry the rank of Colonel which I suppose makes me Army, but it says *Obersturmbannführer* on my nice new identity papers. Best of both worlds.'

Berner slid a piece of notepaper laying on the desk towards himself. Reaching for the General's pen, he started writing whilst keeping the conversation going.

'If I was to put a uniform on, General, which is something I have not done for, oh, a long time now, I would wear that of an *Abwehr Oberstleutnant*. But the SS, for whom I now officially work, well, they've swallowed up what was left of the military intelligence service and like to call me one of their own. They were gloating about my successes as if they were their own only, what, yesterday?'

Berner never normally made small talk like this but having finished writing, he walked the scrap of paper over to Von Kettler, who read it. Berner went on. 'Yet the SS haven't issued me a uniform, which I still find odd as they love a show, don't they? But I can't say I blame them. In my game, wearing a uniform is somewhat of a hindrance. That's what makes me wonder about Sauer sometimes - he's *always* in uniform, it's as if he wants all the agents and resistance in Paris to know he's about. Perhaps he's goading them?'

Von Kettler read Berner's note: *Assume they're*

listening.

Von Kettler visibly hesitated, wondering what to do next, so Berner continued inanely. 'As for me, well, when would a spy-hunter like me need a uniform?'

Berner screwed up the paper, put it in a pocket and sat back down. 'In other words, General, I'm a bureaucratic anomaly and no bureaucracy likes that, especially in Germany where we practically invented it! But I don't think I have answered your question,' joked Berner.

What he wanted to say was '*because I haven't worked it out myself just yet.*'

Crossing his legs, Berner went on: 'But whilst I'm at it, what did happen yesterday? In this headquarters? I mean, you probably had a better view than others. There are so many rumours, so many falsehoods, so many ... *suspicions.* Especially where I work.'

Von Kettler seemed to get the message: *the SS are on to you.* He coughed. 'Well, may I first reiterate, how sorry I am for your arrest. That must have been very troubling.'

'As I said, no hard feelings, General. I'm not sure the Paris SS took it so graciously, however. That spell under arrest is probably going to keep them very agitated and restless for some time to come.'

Von Kettler got the second message: *the SS want revenge.* The General went to say something but stopped himself.

Seeing the man opposite him struggling, Berner leapt in. 'Let's face it; there has been an attempt on the *Führer's* life. It's shocking news. This could have massive implications. What do you think happened?'

'You refer to Hitler as the *Führer* now?' asked Von Kettler in jest, but Berner's commanding expression reminded him the SS was listening. Either way, Von Kettler was thankful Berner had just asked him what he *knew*, not what he *did*.

Von Kettler studied his fingernails for a moment. 'Yesterday was just a normal day for me until about 4pm. I was informed by West Command that an attempt to kill the *Führer* had taken place and the situation was highly confused, which quickly became all too apparent. To get a clearer appreciation of what was going on, I spoke to *Generalfeldmarshall* Weber. He told me Hitler was, in fact, not dead, but he suspected some kind of rouse to sew confusion, to allow a coup attempt to get underway in Berlin. He said how the confusion caused seemed to be working.

'I tell you, this was shocking news, Walter. Look at a situation map in any headquarters you care to choose. Not far from here we face the British, Canadians and Americans - and I still don't know if they will land more troops further up the coast. I mean, Rommel and his men can fight but even he seems to be struggling against this... onslaught. Meanwhile, Paris is getting visibly restless, ready to switch loyalty. To the East, the Bolsheviks attack in hordes. And now this.' Von Kettler shook his head in despair.

'I very much doubt the Parisians have ever been that loyal to us, General. Subjugated perhaps. And where's the choice in that?'

'I'm not sure, Berner. There's no getting away from how the situation is what it is. Maybe Paris is waiting for its moment to turn against us.'

'Betrayal's all a question of timing? I think so.' Berner wanted to get back to the coup. 'So you were surprised, by the news?'

'Of course I was surprised!' blurted Von Kettler, looking towards a window, frustrated. 'People die around here, all over the world, all the time but this...' Von Kettler turned back to look directly at Berner, 'to receive information like this, with all its consequences, it was ... profound. I've never had anything like this before.

'When I was on the phone to Weber,' he continued, 'we discussed what I should do next. Weber was clear: enact Plan *Valkyrie*. You know it yourself: seize military control of all the main sources of power in Berlin and Paris and prevent a coup taking hold. Block main roads, take control of the radio stations; in other words, hold the fort.'

'You arrested SS officers but no Army officers.'

'Yes, immediately. I ... am a senior and well-connected Army officer. I'm probably *the* military key to Paris and most of France with it. That's no brag, you understand, but look at the influence I have across all of France and how linked I am to all the fighting headquarters. I figured that if the Army was behind a coup, I would know about it or at least have my suspicions somehow. There was nothing to suggest to me the Army was behind this - so if the Army wasn't trying to seize power, it could only have been the SS. So I ordered the arrests. Your own included.'

'So it couldn't have been the British, the Americans, the Soviets?'

The General stammered. 'I don't think any of them capable of penetrating that deeply. To do that they would have to get past people like you. Surely we'd have an inkling of what they were planning, here or in Berlin? No. If the Allies had been behind this, they would have needed to use Germans to do their dirty work and so I'm back to my original suspicion: whoever was behind this is German - Army or SS. They must have been to get close enough to shoot the *Führer*.'

'It was a bomb,' corrected Berner.

'I'm sorry?'

'Whoever tried to kill the *Führer* yesterday used a bomb, not a gun.'

'I see.'

Berner noticed Von Kettler's eyes twinkle a little.

Von Kettler continued: 'That doesn't change anything about my view of the situation, and it wouldn't have had the slightest bearing on the reaction. In the absence of any other reliable information, and with Sauer unobtainable - which in itself only seemed to confirm my suspicions - I ordered the arrest of all SS and SD officers and took control of their offices on Avenue Foch. It was a precautionary measure and has since proved an unpopular one at that. But I had to do it.

'I have to be honest, Walter, I'm kept totally in the dark about what you and your new SS colleagues are up to on Avenue Foch. In the absence of any other direction, proof, anything frankly, I had to eliminate the SS as a possible contender for power.'

'Who did you talk to, over the phone, apart from Weber?' asked Berner.

'I can't remember, there were too many calls to list them and the situation was very confused. There may be a log in the operations room downstairs. It was chaos. If I managed to get connected, I had to leave messages with staff officers, who either refused to relay my pleas for more information or couldn't get their calls back to me in the confusion. People were less contactable as the day passed.'

Less alive more like, thought Berner.

'Then, at about 8pm, perhaps later,' Von Kettler continued, 'new information started to come in. The situation in Berlin seemed to be stabilising, becoming clearer. It soon transpired the SS was not running the coup. Sadly, Berner, it now looks as if the Army was behind it all instead. As soon as I was aware, I had the SS and SD officers released. We're lucky no one was killed.'

'So who here knew what was going on?'

Von Kettler almost laughed. 'I don't think anyone really knew what they were doing here yesterday, Walter. You know what it's like at times like this. This isn't a tactical, fighting headquarters, this is an administration; we'd be the last lot to find out about anything like a coup attempt. And so we were, it turned out.'

'Plan *Valkyrie*, the plan you used to orchestrate your reaction yesterday, who wrote that plan?' asked Berner.

'I'm not sure I know, why?'

'A document of that magnitude would have come from the Army General Staff, wouldn't it?'

'Yes, but as to who was the architect of our reaction plans, I'm sorry I can't help you.'

Berner's internal antennae were telling him something was wrong. Berner had felt it ever since Von Kettler said he couldn't remember who he had spoken to only yesterday. Not only that, there was something else: what Von Kettler was saying was completely plausible, but it was not like he was recalling events from memory - it felt more like he was playing out a script.

Berner stood up. 'I'm sorry, General, but it's getting hot in here. Would you mind if we continued this chat out in the garden? It is July after all and it's due to get to 28 degrees later. Don't worry, there are plenty of places where one can talk without being overheard and anyway, I don't want your staff thinking I'm here to interrogate you.'

Von Kettler leapt up, obviously keen to get away from the microphone. 'Let's walk,' he said, reaching for the double doors.

Neither man said a word as they made their way to the courtyard.

Eventually, they found a quiet corner that Berner had used before for private conversations. Surrounded with hedges, it was the only corner in the Hotel Majestic where there were no windows. Sat here, Berner knew no one could lip-read or listen, provided they kept their voices low.

'That's better,' said Von Kettler, settling down onto the bench.

Berner got straight to it: 'What really happened?'

'I beg your pardon?'

'You heard me and don't think for a minute that

your act up there—' Berner gestured in the direction of the General's office, '- will suffice. That felt far too rehearsed to me. Over-rehearsed, in fact. You may not have realised but it's Lemke running the investigation, not Sauer. Lemke will check up on everyone and Sauer is just looking for the chance to get his little pistol out.'

'Lemke's in Paris?' asked the General.

Berner did not give Von Kettler time to ponder. 'Sauer said Lemke's arrival was coincidental, but that's one hell of a coincidence, don't you think? Either way, Lemke is here and he's way more of a threat to you than Sauer could ever be. Someone, somewhere, has probably worked out Sauer hasn't the grey matter for a job like this. You should be *very* careful with what you say from now on.

'Listen to me, General,' Berner continued, 'your first mistake is pretending not to know who you spoke to yesterday. No one will ever believe that. It won't take a moment to check the operator's log to see what offices you called or called you. And if you don't give names and details, they will wonder how it is that a General with literally millions of men under command cannot remember who he spoke to only a day ago. So you need to tidy that up and remember, anything you say from now on that doesn't tally with what you almost certainly have been recorded in your office as saying just then could get you arrested and shot. So if you tell me what you *actually* know, I may be able to help you. Stick to your script and you'll be up against a wall in no time, understand?'

'Whose side are you on, Walter? The way you're

talking, it's as if you are trying to protect me.'

Berner could not give an honest answer to that, so he settled for saying, 'I don't know, I used to work for you. I don't want to see you shot for something you didn't do. Assuming, of course, you didn't.'

'Can I trust you, Walter?'

Berner was puzzled by this. 'Of course you can.'

'No, Walter, I don't think you understand. *Can I trust you?*'

And at that point, Berner knew: Von Kettler was in this up to his neck.

'Go on,' said Berner without committing. The colour was draining fast from Von Kettler's face.

'Yesterday was a disaster for the Army and for Germany. I cannot believe that if someone had gone to such trouble to try to kill Hitler, they would also have not planned a coup to match. It was crazy yesterday, everyone too scared to commit until they knew for definite if Hitler was dead or alive. And anyone who was scared yesterday is going to be *really* scared today.'

'Just how scared are you, General, -or should I say, how scared should you be?'

'Totally.'

Berner blew out hard. He was talking to a conspirator who had confessed with only the lightest pressure. Lemke had been right.

'Now,' said Von Kettler, speaking deliberately, 'you are Admiral Schneider's right-hand man and he is a man I have always trusted completely, without question. Knowing the company the Admiral keeps, I think there is probably more to you than meets the eye, Colonel Berner. I think

Willy Schneider had you working in my offices over the winter so the SS would not find out about what you were really up to and probably still are up to. I think, perhaps, you and I are trusted by the Admiral for the same reason.'

Berner felt himself stop breathing.

Von Kettler went on: 'I'm asking for your help.'

Berner sat completely still, waiting for the General to say more.

Von Kettler was getting frustrated. 'Put simply, Berner, I need to protect myself and I need as many friends as I can get right now. I really do think it's only a matter of time before the SS come for me and if it's Lemke, then I really don't fancy my chances of survival at all. I want out.'

'Curious, you asking me, considering I'm an SS officer.'

'You're not proper SS, are you? You have been with the *Abwehr* for longer than I can remember. You're one of us!'

'I was not in on your little conspiracy, General.' Berner could feel himself struggling to keep his composure. 'Just remember, that sort of talk can get you killed very quickly and let me make one thing clear ...' Berner's voice was suddenly cold and deadly. 'if you threaten my security, then you really are a dead man.'

'Now that, Walter Berner, was a harsh reaction. Maybe you were not in on the plot but who's to say you're not involved in some other plot? Something you are prepared to threaten someone like me for?'

Berner breathed in and collected himself. 'Don't overplay your hand, General. Threatening someone else's life isn't normally a good way of getting them to help you.'

'That's the thing with you spies, isn't it? Happy to blackmail others and get what you want but never happy to be blackmailed yourself. But, Walter, blackmail is blackmail. So, will you help me?'

'That depends. You see, blackmail isn't blackmail. For instance, I know you were a conspirator but what do you know about me? You only have your suspicions and you'll be dead before you get the chance to blurt them out, let alone see them proved. You should walk a more conciliatory line.'

Berner weighed it up. He was certain Von Kettler did not know he was a double agent, but the General still had the means to throw a light of suspicion on him and with Sauer in the mood he was, that would be enough to see the end of Walter Berner. Von Kettler was shrewder than Berner had first given him credit for but wondered if he was shrewd enough. After all, the coup had not gone well, had it?

'You should start by helping yourself,' Berner went on. 'How many people would be involved in a coup attempt like this?'

'In truth, I don't know.'

'Have a guess: ten, twenty, a hundred?'

Von Kettler smiled. 'Perhaps fifty.'

Berner sat back. 'Fifty tongues waggle a lot. So, if it comes to it, you need to throw Lemke the small fry: people who were involved but don't know enough to implicate you directly. If it's a case of them or you, General, make sure it's them and keep Lemke busy. Make the trail lead away from you, not towards you.'

'Thank you, Walter, that's more like it.'

'Just you be careful, General. Threatening my life is tantamount to ending your own. I can get to you any time I want. Mark my words, if you so much as mention my name-'

'I won't, Berner,' said the General earnestly. 'At least I will try not to.'

And that was it. Berner knew Von Kettler could not be trusted.

'I repeat what I said earlier, General, you keep your mouth shut about me and throw Lemke some small scraps if it comes to that. Otherwise, continue to carry on working as a loyal Army officer. I will keep an eye on things and let's see where this takes us.'

Knowing he had said nothing he could not explain away to Lemke, Berner ended the conversation and escorted Von Kettler back to his office politely, keeping up the pretence.

But walking away, Berner felt sick. His biggest secret seemed safe but what did that matter if Von Kettler implicated him in the putsch? What if Berner became one of those 'small scraps'?

One thing was certain: Von Kettler must never be allowed to talk, so reporting him as a conspirator now was not a good idea. Berner needed to make sure Von Kettler never said anything to threaten Berner's own mission and security. Berner needed a plan. And fast.

Sunlight fell, uninterrupted, through the gap in the curtains. It was Eve's first reminder that, for the first time in a long time, she had not woken up in a city full of shadows.

Lying on her stomach, Eve shuffled up onto her elbows and listened. Apart from the noise of the Duval family sharing breakfast below in the kitchen, Eve could hear ... nothing. Wind whooshing through some nearby trees - that was it.

Smiling and keen to get out into the fields, Eve sprang out of bed, washed away the grime of the city, dressed quickly and bounced down the stairs to the welcoming smiles of her hosts.

'It is going to be a beautiful day out there, today, Eve,' said Mr Duval happily as he wished her good morning. 'So make the most of it.'

'Thank you, I fully intend to.' Eve sat down and reached for some bread off the table. 'I will go for a lovely walk and stretch these legs of mine.' Eve paused. 'This is real bread! I haven't had that in months. It's ... wonderful. I want to get out in the countryside for a change; it will do me *wonders.*'

'Does it keep you busy, your work?' asked Chantale, fascinated to be sharing breakfast with a secret agent.

'It has its moments,' smiled Eve.

Jules smiled knowingly. He'd been in the local resistance for a long time and had a pretty good idea what those 'moments' could be like.

But Mrs Duval was not too happy with talk of spying in her kitchen. Wiping her hands down her apron, she said: 'That's enough of all that, I think. We've a farm to run. Who can do what today,

Father?'

'I will give the machines a good once over,' said Mr Duval, 'and make sure they're ready for the weeks to come. It's a shame you're not staying with us longer, Eve; we'll soon need every pair of hands we can get out there, harvesting.' He pointed with his bread knife towards the window.

'Meanwhile,' he continued, 'I think Chantale and Jules should take you out for a walk and show you all around the farm. But stay away from the villages, just in case.'

'I'd love that,' said Eve, brimming with enthusiasm and beaming straight at Jules.

After a short while to tie on her boots, Eve stepped out into the yard where Jules was waiting for her.

'Where's Chantale?'

'She is going to stay here and help Mother. In the kitchen I suppose. That makes me your personal tour guide for the day.' Jules tapped a bag hanging over his shoulder. 'I have bread, cheese, a little wine – it's nothing compared to Paris standards, but it will do – and, a blanket.'

'That'll do me,' smiled Eve and they set off through the expanse of waving cornfields, with only the bird song and their pre-war memories to accompany them as they rekindled an old flame.

* * *

'So, what did he say?' asked Lemke, reclining into an armchair at Avenue Foch, swirling a cognac.

'I'm going to hazard a guess that you already know the answer to that,' replied Berner as he casually took a seat. .

Lemke gave a small, guilty smile..

'All right, I will ask the same question in a different way. What do you think General Von Kettler was telling you?'

Berner narrowed his eyes. Lemke had mentioned both the rank and the name of the man they were now both discussing. That told Berner this conversation was being recorded as well.

Berner played along. 'He told me he did what any officer in his position should have done, carry out the *Valkyrie* plan and arrest anyone he didn't trust. He's pretty shaken up. So I think he told me he suspected the SS was behind the coup initially but now he accepts it was the Army that did it. He seems convinced that the Brits, Yankies and Soviets are not involved but what would he know? Counterintelligence is our job and he isn't privy to information like that. Interestingly, he thought the *Führer* had been shot, not blown up.'

'That it?'

'Von Kettler said he spoke to a lot of people over the phone yesterday. He named Weber specifically but couldn't or wouldn't name anyone else. I'd never fall for that,' Berner went on. 'I can remember everyone I was locked up with yesterday. I may not remember the names, but I remember the basic details and I'd recognise them. So Von Kettler should remember who he spoke to yesterday, shouldn't he? He's always had a good memory as long as I have known him. You'd think he would have just told me, wouldn't you?'

'He's covering something up?'

'In truth, I don't yet know,' lied Berner. 'I want to go through that with him again, if that's fine by you. Have another go. Ease him into remembering rather than scare him into it.'

Lemke stood up, clasped his hands behind his back and began to rise up and down on his toes. 'What did Von Kettler tell you once you two had gone outside?'

Berner lied again 'The same. I went through the same questions to see if there were any anomalies in what he was telling me.'

'And?'

'It was all the same.'

'You're sure about that, *Obersturmbannführer* Berner?'

If Berner needed confirmation this conversation was being recorded by someone, somewhere, there it was.

'Sure. He reiterated how *Valkyrie* was written by the General Staff. Then he went on to say how he and his staff had written the Paris annex to the plan. I should know, I've read it. He confirmed all his usual staff were on duty yesterday; in other words, no one was conspicuous by their absence. Apart from that, he just repeated what he said in the office.'

Berner noticed how easily he was finding it to lie to Lemke. Lemke seemed to be soaking it all up, bouncing merrily on his toes. Lemke turned and walked to an open window and unbuttoned his jacket. 'This heat,' Berner heard him mutter to himself.

'Do you think I should let Sauer have a go at

him?' asked Lemke after a while.

'You seriously think that will uncover something new?'

Lemke seemed to take Berner's point. 'I thought so too. I could speak to the General myself but in a couple of days, see if his story changes with time, they usually do.'

Lemke turned to face Berner. 'I have a list of more pressing suspects if I'm honest. I really am not sure about Von Kettler. Let's see if his story changes once he's had a spell to think it over and over. In the meantime, I will have him kept in the Hotel Majestic under a sort of house arrest. I will certainly want you to have another chat with him, to see if you can get any more out of him but right now, I need you to return to Avenue Foch and get on with your other duties. We need to keep things looking normal to London: all your broadcasts need to continue going out on time as if nothing's really changed here.'

'Sure,' said Berner. 'This attempt on Hitler's life, well we – and when I say we, I mean the SS – we are his bodyguards, aren't we?'

'Implying we failed to protect him from the bomb?'

'The SS has a lot of reputation to get back, hasn't it? We all remember what happened to the SA…'

'Don't you worry, Berner. Starting with Heinrich Himmler himself, the SS is fully engaged on finding and killing the terrorists. All of them. We won't get the same treatment as the SA, of that I'm certain.' Lemke stared at the fireplace for a while and then straight back at Berner before asking gently: 'You fearing for your life, Walter?'

The truth of course was an emphatic yes, but not for the reasons Lemke was thinking of.

'I don't want to see the wrong people accused just to allow the SS to make a point,' said Berner thoughtfully. 'I know I used to be in the Army and a relative newcomer to all this but the last thing we want is another pogrom, surely? Find the guilty but protect the loyal, that's what we're about isn't it? After all, we still have a war to fight.' That last bit was for the stenographer.

'Sounds like you're about to launch into something enlightened about betrayal and loyalty, Walter.'

'No, Horst, don't you worry. Anyway, betrayal and loyalty are two sides of the same coin, are they not? But you see my point.'

Lemke's voice remained calm, deep, assured. 'I see your point, but I don't think you fully understand me. *Fear is what keeps us safe*. You mark my words, Berner – and I've had this from the top – a lot of people are about to remember how *very* afraid of us they need to be.'

'I see.'

Berner got up to leave. He very much doubted fear was going to keep the likes of Lemke safe. At best it might delay the inevitable retribution.

He stopped before he reached the door. 'Do you want me in on any other cases?'

Lemke took a moment to think. 'No, not yet. I will go through your list of acquaintances and if any more of them come up as suspects, I'll get you onto them.'

'Of course. One last question, if I may?'

'Go on,' said Lemke with a tired smile.

'Who's the boss: you or Sauer?'

'*Brigadeführer* Sauer is the senior officer here, Walter.'

Berner could feel Lemke's irritation at having to work for an amateur such as Sauer, and in a way Berner sympathised with him. However, knowing the conversation was being recorded, Berner resisted the temptation to say what they both knew: Sauer being the senior officer was not the same as saying he was in charge. The look on Lemke's face said as much anyway.

Knowing there was a rift between Sauer and Lemke was what Berner had wanted to know, such a schism might come in handy later.

Taking the long way, Walter Berner walked to the Arc de Triomphe and then down Avenue Foch to his office, thinking all the way and for once not caring who was following him.

The temperature continued to rise and Berner felt the sweat stick his collar to his neck. All trace of yesterday's barricades was gone.

Berner concluded that for now, he was off the hook as long as Von Kettler was kept quiet. Keeping Von Kettler's mouth shut was the objective.

Berner walked on, studying the people he passed. That same resolute look haunted their eyes, maybe even more than before. Paris may not have known someone tried to kill Hitler yesterday, but they certainly knew the Americans were in Saint-Lo and the British in Caen.

Berner wondered what was stopping them attacking him now, as he walked along the street. Surely, someone must recognise him as one of the officers working out of the SS HQ? He was used to being afraid of detection, that nagging fear pulling permanently at his sleeve. But to have to be frightened of a threat from anywhere was new. Everywhere he looked, there was a threat in front of him - and they were getting deadlier by the day.

As if to make the point, Berner got more suspecting looks from his own side as he entered SS HQ at Number 84 and climbed the main staircase to his office. Having worked here for months and shared incarceration with some of Paris's most loyal SS officers, he still felt he was very much the outsider here.

He collected some files from the desk clerk and continued along the corridor. After unlocking his door, he opened a window to let in some much-needed air, threw the files unread on the desk, sat down and stared at the ceiling for inspiration. The ceiling did not oblige.

His thoughts could not be forced and so Berner smiled a reminiscence or two as a distraction before getting down to the real thinking. He was a double agent for the British, there was someone as acutely suspicious as Lemke around, keen to boost his own reputation, and Von Kettler threatening to make Berner appear as guilty as he was. Berner was regretting advising Von Kettler to throw some dispensable people to the lions.

He got up and began to pace, stopping every now and then to consolidate his own thoughts. Up and down the room he went. Those working on the floor below soon grew tired of Berner's steps, back and forth, back and forth, faster then slower, faster then slower.

For the next two days Berner went about his normal duties but his heart was not really in it, he was still too distracted with his Von Kettler problem.

And Eve, of course. He had had no reports of an arrest, so he guessed Eve was away and safe somewhere. He knew he missed her and smiled as he remembered her, which, he noticed, was becoming more frequent.

Saturday

Jules stood guard at the edge of the wood and watched the sun begin to set whilst Eve sent a message to London. Every now and then, he would watch her push her hair back over her ears as she tapped away at the Morse key and jotted down the reply. He let his eyes wander over Eve's body and legs and the look of concentration on her face.

He really couldn't believe it – he'd been brought up to think war heroes should be tall, broad-shouldered, gruff and above all, men. And yet here was Eve, the elegant girl returned from Paris, slender, talented, resolute. He'd loved having her to himself for the day, listening to her talk of Paris and London, of parties, of family outings, anything except the war and her part in it.

Eve packed up the radio and fished the antennae wire from out of the trees. She sat on the suitcase, decoded her message. It was long enough to make his legs ache, and he was glad when eventually she arrived by his side with one shoulder hunched higher to counter the weight of the radio.

Eve put the suitcase down, took the cigarette from Jules's mouth and set light to the notes she had made from the broadcast.

She smiled: 'I have to go back to Paris on Monday morning. Early.'

Jules looked away to the horizon, crestfallen.

'So best we make some good use of those woods

and that blanket whilst we still can,' she said with a grin.

* * *

Sergeant Major Stan Morgan looked out towards a ramshackle-looking convoy of cars and trucks making its way along the road towards him.

'Here they come, Fred Karno's Army,' he said, unimpressed.

'Here they come, indeed.'   Major Mike Slater looked out to where the Sergeant Major had been pointing. 'You're not wrong in your assessment, are you? What an assortment.'

At least ten cars of all sorts and a matching number of trucks lumbered towards them kicking up a cloud of white dust. Some of the trucks looked like furniture vans, the rest were open topped and filled with Resistance fighters, some looking out as sentries, the others facing in, their heads swaying with the roll of the road. At the convoy's head and tail was an Army Jeep. Slater focussed in on the lead one.

'Agent Saxon, as I live and breath!'

'I'm sorry, Sir?' asked the Sergeant Major.

'There's a British officer in the lead Jeep. He's an old mate of mine. We were Commandos together in fact. Saxon's his name, good bloke. Last I saw of him he was in London for a bit of R&R. He'd got separated from the rest of us in the Dieppe raid and went on the run in France. Linked up with the Resistance down near Rouen and he's been out here a lot since then, apparently. He's a bit cagey, like all those secret agent types but he's sound enough. You'll like him.'

The Sergeant Major nodded appreciatively. 'If you say so, Sir. I reckon those old trucks will be thirsty. I'll get some of the petrol off-loaded so they can refill.' Morgan slunk off deeper into the woods.

The convoy slowed to a halt and Slater could see Saxon looking down at his map.

'Ellis?' Slater said to his second in command.

'Yes, Mike?'

'They won't be able to see us up here, take a Jeep and show them the way in will you?'

'Certainly.'

Slater heard a Jeep cough into life behind him and soon enough, Ellis was driving across the field towards the crossroads. Slater smiled as he watched Saxon wave, put his map away and wave the rest of his convoy on.

'You didn't make bad time, Saxon, not bad at all, considering.' Slater gave a quick and disapproving look at some of the vehicles lurching their way into the woods.

'Mike! I had no idea it would be you here, how are you?' The two shook hands as Saxon stepped from his seat.

'Good actually. We dropped in on the night of the invasion, the Jeeps were landed in the day after, and we've been roving the French countryside ever since, making a right old nuisance of ourselves. Jerry's petrified: the Germans around here are mostly logistics and admin types. They don't know much but they know we're on the prowl and they just don't want to fight us.'

'They are certainly on edge, that's for sure,' said Saxon pushing his goggles up, showing just how dusty his face was.

Slater watched a hard and uncompromising-looking Frenchman approach. His hair and bushy beard were white, his eyes sparkling with mischief and a pipe clenched between his teeth.

'Hello, I'm Clement, *Chasseur Alpins*,' he said.

'You're a long way from the mountains, if you don't mind me saying,' smiled Slater in reply.

'I wanted my wife to live safe in the mountains, so I moved to somewhere a long way from home, Rouen. I formed a Resistance group and that's how I came to meet Saxon here. Now, we are driving eastward to inspire others to rise up against the Germans. This is a wonderful time, is it not?'

'Certainly is, although it does have its moments. How many men have you got with you?'

'Well,' Clement took his pipe from his mouth for a moment. 'There were fifty-one of us last night but now only forty-eight. We bumped into the SS. They were not expecting us and we killed many but they also gave a good account of themselves.'

'Was that far away from here?'

'Oh yes and they were headed north. Don't worry, Major, they're no threat to you,' replied Clement matter-of-factly.

'They're headed north here as well are they, the Germans?' asked Saxon.

'Very much so,' replied Slater. 'Jerry's in a real hurry to get up to the coast. That's why we're here, of course, to cut the railway lines and hit the convoys on the roads. Mind you, Jerry's only moving at night now. Too scared of the RAF.'

'The Americans are up there too.' The officer who had been travelling at the rear of Saxon's convoy approached, wearing an American uniform. 'Let me introduce myself, I'm Lieutenant Jim Jackson, OSS.'

Slater smiled a welcome, impressed. 'Pleased to meet you. You sound like you have travelled a long way to be here.'

'All the way from California.'

'That is a long way!' replied Slater. 'So you're here learning the ropes from Saxon, are you?'

'That was the plan,' Jim smiled ironically. 'Although the passage of information isn't always going in just the one direction. Sometimes Saxon here allows me ideas all of my own.'

'So it's the two of you and Clement's private army, is it?'

'I have a Frenchman with me as well,' said Saxon. 'Maurice over there used to be in Clement's group but I got him back to Britain where he joined up and I insisted on getting him trained up to come back over with me.'

'Very cosy,' said Slater with a laugh. 'Honestly, you SOE lot; you just make it all up as you go along, don't you? But who am I to complain: some of the stuff we used to get up to in the desert was purely by the seat of our pants.'

'I'll bet it was. Look, I know we've only just arrived but we won't be staying long, Mike, if that's alright,' said Saxon. 'We'll overnight here and then head off again in the morning. I need to get further east than this if at all possible.'

'Sure. I've had my Sergeant Major put some fuel aside for you. We can't spare you much ammo I'm afraid, we're going to need that for ourselves.'

'Understood.'

'Although,' said Slater with a look of adventure in his eyes. 'You may want to accompany us on a raid tonight. I could do with the extra manpower, it'll make the Germans think the whole Army's here.'

'What did you have in mind?' asked Jim.

'A few of the local Resistance have been in touch,' said Slater pushing his beret back on his head a little. 'It looks like there's a Panzer division booked to head north by train this evening. The main line's over by Bouchevilliers, which isn't too far from here at all. We're going to drive over later and shoot up the trains as they go by. We'll be back before it's dark so you'll be able to rest up before the morning. Up to you but as I say, one hundred men will look a damn sight more impressive than just my fifty.'

Saxon looked at Clement and then Jim. They were clearly in the mood for ambush.

'Alright, Mike, we're in. What's the plan?'

Gefreiter Alfred Bohler of the *Wehrmachtnachrichtenverbindungen Funkwesen*, unsurprisingly abbreviated to the WNV/FU, put his earphones on his desk and pushed his chair back, tired. He lumbered across the dark and stale room to some filing cabinets. Passing 'C' and 'D' to settle on 'E' for Eve. Pushing his thick glasses back onto the bridge of his nose, he located Eve's index card, which cross-referenced him to a file, the number of which he jotted down onto a request form with an annoyingly blunt pencil.

He checked his watch. Perfect. He had an hour left of his shift and he could spend that time pretending to study a file in the library rather than sit around wearing uncomfortable headphones.

No one around here seemed to care like they used to any longer and Bohler was in no way immune to the indifference. The WNV/FU had been a part of the *Abwehr,* but since the SS had taken it all over, the juicier radio intercepts went to Bohler's rivals in the *Funkmessstelle.* Once credited as being a genius with the radio, Bohler was reduced to spending his time checking what known British agents were signalling back to Britain. He was checking the work of people he already knew were working for the Germans.

This was a far cry from looking out for real agents. This wasn't the hunt, the search for clues, following an invisible, electronic trail to the enemy. No, this was just routine, mundane, checking.

The work was easy and dull. But Bohler decided that since the WNV/FU had been disbanded, he could do dull. He was one of life's pedants and this work was ideal for someone with his eye for the small points. That was what had made him dangerous through most of the war: he was the devil in the detail.

Having exchanged pleasantries with the library clerk, Alfred Bohler signed for the Eve file and walked slowly to the desk allocated for reading such secret files. He took out the cipher book, checked it against the serial number given to Eve's message, ensured he had the right cipher sheet and then, having licked the end of a new and sharper pencil, began to decode Eve's last message and the reply from London. Every now and then, Bohler's eyes would flick across to the official photograph of Eve.

The message read innocuously enough: send instructions, get back to Paris *et cetera*. Bohler went through Agent Eve's more recent messages and they all looked pretty tame too. Plenty of instructions but never giving any real detail except perhaps some details about troop movements in the north. Bohler thought them harmless enough. The SS had decoded them correctly; there were no mistakes.

Satisfied, Bohler put the message back into the file, annotated the cover sheet to document his check, and placed the cipher booklet back into the little pocket where it belonged.

He was just about to stand up when something stopped him. He sighed, wondering what was niggling at him. With ten more minutes of his shift to waste, Bohler sat back down and compared Eve's last message with her broadcasting schedule.

Suddenly Bohler frowned. Eve's last message could not have been a planned broadcast. The file said Eve sent messages on Sundays, Tuesdays and Thursdays but never on a Saturday, except once in late January.

Bohler checked back a little further in the log and it got still more interesting. This was more like it! There was no record of a transmission by her this Thursday. Something was wrong – an agent who was working for the Germans would normally have no reason to disrupt their broadcast schedule and yet here was Eve missing one broadcast and sending another on a non-routine day.

The answers always lay in the anomalies.

* * *

Berner still wasn't sure if he had a plan or not. In the past, he used to run his schemes past Sergeant Brunswick who would, normally with only the movement of an eyebrow, let him know if he'd had a good idea or was in need of another. With Eve still in hiding, Berner had no one but himself to share his plans with.

Berner jumped as his phone rang. It was Lemke.

'I think it's time you came across to the Majestic for another chat with Von Kettler.'

'Why, are you onto something?' fished Berner.

'No, not really. I just want to keep him on his toes and I really do think he'll talk a lot more to you than me.'

'You said I needed to come across. Where are you?'

'Ah, yes, I've decided to base myself in the Majestic for a while, so I can keep an eye on Von Kettler, just in case.'

'That the only reason?' asked Berner cheekily.

'What other reason could I possibly have?' asked Lemke. Berner decided not to say "because it's salubrious and Sauer doesn't work there".

'How's the General doing? What's he been up to?' asked Berner.

'His job,' replied Lemke in a matter of fact way.

'Nothing else?'

'Let's not discuss this over the telephone. It's not urgent so come and see me Monday, sometime after two. You can chat to Von Kettler after that. All right?'

Berner said yes and slowly put the phone down. Berner knew how other senior-ranking suspects had already been shot, poisoned or sent back to Berlin for a show trail and then be shot or poisoned. Maybe Lemke didn't have that much on Von Kettler after all and not having to put too much pressure on the General meant Berner's little secret could be kept.

And then it happened, it always happened like that with him. Despite days of thinking and pacing, suddenly his thinking was clear. Suddenly, he knew exactly what to do. That certainly gave Berner his confidence back. He smiled contentedly and reached for his coat.

Clement's men had already set off. Being in civilian clothes and - more importantly - French, they had the job of guarding the junctions between the SAS camp and where the trains were to be ambushed. Amateurs and volunteers, Clement watched with pride how his men fitted in so easily with the SAS soldiers, fighting their unconventional war. He'd trained them well, he smiled to himself, and he wanted to see as many of them through to the end, to see France free of the invader.

With a pistol at his belt and a Thompson sub-machine gun tucked under an arm, Sergeant Major Morgan pulled on some driving gauntlets. 'We're all set, Sir,' he said.

'Excellent. Right then, it's time to go.' Slater pulled his goggles down onto his eyes. 'You all set, Saxon?'

Saxon gave a quick look to Jim and Maurice. Jim was driving and Maurice was manning the twin machine guns in the back. They both looked grimly prepared for the task in hand.

'Yep, we're ready.'

With that, Slater nodded his head and the engines of ten Jeeps came to life. Slater's men were a mix of those new to life in the SAS as well as the craggy-faced veterans of raids in the African desert and the Mediterranean. Their Jeeps looked like open-topped mobile fortresses, each fitted with five Vickers machine guns, with small bulletproof windshields for the driver and passenger. Any rear-echelon German soldier armed only with a rifle did not stand a chance against this lot, Saxon thought.

Slater's Jeep lurched out from the tree line, across the fields and down onto the road through a gap in a hedge. Once on the road, all the drivers settled into the journey, keeping a regular fifty yards between Jeeps. After a minute or two, Saxon saw Slater turn around and stand up a little, looking back to check everyone was on the road and when satisfied signalled to his driver to put his foot down. They raced off to battle. Their tyres whined on the tarmac.

Saxon still could not quite believe it: here he was on a beautiful sunny afternoon, driving boldly through enemy territory on his way to ambush a train. The speed and the pre-battle nerves were exhilarating but how things had changed since January, when he could only attack the railways with plastic explosives at night after a slow, stealthy approach.

Feeling the convoy slow down, Saxon looked up. Sitting up high to look forward, Saxon spotted Clement, waving the convoy to a halt at a junction with an unmistakably roguish look about him. Something was up.

Jim pulled up behind Slater's Jeep. Saxon got out and walked over.

'What's the matter, Clement?'

'I've found you a much juicier target!'

'How do you mean?' asked Slater, clearly intrigued.

'Some of the boys got chatting and smoking with the locals over there. They said that we could go and ambush the trains if we wanted but there's about ten petrol trains in the marshalling yards just up the road. They won't move until nightfall. I thought perhaps you would be more interested in those!'

'My God,' said Slater slowly, turning to Saxon. 'What do you think, happy to continue?'

'Of course!' said Saxon, 'I'm very happy to change the plan if you are.'

'I thought you'd say that,' said Clement. 'So I have already moved some of my men onto the junctions between here and where I think we could attack the marshalling yards. The rest of my men are parked up behind that farmhouse over there.'

'Right,' said Slater, alive with the prospect of more action. 'You don't hang about, do you? Clement: you jump in with me. Saxon, you come along too, please. Let's go and take a quick look at the marshalling yards. Sergeant Major?'

'Don't worry, Sir,' said Sergeant Major Morgan with mock weariness, 'I'll stay here with the men whilst you go off gallivanting.'

Slater raced off with Saxon in tow.

Having parked up, Slater, Clement, Jim and Saxon climbed a slight incline in the cover of some trees to approach the marshalling yard. When they saw it, they all halted abruptly.

'Will you look at that,' Slater's sense of awe was tangible.

Saxon looked out. The rise they stood on was the top of a wide embankment which sloped gently back down towards the railway tracks. Crossing his front from right to left was what looked like the main line to Paris. Behind that was a number of parallel sidings under camouflage netting where eleven, not ten, trains full of petrol tank wagons stood.

'I don't know about you two,' said Clement knocking the tobacco out of his pipe, 'but I can smell the petrol from here.'

'Me too,' said Slater, slowly lowering his binoculars.

Saxon continued to scan the scene. Off to each side, where the sidings began, was a hut surrounded with sandbags, manned by German soldiers. Saxon could just make out the roof of another sentry hut on the far side of the sidings.

'Have they really parked up what must be, what, a week's worth of fuel for Rommel's Panzers all at the same spot? Pretty damn careless, wouldn't you say?' asked Jim.

'Especially with us lot around.' grinned Clement.

Slater glanced at Clement. 'Quite.'

'I think we can attack this alright, don't you?' asked Saxon.

'Certainly,' replied Slater. 'Actually, I think we can kill all our birds with one stone, so to speak. Right, here's a plan, tell me what you think of this.'

Once again, Clement's men went on ahead to set up ambush positions to make sure no Germans got in or out once the attack began. Clement took the rest of his men to the next village to look for trouble and make some noise.

With the Frenchmen underway, Slater led the Jeeps slowly towards where he, Saxon, Jim and Clement had been parked half an hour earlier. They drove slowly to keep down the noise and the dust. With their engines purring, they sat and waited.

With a mouth dry from the journey and the prospect of a gunfight, Saxon took a small swig from his water bottle before handing it back to Maurice.

The minutes passed slowly.

Then Saxon heard a crack in the distance, then another.

'That'll be the distraction playing out, then?' asked Jim quietly.

'Sounds like it.' Saxon looked at his watch. 'You have to admire their timing, don't you?'

They heard the shooting by Clement's men intensify; a firefight seemed to be starting. A grenade popped loudly.

Slater turned round, Saxon could see his big grin visible from under his goggles. Saxon smiled back.

Slater's Jeep lurched up the incline, weaving amongst the trees. Jim followed. Slater came to a halt at the top of the incline and Jim pulled up next to him, a few yards to Slater's left. Sergeant Major Morgan, with three other Jeeps behind him, continued down the incline, bumped over the main railway lines and sped out to Saxon's right.

Then Ellis appeared, hurtled down to the railway tracks and veered off to the left with another two Jeeps.

Saxon watched one of the German sentries as Ellis approached. Realising at last what he was seeing, the German shouted something, raising the alarm and began to swing his rifle off his shoulder. Ellis opened up with his twin Vickers guns and the force of the machine guns began to rip the sandbag wall the soldier stood behind in two. Ellis's Jeep moved over a little so the Jeeps behind could also bring their guns to bear. The sentry shed began to break apart in big splinters under the weight of fire.

Meanwhile, Sergeant Major Morgan hurtled straight passed the sentry post to Saxon's right and kept going. Saxon could see Morgan hunch his head down into his shoulders. Morgan swept on, taking another Jeep with him, to attack the sentry post beyond the trains. A stray round in amongst that lot could kill them all. Two of the Jeeps behind Morgan stopped and poured fire into the sentry hut to

Saxon's right.

The German sentries tried their hardest to get a few rounds off at their attackers but it was no good.

Saxon was briefly distracted by the remaining Jeeps as they formed up in a long line stretching out beyond Slater and Saxon, dominating the small ridge. From their height, they too poured fire into the sentry huts in support of Morgan and Ellis.

Jim, from the driving seat of the Jeep fired off a few rounds from his gun.

'Hey!' shouted Maurice from the back, 'what about me?'

'You've been here for years, Maurice, I'm the one who needs the practice!' shouted Jim, brimming with the joy of impending victory.

Slater waved his arms above his head and the shooting stopped.

Echoes of the gunfire reverberated off the trains. And then, there was silence.

Slater reached into his smock and pulled out a metal whistle, giving two quick 'peeps' on it.

The Jeeps who had attacked the sentry posts jolted into life, reversed, turned around and hurried up to the growing line of Jeeps on the ridge. Everyone turned off their engines and the silence returned. Clement's men could not be heard. Saxon assumed the Resistance fighters must have killed off any opposition.

Slater pushed his goggles back on his head and looked at his watch. 'Couple of minutes and the first train will be here,' he shouted.

And so they all waited. Saxon could hear nervous chatter amongst the Jeep crews.

The rail tracks started to sing gently. Saxon recognised the sound straight away

'Here it comes!' he shouted.

He heard a few machine gun cocking levers snap back and forth. Then he heard the train puffing towards him, hidden somewhere off to the right behind some trees. Then he saw smoke pulsing up into the air as the train approached. Saxon could feel the sweat in his hands against the pistol grips of his machine guns.

The train came into view. In front of the locomotive was a flat wagon with an anti-aircraft gun on it. Its crew looked tense and alert. As the train moved forward, carriage after carriage packed with soldiers came into view.

Slater took his time and waited until the locomotive was level with him before opening fire. The anti aircraft gun crew seemed to jump and jolt as bullets poured into unprotected bodies. Further down the train, windows smashed as twenty Vickers machine guns ripped into the carriages.

Saxon pumped fire into the train, round after round into carriage after carriage. He watched men stand, scream, scramble for cover, and die.

Saxon watched the train begin to accelerate as the driver tried to escape with his life.

The machine gunners continued to pump rounds into the carriages until the train disappeared from view. All that was left was dust and some German soldiers who had jumped down in an attempt to escape. Any that moved were finished off with a quick burst of 0.303.

All was silent.

'Do you reckon they were SS?' asked Jim. 'I could see some black uniforms in there.'

'Unlikely,' said Saxon. 'The SS tend not to wear black out in the field. No, I reckon they were tank crews. They probably crew the tanks that are supposed to be on the next train.'

Then more firing could be heard off to the left.

'That must be Clement having another crack at that train,' said Slater. The excitement had made his voice shaky.

'Five more minutes and then the next one should be along. All yours, Saxon!'

Saxon clambered out from his Jeep and grabbed the haversack slung down by his knee. 'You ready Maurice?'

'Oh yes. It's about time I got a share of the action,' he said as he picked up a haversack of his own and gave Jim an amused look. 'Coming with us?'

'No, I'm sitting this one out. Literally. I am going to sit here and watch you two do your trick.'

'Our pleasure,' said Maurice as he and Saxon ran down to the tracks.

Saxon stopped at the first track. 'Here?'

'No problem,' said Maurice, a professional at work.

Like Maurice, Saxon knelt beside the railway line and they each pulled out a pre-package explosive charge, made back in Britain to fit a French railway line perfectly. Saxon held his charge in place with his knee and fastened it to the rail with a small canvas strap, supplied for just this purpose. About a yard down the track, Maurice did the same.

Saxon then reached back into his rucksack and pulled out a length of Cordtex, plugging one end into his explosive charge and handed the other to Maurice, who plugged it into his explosive charge.

Saxon then moved one pace beyond Maurice, in the direction the train would approach, and unwound a cable with a fog-signal detonator fixed at one end. Stretching it out, Maurice grabbed the other end of the cable and pushed it into his explosive charge. Saxon pulled the cable taut before placing the fog signal on top of the rail and fixing that in place with another thin canvas strap. When the train wheel ran over the fog signal, it would detonate, sending an explosive shock up the Cordtex, which would set of the explosive charges. Simple, really. The whole thing must have taken no more than two minutes to set up.

Saxon and Maurice both stood up and clapped the dust from their hands.

'All done?'

'All done,' replied Maurice.

'Even blowing up trains is easier now, isn't it?' Saxon asked as the two men made their way up to the incline to the Jeeps.

'All set,' said Saxon as he clambered into his Jeep.

'Jolly good,' said Slater, with one eye on his watch.

Saxon shared out some more water with Maurice and Jim, checked the ammunition levels on his two machine guns and prepared for the arrival of the second train. After a couple of minutes, he could hear it approaching. It sounded to Saxon like this train was labouring a bit more, probably pulling more weight. That meant it was the train with the tanks on.

This time it was a bit different: the anti-aircraft gun crew, having seen some dead bodies laying out by the tracks, swung their gun towards the embankment where the Jeeps were and opened fire. Saxon felt his Jeep sway as an 88m round thudded into the ground just in front of him. Saxon, like all the other British machine gunners, poured fire onto the first wagon. Jim watched open-mouthed as he watched the gun crew be ripped apart in the hail of SAS bullets.

Saxon felt nervous as he watched the train accelerate towards the explosive charges. He watched intently as the front wheels of the *Kriegslokomotive* rolled over the fog signal. He watched the small puff of the signal exploding and then a blinding white flash along the track as the Cordtex ignited and then BANG! Up went the plastic explosive.

The locomotive jumped a couple of feet up into the air before crashing back down at an angle. The coal truck rammed forward, crushing the back of the locomotive as it weaved forward, ripping the sleepers up into matchwood. The wagons behind jolted back and forth and side to side, their momentum pushing them forward. A Panzer Mark IV tank snapped free from its tethers and fell nose-down onto the track. The wagon behind clipped the back of the tank, forcing it instantly to jack-knife. The third wagon crashed into that and the fourth rode up and ploughed straight into the tank ahead, ripping off the turret.

Amongst the dust and the chaos, the train ground to a halt.

The guns remained silent; there was no one to shoot at.

The only noise left was the idling of the steam engine. Everything else was still.

'What do you reckon, Saxon, OK for us to move down?' asked Slater.

'Sure.'

Jim pressed the starter button and they set off towards the train. As planned, each Jeep pulled up next to a train wagon or a tank. The passengers of each Jeep leapt out and bent down to pick up a handful of earth before climbing up onto the tanks.

Saxon let Jim have a go instead of doing this bit of sabotage himself.

'You get up on top there and the petrol cap is on the top of the decking, can you see it?' said Saxon as he watched Jim clamber up.

'Sure can.'

Jim unscrewed the petrol cap with his free hand and poured in the sand and soil.

'That'll do the trick. Jerry'll try to salvage some of these and boy will they be annoyed to find the engine seizing up after a couple of minutes!'

Jim jumped down. 'They certainly will. I can almost see the look on their faces now.'

Like the other crews, Jim and Saxon mounted up and drove back up the incline but parked facing away from the marshalling yard.

'Looks like you're going to get your fun after all, Maurice,' said Jim as he brought the Jeep to a halt.

'Oh, yes,' replied Maurice with more than a hint

of malevolence in his voice as he worked the cocking levers of his machine guns.

'We all set?' shouted Slater, looking up and down the line of cars.

'Fire!'

The rear gunners fired into the fuel trains. As the rounds landed the first fuel tank blew up, taking a few others with it. Then a chain reaction began and all the petrol wagons erupted in turn, like giant firecrackers. The noise was incredible. Saxon, having turned to watch the spectacle, felt the intense heat on his face and the sudden, hot draught rush through his hair.

The whole area erupted in flame. The sky began to fill with black smoke.

Saxon had a better look. There was nothing left of the petrol trains except twisted, black metal. The tank train was still there but many of the wagons had shattered into bits, strewn all over the tracks. The tanks had survived the blasts by the look of it but many had black burn marks on the side that had faced the inferno.

The men looked like they could not quite believe it. They all looked on silently.

'Right, everybody, that was all very entertaining but we need to get out of here fast,' shouted Slater, his Jeep bursting into life. He led the convoy off, with all the others following out in the same order they had arrived in.

After a couple of minutes, Slater slowed a little as they reached Clement. 'You all alright?'

'We sure are,' beamed Clement. 'That explosion! I have now fought in two great wars but I haven't seen anything like that before. Magnificent! What happened to you?' asked Clement on Maurice.

'What?'

'Your face,' persisted Clement, 'it's all red.'

'It must have been the blast,' explained Jim as Maurice put a hand gently to his face. Clement was right, he looked sunburned.

'Well, yes, quite,' said Slater, not quite sure how to take Clement's exuberance. 'All your men ready to get going?'

'What? Oh yes, all set. We bagged a few Germans ourselves. I even took a couple prisoner. We can ask them a few questions later, no?'

Clement could sense Slater's impatience to get moving.

'Alright, alright, I'll just give them the signal,' said Clement walking off to a nearby barn and started beckoning.

A truck pulled out and the passenger door flew open. Clement embarked and the convoy took off.

'What now?' asked Jim above the noise of the engine, the wind and the tyres.

'We get back and get something to eat whilst Maurice gets the radio set up,' said Saxon. 'We need to report in. I also want to know what London wants us to do next.'

The convoy sped on unhindered.

PART TWO

Monday

Berner set off early, doing his usual back and double-back and checking in shop windows to make sure no one was following, before nipping into the cemetery to leave a chalk mark against a certain headstone. He then returned to the office to spend the rest of the morning reading pointless files, had a leisurely lunch and was knocking on Lemke's door a little after two.

Lemke made a point of checking his watch to let Berner know he had been a few minutes late. Sauer was there too and just smiled weakly, the senior rank but no longer in charge. The fact they were in Lemke's office rather than Sauer's said enough for Berner.

'Come in, Walter. Take a seat, please,' said a cheery Lemke. Lemke stood by the window, bobbing happily on his toes.

Berner could not help but notice how things were not quite right between Lemke and Sauer. Something was up.

Berner went into high alert.

Lemke was composed but Sauer looked like a scolded child, playing nervously at his fingernails. Something told Berner Sauer had just been put in his place and Sauer did not like it one bit. Sauer always wanted to be top dog wherever he went, whether he deserved it or not.

With Lemke more soundly in charge, thought

Berner, Paris was a much more dangerous place for a double agent.

'We have made over a hundred arrests already,' said Lemke proudly, getting the ball rolling.

'Over a hundred?' asked Berner, a little shocked. That was double the number of conspirators Von Kettler had hinted at. 'And what's happening to them?'

'The *Führer* wants those arrested kept alive wherever possible,' replied Lemke. 'Some of the main conspirators were shot out of hand and that seems to have been the wrong thing to do. I understand the *Führer* wants any conspirator to suffer *a lot of pain* before they die. So no summary executions.' Lemke was looking at Berner but seemed to be talking to Sauer.

'So not just an execution,' said Berner settling into a chair, 'more of a message.'

'Precisely. Now, about your old boss Von Kettler,' said Lemke.

'Yes?'

'Well, I had a chat with him.'

Berner felt his pulse quicken.

'I've had everything he said to both me and you double-checked: every name, every detail, every timing.'

'And?' Berner was dreading the answer.

'It all adds up.'

'What does?' Berner was rigid with fear.

'His story. Do you know what, I think he might be one of us after all.'

Berner breathed out a little too obviously and Lemke spotted it.

'You look relieved, Berner, why's that?'

'As you said, I used to work for Von Kettler. I didn't have him down as a conspirator, so I'm glad he is not a suspect-'

'Yet,' blurted Sauer before returning to studying his fingernails.

'Yet,' replied Berner, warily but recovering quickly, 'the way I see it, it wouldn't be a good reflection on my abilities if it turned out he was a conspirator, would it?'

'True,' nodded Lemke.

'Also,' Berner continued, 'more personally, if Von Kettler's a suspect, then that could make me a suspect simply by association and I certainly don't want that either. Do you still consider him a suspect then?'

'What's going against him,' Lemke said, tapping his new desk grandly and not answering the question, 'is how old-school *Wehrmacht* he is. Most of the other conspirators we've picked up are just like him in outlook - too snobby to be a Nazi, know what I mean? Mind you, von Rundstedt is checking out and he's as old-school Prussian as they come. So maybe Von Kettler's clean too.'

'But then again,' said Sauer, 'maybe not, right?' Berner noticed how the question was aimed at Lemke. Did Sauer have to have his statements censored and approved by Lemke now? In which case, thought Berner to himself, the takeover here is complete. 'Do you still want me to have a chat with him again? You think I'll be able to uncover something new?' asked Berner.

Lemke grimaced. 'Unlikely but it's worth a try.

Keep it conversational..'

'Easy.'

'Precisely.' Lemke showed his pointed teeth in a grim smile. 'Oh, and Berner, there's something else.'

Berner's heart plummeted back to his stomach.

'Oh no, don't worry, it's nothing sinister but you were in the 124th Regiment with Rommel in the last war, weren't you?'

'Oh no, not Rommel, surely?' asked Berner, astounded.

'What? Oh no, no, Berner, it's not that at all.'

'Not yet,' chipped in Sauer.

Lemke ignored him.

'What I mean is, Berner, the Field Marshal's car was attacked by a British plane and he's been hit. His driver was killed but Rommel's still alive.'

'Ah. Not good,' Berner was still adapting to the change of subject whilst maintaining vigilance for any attempt to trip him up. 'Where is he now?

'In hospital, recovering not too far from here.'

'Well I'd like to go and see him at some point if that's all right? Us old comrades have to stick together, don't we?' asked Berner.

'You have to be careful saying things like that this week, Berner.'

'Sadly, that's true,' said Berner, sadly. 'But my acquaintances may prove to be a strength.' Berner was back on the offensive.

'True,' said Lemke thoughtfully.

'As long as you're not in amongst them, Berner,' spat out Sauer with a nasty little grin on his face and eyes that burned malice.

Lemke allowed Sauer this tiny contribution, like an owner smiling at their cat playing with a mouse. Lemke grinned and said, 'Go and have another chat with Von Kettler, Berner. You can tell him about Rommel if you like, although he probably already knows. And please remember that cosmetically, Von Kettler is still the Military Governor of Paris but mark my words, everything, and I do mean everything that man does at the moment is done only with my express permission. He doesn't like it, but he knows he has to play along or else…'

'Understood. Anything in particular you want me to try to get out of him?'

'A few more names for us to check out would be good. And if you want to interview him in the garden like last time, feel free.'

That told Berner the bench in the garden boasted a new microphone.

* * *

Berner had them sit on a different bench.

'They have barely touched me or spoken to me, Walter,' said Von Kettler quietly. 'I really don't know what to make of it.'

'Keep your head pointing down a little more, General, please. I don't want you being lip-read.'

'Ah, yes, of course.' Von Kettler bent a little more towards the ground, clasped his hands together and leant on his knees.

'What do you think, what have they told you? I'm getting reports of arrests being made everywhere,' he said earnestly. 'People who, to my knowledge, have no connection with the plot at all.'

'And how would you know that, General?' asked Berner.

'All right, people who I would consider it impossible for them to be a conspirator.'

'That's better,' chided Berner gently. 'This coup is giving the Nazis the perfect excuse for a bit of a clear out. An opportunity to get rid of those who they don't consider Nazi enough. So just being suspected of involvement is good enough to warrant an arrest at the moment. According to Lemke, anyway.'

'So why am I still here? Do they suspect me?'

'I don't know. From what Lemke's just told me, maybe you can be trusted, like von Rundstedt.'

The General gave Berner an imploring look.

'Trust me,' said Berner, spreading his hands wide, 'I have no idea. They're not really telling me anything but don't read anything into that, it's standard operating procedure to keep all your cards close to your chest in this game.' Berner looked up and gave a little snort of a laugh.

'What is it?' asked Von Kettler.

'Don't look up but we're being watched.'

Von Kettler looked up..

'I said don't look up, didn't I? Don't start making mistakes as simple as that, you'll get me worried,' said Berner. 'Mistakes will get you and possibly me killed.'

Dropping his head, Von Kettler muttered quietly: 'Walter, I'm worried about my family. Berlin has declared *Sippenhaft*: the family is also made to pay the price for any transgressions an officer makes - or is accused of, at least.' Von Kettler paused for a moment before saying, 'Could you get them out?'

Berner blew out hard. 'Why would you want that when your story is you're clean?'

'It's not that simple though, is it, Berner?'

'What?'

'We were so confident of success, Walter. *So sure* of victory. We had a cabinet all worked out with a President, a Chancellor…'

Berner gazed at him, utterly astounded.

'I know, Berner, the thing is, the more I have thought about this, whatever I say or do isn't important. There are plenty of people out there who knew I was involved. As soon as they mention my name…' Von Kettler stared down at his boots. 'You tell me Lemke does not suspect me,' he continued, 'but the situation is still too precarious for my liking. I will face the music if I have to, but I'm scared for my family. I'm asking you to get them to safety.'

'And don't tell me, if I don't, you'll be threatening to tell Lemke you think I was involved in the plot somehow.'

'What would you do in my circumstances?'

'As I said, keep my mouth firmly shut.' Berner said.

He paused, thinking. It was time to bring his plan into play. 'I might just be able to help you.'

'You can? Oh my God, Berner, thank you, thank you.' Von Kettler placed his hands together, imploringly.

'Before we get into that, however,' asked Berner, 'I want to know just how involved you were in the coup. When did you first start thinking about it?'

'Before the war even started, Walter. I was in the *Schwarze Kapelle*, heard of that?'

'Of course. So you're not just a conspirator, you're an originator.'

'Pretty much. I believe, and I'm not the only one, that the Nazis will have their day. Then what? There still needs to be a Germany left after all this.'

Berner was on the same path as the General but wasn't going to say as much.

'There's something else I want to know. My boss, Admiral Schneider, was he in on this also?'

'That I don't know; he always keeps his options open, his mouth shut, and his opinions to himself. Like you.'

Berner could see he was telling the truth. 'Well, you would do well to learn a lot from the Admiral, as far as keeping your opinions to yourself is concerned,' said Berner.

Von Kettler smiled. 'Fair point.'

Berner thought for a moment and then began to speak. 'I think I can get your kids out, but I want something in return.'

'Every bit the counterintelligence officer, aren't you Berner: I scratch your back…'

'Do you want your kids to live or not?' asked Berner impatiently.

'I'm sorry, I-'

'I don't often tell generals to shut up but if you want your kids to see Christmas, you march to my tune from now on. Understand?' Berner's head was clear, his mind set - and, it gave him confidence.

Von Kettler nodded like a scolded child.

'I want a list from you. All those who you know are in on the conspiracy, including the bigger players. *Especially* the bigger players, the ones who knew you were involved from the early days.'

'Why on earth would I do that?'

'It's simple. It will allow me to keep an eye on who's getting arrested. It will help me make a judgment on whether the net is closing in around you or not. Then we can make a decision on whether we have to get you out of here to stop you blabbing away at the first sign of a pair of handcuffs.'

'And what if you hand that list straight to Lemke?'

'I thought you said you trusted me.'

'I do, but you could buy your own freedom with that list if ever you were implicated...'

'Don't be ridiculous. Once you're implicated in this, you're dead, no matter what you offer to tell them. Hitler's not in a bargaining mood. And there's something else,' said Berner, looking Von Kettler straight in the eye. 'You listen to this and make sure it sinks in because from now on, your life depends on it. If *ever* I tell you to get out of here, no matter how, whether it's over the phone, a telegram, a messenger, or someone you've never seen before in your life walks up and tells you to follow them out, it doesn't matter – the moment I tell you to get out, you drop everything and you go. Understand?'

'Where?'

'Wherever you're told. and if no instructions come, you go straight to Passy Cemetery.'

Von Kettler's mouth fell open.

'I'll find you there. Make sure no one follows you. Bring no one with you.'

'No one.'

'Meanwhile, I'll see what I can do for your family. Don't say *anything* to them: assume your phone at home is tapped and your mail is being read. Don't tell them to do anything, leave it all to me. So, when the time comes, go to Passy Cemetery and wear a coat that makes you look less military. Spend your time planning how you would get out - as the commanding General, I'm sure people would understand if you said you wanted to get away and … I don't know, get some exercise or something. Anyway, devising that bit is your job, I do the rest. And when you get to the Cemetery, if the locals recognise you, they'll inform the Resistance who can get you out of Paris and over to the Allies.'

'The French! Are you crazy? They'll have me strung up.'

'Not if they're expecting you, they won't.'

'How…'

'Never you mind. Trust me, you don't want to know a fraction of what I do and how I do it. But you'll be bloody grateful if it gets you off the hook, won't you?'

Von Kettler nodded, impressed. Berner was back on form.

'You could betray me at any time, couldn't you, Berner?'

'And you, likewise, so we work as a team from now on. Now, start getting that extra list ready and get your escape plan ready. I'll be in touch again soon.'

Berner reached into a pocket.

'What's this?' asked the General.

'It's a suicide tablet. Use it if you must. All you have to do is crush it between your back teeth. You'll be out in a second or two, dead in less than a minute. You won't feel a thing.'

Von Kettler studied the white pill now in his hand before putting it into a tunic pocket.

'I suppose I ought to thank you for this,' he said slowly, getting up.

'Stick to the plan and you'll be fine. You won't need what I've just given you.'

The General looked genuine when he thanked Berner before walking away, subdued.

What was annoying Berner was how quickly, how easily, Von Kettler spewed up his secrets. If Von Kettler was put under real interrogation, he'd sing like a canary in no time.

It was clearer to him than ever. Berner had two options: spring Von Kettler from the Hotel Majestic, or kill him.

Tuesday

Not overly pleased to be back in Paris, Eve dangled one leg over the other, sipped ersatz coffee, and cast her mind back to a farm near Orléans and Jules. She smiled playfully to herself.

She looked up to watch Berner walk towards her with a big smile on his face. He kissed each cheek and then took a seat at the café table. Eve ordered more coffee.

Berner beamed a smile but Eve detected a nervousness in his voice. 'It's good to have you back, Eve. You look great, by the way.'

'Thank you. It's good to have you out of jail, Walter.'

'Yes and it's great to be out. Gave me quite a turn when they came to arrest me, as you can no doubt imagine. I really couldn't believe it. I thought they'd got me for a moment. I must have been sat in that cell for a few hours before it started to become clear that I was not under arrest for … our activities but because of everything else that was happening that day. My God, Eve, I was dreading it, the thought of an SS interrogation. I just kept hoping upon hope that you were out of Paris and safe.'

'I know. You'll be pleased to hear I was out in no time; you need not have worried. So come on then, what happened? You getting arrested like that frightened the daylights out of me.'

'Are we being listened to?' asked Berner, checking

around.

'Definitely not.'

Berner leaned forward. 'The German Army tried to kill Hitler on Thursday.'

Eve swore.

'I know, it's shocking but true. Von Kettler thought it might have been the SS behind it all, so he had them all arrested. I'm an SS officer, so I was rounded up like all the others. That explains my arrest. Thankfully, I was released only a few hours later but I assume you were well and truly gone by then.'

Eve looked incredulous. 'They tried to kill him here, in Paris?'

'No! Hitler was out East of Berlin. The plan had always been that if there was an attempt to take power, the Army's job was to take control and defend the big cities like this one.'

Berner let it all sink in.

'Since then, it's been pretty lonely for me here, so yes, it is very good to see you. And I'm glad you got away all right: the plan worked, eh?'

'It certainly did, Walter, I got a long way from here very quickly. Had a little holiday, actually. I could have stayed there for ever if I'm honest.'

'Well, you look good on it. Refreshed.'

'Something like that, Walter, something like that.'

Berner put his newspaper on the table. 'Rolled up in here are some new travel documents for you to replace the ones you used the other day, and addresses of new safe houses should you need them. You'll need a new safe house to run to if I get arrested again. The travel office rubber stamp I gave you is still valid, they haven't changed them for a while, so you should be able to stamp all your papers just fine.'

'Thank you, that's very thoughtful. No chance of me being able to go back where I went last time then?'

'Of course not,' smiled Berner.

Eve's eyebrows dropped. 'You don't normally talk about escape plans first. What's the matter?'

Both stopped talking to let a waiter set their drinks down.

'Something's come up. It could be good, it could be trouble, but either way I'm going to need your help.'

'Here we go again.'

Berner smiled. 'You're still due to broadcast tomorrow night, aren't you? OK. So also rolled up in that newspaper is information regarding troop movements towards St-Lo. It may be of some use to the Americans there.'

'All right. But that's not all, is it?'

Berner smiled. 'You know me too well. The truth is, I need your help in arranging an escape.'

'Yours? Mine?'

'The Military Governor of Paris. He wants to defect.'

Eve sipped her coffee slowly. 'This is an afternoon full of surprises, Walter.'

'I know, I'm sorry.'

'Anything else whilst you're at it?'

'As a matter of fact, yes. I need you to get in touch with your old friend Oberon. We're going to need his help with the defection.'

'That, Walter, is the worst idea I've heard for a long time.'

'I know, sorry again. That you two don't get on is both obvious and understandable and I know how much you despise his little helper, Franck. But the truth is I need to stage something very big here in Paris as a distraction and that's where they come in.'

Eve waited patiently for Berner to stop talking. 'It's not that, Walter. What I don't think you know is how much Oberon wants you dead.'

'*What?*'

'The day you were arrested, Thursday? Well, just as you turned up at that café, I had to make sure his little helper - as you called him - didn't put a bullet straight through your head.'

It was Berner's turn to look incredulous.

Eve went on: 'Oberon doesn't know what I know about you. He considers you just another spy-catcher and that makes you his worst kind of enemy. I get the impression he's quite keen on getting even with as many of you lot as he can before the Allies arrive.'

'I don't know what to say, Eve, I'm stunned.'

'That's why I'm here, Walter, to keep you alive.'

Berner started thinking; Eve knew at times like this, it was best to let him crack on.

Coming back from his thoughts, Berner said, 'You know what, Eve, I think my new enemy Oberon could still come in quite handy. Sorry, but I still need you to talk to him. I think he will need significantly less encouragement to help me now than I thought he would.'

'Because…?'

Berner quickly explained his plan. Eve's leg began to bounce playfully once more. Once the plan was agreed between them, Berner ordered more coffee and the two of them chatted like old friends, enjoying the sunshine.

* * *

'No way, it's too dangerous,' protested Oberon, waving his hands as if to make Eve's plan go away like a bothersome wasp.

'The Allies are attacking again in the west. They'll be here soon enough, which means people like Berner will be heading East soon. If you really do want to get at them, you need to get them while you can. I say it again, you can do what you like to Berner once I've got the man I want away. Berner's the only one who can get this part of the mission done and I need you to help him help me.'

'That's what you've been up to?'

'I'm sorry?'

'You disappeared on Thursday, just like he did.'

Eve breathed in patiently. 'I went on the run and who would blame me in circumstances like that. He, on the other hand, was arrested and locked up with a load of other SS types. But you're right, whilst I was away, I got briefed up for this particular job.' That's eighty percent true, thought Eve, which in the circumstances was more than good enough.

'One week you're telling me not to kill him, the next week you are. You're making no sense, Eve.'

'That's the sort of work we do,' said Eve,

sufficiently nonchalant to be convincing. 'Once the war in the west is won, you have to ask what value a counter-intelligence type like Berner would have to us? Anyway, I'm sure London's looking to the future and doesn't want ex Nazis on its hands. Having people like him around could prove … unhelpful.'

Oberon took this in and looked to believe it.

'But Eve, you don't know what else is beginning to take shape here in the city. The Resistance are almost ready to take over.'

'Great, let's use that as cover.'

'Just hold on. I don't want to jeopardise Resistance plans by setting off an ambush in the middle of Paris. The Germans are still strong enough here to take hostages and kill many as a punishment. Trains with cattle trucks full of people are still leaving Paris, remember?'

'How ready are the people for revolution do you think?' whispered Eve.

'That's the problem, the Resistance is ready, but the people are not. Not yet anyway. A few of us are saying we should wait until the Americans and the British get close enough to the city before it begins. They're getting closer and closer. The Free French want a Frenchman to take over Paris, not some American. But whoever is going to be in charge when the time comes, the city is not ready for it yet. A lot of people still think it too early, too risky to turncoat. And then there are the Germans, of course. No one knows what they will do when they're forced to leave. They could raze this city to the ground.'

Eve was determined to enlist Oberon whether he wanted to help or not. 'If hostages were taken, though, that may incite the city to revolt and perhaps all of France with it, to save them?'

'Maybe, Eve, let's not plan on getting lots of citizens rounded up by the SS or the *Milice*, just to spark a civil war, eh?' He grimaced. 'As soon as the *Milice* think their days are numbered, they'll just start machine-gunning at will. They're the only ones with nothing to lose.'

After a while contemplating, Oberon said, 'Eve, I'm just not doing it. Sorry but that's that.'

But Eve was determined to get her way. 'Well, maybe right now's too early for an attack like that - but what about a bomb?'

'Eve, it's still too-'

'How's Franck?'

'What?' said Oberon, surprised.

'Still difficult to control? Someone you could do without?'

'He's someone certainly *you* could do without.' Oberon knew only too well how Eve hated Franck's lecherous glares. 'If you think I would sacrifice Franck for you and your German friend, you've got another thing coming. I admit, he's not been good to you, but he's been good to me and loyal all the way since I got here in, what, 1940? Sorry Eve, but I won't do that and … now I come to think of it, I think you making a suggestion like that means we should break contact, you and me. From now on, you're on your own.'

'Not so hasty, Oberon.'

There was a real aggression in Eve's voice and

Oberon picked it up instantly.

'You're forgetting where my orders are coming from. London accepts people may withdraw from taking part in an operation for reasons of personal security, but you're refusing to help get a key German officer over to our side when the war here is almost over. Think about it. Von Kettler's got all the German plans in his head. *We've got to get him out.* And let's face it, what's your future going to be once Paris is liberated? You won't be so valuable to London then yourself, will you? And just in case you've forgotten,' she persisted, ramming her point home, 'my German colleague is a counter intelligence officer and would gladly arrest you, Franck, in fact the whole lot of you, before he heads off back to Berlin. It's only me that's stopped him from doing it so far. So best you find a way of helping or maybe London can be convinced we don't need you any more.'

'You wouldn't!'

Eve just stared straight into Oberon's eyes.

Oberon blinked first and bit a nail. 'All right. I'll think of something but because London says so, not you. I have my future to think of and for that I will need London's help one day soon. My people have survived this long and I want them to survive the war, especially now we're so close to the end. Come back on Thursday. I should have something for you by then.'

Eve knew from Berner that there were probably a few more days before they needed to get Von Kettler out, so she acceded gracefully. 'That's fine by me. Same time Thursday, then?'

'Same time, Thursday,' said Oberon dejectedly.

At eight on the dot, Eve started to send her message. She was an old hand at it now, tapping away at the Morse key in bursts, and was done in good time. She wound in the wire antenna, locked everything away and went down from the roof to share a bottle of wine with her old friend, Lotti. Eve was safe living here with Lotti all the time Berner kept it that way. The SS probably knew where Eve was staying and who with but all the time she was considered to be an agent of Berner's, she could enjoy life as much as she liked.

'All done?' asked Lotti as Eve closed the roof hatch behind her.

'All done.' Eve gratefully took a sip from the glass Lotti passed her.

Lotti smiled. 'One day, Eve, this war is going to end and all those German soldiers are going to leave their Lotti behind.'

'Only to be replaced by a load of British and Americans.'

'And French of course. Hm. Americans, Eve, think about it. They're all big and tall, and we could do with some big spenders around here once the Germans go. Get me back to the lifestyle I was accustomed to before this all started, eh?'

'Aren't you worried, Lotti? I mean, being seen with all those Germans?'

'Not in the slightest. I'm doing my bit for the war, am I not? I'm housing a British secret agent and telling her all the little secrets those German officers tell me in the small hours. You should write me up for a medal for what I have been through for France.'

'Who you've been through, more like.'

They both burst into laughter. Eve knew this was her moment.

'Do you know what, Lotti, perhaps we should arrange one last big party before the Germans go. A final blowout to shift all that Champagne they've got. Let's face it, they won't leave it behind when they go, so we should lighten their load for them, no?'

Lotti had arranged plenty of parties for the senior German staff and their more aristocratic flunkies since the occupation began. She had been hitting all the high spots in town, even bars the Germans usually reserved only for themselves. They were always willing to make exceptions for someone like Lotti and her friend, Eve.

'You sure?' replied Lotti, 'I doubt the German Army will want to celebrate its own defeat, forced to leave Paris of all places.'

'Ask them. But if you'd like to do something, I suggest going to the Hotel Majestic again and sometime soon.'

'Do you know something I don't, Agent Eve?'

'I know a lot of things you don't. That's why we're both still alive.'

Lotti took a moment to appraise her housemate. 'Do you know, before the war you were just happy to go along with the crowd but never really draw attention to yourself. Now look at you. Walking tall, calling the shots and winning a war.'

Eve shrugged casually.

'I don't know what you're up to, Eve, but I'm as game as ever. I'll call the boys tomorrow and tell them they need some cheering up.'

'Perfect,' said Eve. Walter will be pleased, she thought.

Alfred Bohler watched the seconds tick away and then, on time, his headphones crackled a little as he heard Eve starting to send her routine Tuesday message. He recognised the cadence of her dots and dashes and jotted down the message as it came in through his left earphone. A little while later, his right ear took in London's reply.

Content the messaging was complete, Bohler took his notepad to the main desk, signed out Eve's file and decoded both messages.

Eve's message began by saying how the reinforcement of the 272nd Infantry Division was cancelled owing to concerns about a potential American advance from St-Lo, where the German line currently looked vulnerable. Then it got more interesting, as Eve said how she had chanced upon an unexpected target of significant intelligence value that she may need help in getting to British lines and that 'S', whoever this 'S' was, should stand by.

'Significant intelligence value,' said Bohler to himself. 'What's Berner up to now, the old fox?'. Bohler had helped Berner infiltrate an entire British and Dutch network of agents, using every trick in the book. It looked very much like the master was up to his old tricks again. *Dangle the prize, Bohler,* he remembered Berner saying, *dangle the prize right in front of their eyes, they can't resist it!* Bohler shook his head and smiled.

'Berner's dangling Rommel again, I'll bet.'

Bohler turned his head back to his report which he soon finished. Having cast another appreciative eye over the photograph of Eve, he updated her index card and put all the documents back into the file.

He stood up and passed the file to the waiting librarian.

'How are you settling in, Wolfgang? You've been here, what, two or three days now?' asked Bohler.

'Three days,' said Wolfgang cheerily. 'I'm getting used to the city now and I like being here, and a few more of the old team from Germany have arrived. It's good to have them around. *Standartenführer* Lemke likes to take his team with him wherever he goes, so here we are. I am enjoying being in Paris even if I can't see it: there's not one window to look out of in this basement.'

'You're right, we don't see a thing down here but in so many ways we see everything, don't we? It's such a privilege to work here.'

'It is,' smiled Wolfgang politely.

'I'd best be going, I'll see you later,' said Bohler.

'Good night.' Wolfgang watched Bohler lollop along the corridor and turn to climb the stairs. Once he was certain Bohler had clocked off and away, Wolfgang opened the file and, checking no one was watching, he read Eve's message:

REINFORCEMENT OF THE 272 INF DIV CANCELLED OWING TO POSSIBLE AMERICAN ADVANCE SOUTH FROM ST-LO. GERMAN LINE ASSESSED TO BE THIN THERE. HAVE CHANCED UPON AN UNEXPECTED TARGET OF SIGNIFICANT REPEAT SIGNIFICANT INTELLIGENCE VALUE. I MIGHT NEED HELP IN GETTING TARGET TO BRITISH LINES. STAMD BY.

In the margin, Bohler had written 'Target referred to is probably ROMMEL.'

Wolfgang pulled a notebook from his draw and copied out the last sentences of Eve's message and Bohler's comment. He'd made many notes since taking up a job spying on the Bohler and his friends but this had the feel of something important about it. As soon as his shift was over, Wolfgang grabbed his notebook and went straight to the Hotel Majestic.

'What's this, Wolfgang?' asked Lemke an hour or so later, annoyed at having been pulled away from dinner.

'I don't know for certain but it's possible the Allies know *Generalfeldmarschall* Rommel's whereabouts and they may be planning to steal him back to their lines.'

Lemke briefly laughed out loud.

'Show me that,' he said, holding his hand out for

the file.

'"Probably" it says here, Wolfgang. Look: *probably* Rommel.' said Lemke.

'That's quite correct,' said Wolfgang. 'I'm sure France is teeming with items and people of high intelligence value right now. How or why the WNV/FU have come up with Rommel, well, that I don't know. There's been no other mention of this that I have seen. But it's not just the message or what it seems to be saying. It's Bohler.'

'Who or what is a Bohler?' asked Lemke, springing up on his toes.

'Well, Sir, Bohler is a who, a *Gefreiter*, one of the radio watchmen and he is the one who wrote down that it's probably Rommel.'

Lemke looked puzzled: 'Do you know why *Gefreiter* Bohler, a Corporal, would be making assumptions like this, about a Field Marshal?' Lemke paused. 'But Wolfgang, you wouldn't have me stood here talking about the wild ravings of an *Abwehr* Corporal for nothing though, would you? Did the *Funkmessstelle* pick this up?'

Wolfgang shuffled uncomfortably. 'It would appear not.'

Lemke pushed his lips together in frustration. It looked like the *Abwehr* was doing better than the SS.

'If I may,' Wolfgang was still looking pretty uncomfortable, 'this *Gefreiter*, Bohler, isn't like your average radio operator, I think that's why this message stands out to me.'

Lemke visibly stiffened.

'Please, bear with me,' said Wolfgang, 'what I mean is that in the short time I have been down in that basement, I get the impression Bohler could be pretty much *any* rank. He sits and listens with those earphones on and he detects Allied agents in a way I haven't seen before. He's good. I've watched him mimic them when broadcasting in Morse, which is, as I'm sure you are already aware.'

'Get to the point.'

'Bohler is a first class watchman and he used to work for Colonel Berner. Berner's a bit of a hero to the boys and girls of the WNV/FU and Bohler was one of Berner's radio operators in the *Englandspiel* of '42 and '43. I suppose that's why I say Bohler's observations stand out to me. Anyone working for Berner you've had me tail in the past has usually been a bit special, haven't they?'

Lemke's eyes seem to turn to steel.

'Tell *Gefreiter* Bohler I would very much like to see him. Now. My office.'

Lemke stopped to think quickly before going on: 'Also, go and find Sauer, he'll be in one of the bordellos by now. One of the licensed ones no doubt. Find him and tell him I want him in a little earlier than usual tomorrow.'

'Or should I ask him? After all, he is a *Brigadeführer*?'

'Of course,' said Lemke remembering himself, 'please ask the *Brigadeführer* to very kindly get to work early tomorrow morning.'

Wednesday

Wolfgang was right, thought Lemke to himself as he studied the soldier stood in front of him, Bohler was no average *Gefreiter*. It was certainly not usual for a corporal to not be available to someone like him until the morning.

Bohler was tall and had had one Bratwurst too many over the years, by the look of it. Lemke marvelled at how such thick, round lenses could stay fixed in their spectacle frames.

Bohler stood in front of Lemke's desk and fiddled with the peak of his field cap, which looked like it had had very little wear.

Lemke pushed the WNV/FU file across his desk at Bohler.

'You took this message and you made these notes?'

'May I?' Bohler gestured towards the file for a closer look.

Lemke rolled his eyes at Sauer. 'Be my guest, *Gefreiter.*'

Bohler squared his glasses on his nose and read, his head quite close to the file. With a smile hinting at self-satisfaction, Bohler said that yes, it was he who took intercepted the message last night and did indeed make those notes. Bohler had a deep but soft voice and sounded like a university professor, or a monk.

Not your average *Gefreiter.*

Bohler's smile changed to a full beam.

'Yes, Sir, I deciphered that message yesterday and made the note about Rommel.'

Lemke was surprised to find himself smiling back. 'May I please ask why it is you're smiling so much?'

Bohler beamed back, 'It's Colonel Berner isn't it? This has the Colonel's hallmarks all over it and you want me to tell you what he's up to?'

Lemke shifted in his chair. 'Well, yes.'

The smile continued. 'Ah, good,' he nodded, pleased to have had his recognition of Berner confirmed. 'And that's where I'm going to have to disappoint you. Sorry, Sir, but as I'm sure you are already well aware, I used to work for the Colonel. A real professional and a pleasure to work with if you don't mind me saying. You have to admire his mind, don't you think?'

Lemke clearly wanted just the edited version of this story.

Bohler continued at a faster pace: 'Yes, I know Colonel Berner's methods intimately, but I'm very sorry, I'm forbidden from saying anything about his operations without his *express* permission. But I'm sure that can be arranged if required. He's a very amenable chap, is the Colonel.'

Bohler looked sincere - the kind of sincerity that is polite but utterly uncompromising.

Lemke breathed in, struggling to keep his composure. 'Well, I'm so very sorry, my dear Bohler, to tell you that Colonel Berner is not available to give that express permission you so desire.'

'Oh,' said Bohler, 'that gives you quite a problem,

Sir, doesn't it?'

Under normal circumstances, Lemke would have threatened Bohler with violence, but Lemke felt somehow disarmed by Bohler's intense *reasonableness*.

'Bohler, you have heard, haven't you, about obeying orders?'

'Of course, I'm obeying them now. Express permission, that's my orders, Sir. So I would need *Abwehr* approval to proceed and, forgive me, but you are wearing a Nazi party lapel badge and I don't know for certain but I think you are *Standartenführer* Horst Lemke. That means you are not an *Abwehr* officer, you're SS or SD. I'm sure you understand how security is maintained in operations such as this and my orders are very clear. I'm so sorry and I do hope you understand my predicament.'

'I do. Operations such as what?'

'Ha ha, very funny, Sir, but I'm not saying a word,' said Bohler, nodding warmly at what he considered a joke.

Lemke could not help but notice Bohler's earnestness. Intelligent, loyal and good at his job. Lemke looked over at Sauer and felt a deep sense of depression.

Then, quite unexpectedly, Lemke sat upright in his chair and changed tone.

'Bohler, let me solve both our problems in one go for you. For your painstaking work and, being one of Berner's specials, you are to be transferred immediately to the *Funkmessstelle*. They get all the good cases these days and by the sounds of it could do with making some improvements.

'I will see to it that you get all of the most

interesting cases to monitor. That means you would now work *for me*, you understand?'

Bohler understood and shifted uncomfortably in his boots.

'The only real way for a soldier to beat bureaucracy is with bureaucracy, I've learned,' Lemke continued. 'Colonel Berner works for me as well, so from now on, you both will. The old team will be getting back together, which is good. Colonel Berner's work interests me *greatly*. He's a busy man, so keep me personally informed of his messages to and from London via Eve.'

'But I-' Bohler tried to interrupt.

'Oh, and I forgot to say congratulations, Bohler. You have been promoted to *SS-Scharführer*, or Sergeant if you insist, and your transfer to the *Funkmessstelle* is effective as of now. Congratulations, and welcome to the SS.' Lemke stepped forwards to shake hands.

'These are your orders?'

'Yes, Bohler.'

Bohler was clearly not overly impressed with this news but went on to say: 'That does change things, doesn't it, Sir. But I will, however, first need to return to my desk to collect my books and reference material. Also, I assume that file you have on your desk there will need to be returned to the WNV/FU library? Anything less would be quite improper. I would like you to arrange for a copy to be sent to my new office. And thank you for the promotion. Frau Bohler at least will be very pleased.' He turned to leave.

Lemke realised that a very newly promoted

Sergeant had just given him, *him*, instructions. 'One last thing, Bohler, before you go, if you don't mind.'

'Yes, Sir,' said Bohler turning back.

'Frau Bohler won't live another week unless you tell me now why you wrote 'probably Rommel' on that file entry. So best you get talking. Right now.'

'Sir, this is most irregular.'

'I don't care.'

'You have made that obvious, Sir. You really are not willing to negotiate on this, are you?'

Lemke just glared.

'I see. All right then. You're quite sure I now work for the *Funkmessstelle?* Good. Then it's very simple, actually, Sir, if you don't mind me saying. You see back in, now let me see, January, this year, Berner recruited Agent Eve - that's her portrait there—' Bohler smiled. '- to be his go-between with London by using Rommel as bait. Berner said that, to prove his reliability as a source of good intelligence, he would arrange for Eve to see Rommel up close at exactly the time and place Berner said he would be there. Eve made the rendezvous, Rommel arrived on time – anything to help a fellow *Wurttemberger* like himself – and Eve was hooked. Simple.

'So, in my estimation, Berner may be dangling Rommel like bait once again. This time to convince the British to do something else. It has to be something important. London would love to have the Desert Fox in their possession, of course they would. What a propaganda coup that would be? Rommel is a great general and a threat to their invasion plans, has to be. Maybe Colonel Berner wants something really important from the Allies and he's baiting them again. Information perhaps, *plans*. As I say, this sort of thing has worked for him before; I can't see any reason why he wouldn't try it again if he felt he could get away with it.'

Lemke nodded his thanks.

'Sir, if that will be all?'

'When does Eve next broadcast?'

'Tomorrow, Sir. Her routine is Sundays, Tuesdays and Thursdays at 8pm. I have not routinely listened into her messages, but the file suggests that with only a couple of exceptions, she's minute-perfect every time.'

'Thank you, *Scharführer* Bohler, and yes, that will be all.'

Bohler nodded at the promotion, began to turn and then paused. 'And Frau Bohler?'

'Off the hook completely.'

Bohler was through the doors before Lemke could change his mind.

Sauer pushed himself off the wall and sat down opposite Lemke.

'So we need to protect the Field Marshal whilst he's recovering?' Sauer asked.

'Of course. I mean, Berner's not stupid: he's not going to actually give them Rommel, is he? But I don't want the British getting ideas. I'm assuming, Sauer, you haven't paid too much attention to the minute details to Berner's counterintelligence work in the past? He tells you what London has told him and you leave it at that?'

'Yes.' Sauer felt chided. 'I did try asking him once and he made it clear he doesn't share his agents with anyone. He's still smarting about having all his agents killed in Holland. And,' Sauer shifted uncomfortably in his seat, 'it was the SS that killed them.'

'What Berner gets in return from London, is it good?'

'It was never specific, as far as I could tell. Berner was never be able to tell me that such and such an American division will attack at such and such a place on such and such a day. Nothing like that. It's always *suggestive*. Something like 'agents being sent to Cherbourg, Tours, Montpellier …' that sort of thing. Sure enough, sometime soon after messages like that came in, there was a battle, or the Resistance did something big. So all Berner can give us is a suggestion that something in a certain area is about to happen. As I said, vague. It's more strategic, than tactical.'

'Those last words were Berner's, weren't they?'

Sauer looked embarrassed. 'Yes.'

'It's a good job I'm here, isn't it, Sauer? To do the thinking.'

Sauer obviously took that to be the rhetorical question it was and left it.

'I can't ask Berner directly what he's up to, he'd be instantly – and correctly – suspicious. No, we will use Bohler to monitor his old boss but make sure Bohler thinks this as more a *celebration* of Berner's work, not an investigation.'

Sauer's head shot up.

'That's right,' continued Lemke, 'you and I need to keep a very careful eye on Walter Berner from now on.'

'Because?'

'Because Rommel isn't the only 'target of high intelligence value' Berner knows, is he? The other one is Von Kettler.'

Thursday

Oberon hadn't changed, he still looked like a bag of nerves whilst Eve sat opposite him, sipping her coffee calmly. She saw how Oberon's fingernails had been bitten right back again.

'I can give you the distraction you want but I don't like it, I still don't think the timing's right,' he said, having checked around for anyone listening a few times more.

Eve overplayed it. 'Oh, thank you, thank you so much. I'm very grateful for this, as it's so important.'

'I understand London thinks it's important,' he said haughtily. Eve took that to mean that Oberon didn't. 'What makes this a little easier for me, Eve, is the liberation is about to start. Of Paris.'

Eve put her cup down. 'Meaning?'

Oberon checked around for listeners again. 'The Americans are breaking out. The Germans are being slaughtered near Falaise, the British are well out of Caen and getting a move on at last. Eve, they're on their way *here*. The Germans moved their women soldiers west yesterday, and some supply troops have gone as well. The Germans are getting ready to leave.'

'So…?'

'We think it's likely the sort of distraction you have in mind might trigger the people to come out onto the streets thinking the liberation has begun. If we fire the starting pistol too early, the fighting will start, the Germans will fight us and there won't be any Resistance fighters left to hand the city over to the Americans when they get here. I can have your distraction go off for you, but it needs to be well timed. I'm not taking chances on this and so this part is non-negotiable.'

'Fair enough.'

It was clear from Oberon's fidgeting that he had more to say.

'The Resistance is almost ready to start the uprising. When the Americans are about 70-80 kilometres away, that is when it will begin. That is when you can have your distraction.'

'That's a very accurate figure, seventy to eighty.'

'It means the Americans could be with us in a day, maybe two. We think we have enough weapons to hold out that long. We don't want what happened in Warsaw to happen here. We've been stock-piling it, but we will need a lot more ammunition.'

This is where I come in, thought Eve.

Oberon continued: 'I've been asking London for ammunition continually. My problem is that the Germans around Paris are starting to dig in near my landing grounds. I can't get anything in by air anymore. You can't drive out without a permit and the Germans are deliberately changing the format of those permits every day so we can't forge them. In other words, Eve, I want you to tell London to get ammunition to us as a first priority. This is my pre-condition for giving you what you want. They can have their victory parade later.'

'I can ask for that, of course.'

'And remind them, Eve, that I'm no communist. There's plenty of them here wanting to take over the city and France with it. I can help you lot stop that. So if I get what I want, you'll get what you want. You see, I think all the clues are that the Germans want to fight it out. Trucks of explosives were dropped off at the Engineer barracks last night. Tons of the stuff. They're getting ready to blow this place sky high.'

Eve looked around, her earlier exuberance wearing off.

'So let me get this right,' she said carefully. 'You provide me a distraction near the Hotel Majestic, on a date to be agreed. Meanwhile, I ask the Allies to fight their way into the city carrying truckloads of ammunition just for you, not the communists.'

Oberon hesitated before smiling weakly. 'You get to the point very quickly, Eve, don't you?'

'I do. Now, tell me all about this distraction you've got planned out for me.'

'All right, Eve, we think it needs to come in two parts...'

* * *

'What's this?' asked Berner as Eve slid a piece of card across the table, parking it beside his coffee cup.

'I'm inviting you to a leaving party,' replied Eve convivially.

'Who's leaving?' he asked.

'You are.'

'What?'

'Not just you,' Eve smiled, 'all of you. All you Germans. On your way back east.'

'I'm sorry, Eve, but I just don't understand.'

'You remember my friend, Lotti?'

'Eve, every officer in Paris remembers Lotti.'

'Her, exactly. I've asked her to convince a few of the captains and majors to run a party at the Hotel Majestic. Have a bit of a blow out before the Allies arrive. If we have the party on Saturday night, there should still be enough of you lot around to make it worthwhile.'

'I thought all these parties would have stopped.'

Berner still didn't quite understand how a functioning military headquarters could still host such shindigs. Keeping the word 'Hotel' in the title probably had something to do with it: once a hotel, always a hotel; once a ballroom, always a ballroom.

'And you say we're leaving?'

'Only a matter of time, Walter, and I think I've judged the mood of the staff well, from what Lotti has since told me. They need perking up before they pack up. No one has said it directly, it seems, but with Von Kettler under house arrest and the SS watching every move the Army makes, the atmosphere is tense.'

Berner simply nodded. 'That sums up the atmosphere nicely, I think.'

'You're in there quite a bit, the Majestic. What do you think?'

'It's a powder keg, Eve.'

'Good. Then let's light the fuse. I have our distraction all booked. It'll happen the night of the party; catch 'em with their arms on the bar.'

'Oberon agreed then?'

'He took a bit of convincing. Initially, I offered you as bait, but I don't think he's that interested in killing you any more. He has bigger things on his mind. Things like liberation.'

Eve went on to say what Oberon had said in a different café earlier. Berner was impressed.

'Saturday night then?' he asked, turning the invite so he could read it.

'Saturday night.'

'How did Lotti get into all this in the first place?'

'Lotti lives for high-society events, she's the light every party needs. She was like this when she was a student and she's never going to change. She's already looking forward to giving the Americans a jolly good hosting.'

'You modern girls, eh?'

Eve smiled. Her foot wagged cheerily again.

'Well, it would seem you have arranged for a party none of us will forget in a hurry, thank you. You are very good at this game, aren't you? At this rate, you'll soon be better at all this than me, if you're not already.'

'I'm enjoying playing my part, Walter, that's all. I'm happy doing my bit in bringing about the end of this war.'

'And what then, Eve?'

Eve stopped and went into a faraway look. 'I don't know, something … peaceful, something where I can be out in the open any time I like.'

'Or more of this?' asked Berner optimistically. 'You're good at it. I'm sure we could work together again in the future.'

'We could,' said Eve without committing. 'The problem is that I'm a French-speaker, whereas I doubt you'll need someone who can speak much French in the near future. Russian perhaps…'

Berner smiled. 'Could you learn German?'

'I could certainly give it a go. I did a little at school, but Germans weren't that popular in Paris then either.'

'Well if ever you want to come to Germany and work with me after the war, I would be delighted.'

The smile on Berner's face told Eve what he had just said was true, but Eve had no real time for the future.

'Are you going to tell Von Kettler?' she asked.

'No.' Berner returned to business with a snap. 'If he changes his routine or starts acting strange, Lemke is likely to pick it up. The General has been told what to do if he is instructed to move immediately. Telling him anything else is too dangerous at the moment. No, it's best we keep him totally ignorant for the time being.'

'You're the boss,' said Eve smiling as she adjusted her sunglasses.

Eve and Berner sat for the next hour chatting. Berner would ask her questions about her youth, growing up, boyfriends, university and Eve would merrily chatter away. He barely spoke about himself at all, happy just listening to Eve and taking it all in.

Having both had their fill of ersatz coffee, Eve got up to get ready for her broadcast, carrying Berner's newspaper with the message she was to send inside it.

Berner knew she needed to go but he did not want

her to. Instead he just wanted to spend the afternoon talking freely with her. He watched her go with a smile on her face, ready to plan a party, an attack and the first moves of liberating the city.

The big issues seemed unimportant right now. Right now, his head was filled purely with the woman striding confidently off to the Metro station in the sunshine.

* * *

Scharführer Bohler stroked the shiny new chevrons on his arm as he waited for the seconds until 8pm to tick by. His SS uniform hadn't arrived yet and so Bohler had the misfortune of really standing out from the crowd. He felt very new and his colleagues were keeping their distance. They definitely did not like how Bohler had come across from the WNV/FU. In their opinion the signals intelligence were poor relations, only to be given a special assignment by Lemke of all people. His new colleagues, thought Bohler, really did look down their nose at him.

Bohler heard the crackle in his earphone and picked up his pencil.

And there was Eve, exactly on time, tapping out her callsign. He had already come to recognise the patterns in Eve's signalling, the beat that she used to keep time for the dots and dashes. That beat was like a fingerprint - everyone's was different - and he knew instantly it was Eve pressing that Morse key and no one else. He scribbled down the letters in the five-letter groups Eve sent them in.

London's response did not take much de-coding, it was very short: 'Roger, out.'

So this was not a radio conversation, this was a message going one way which meant it was something for London to think about. He set to decoding, but it was not as exciting as he thought it would be.

MOOD IN PARIS CHANGING AS AMERICAN FORCES APPROACH. ENGINEERS HAVE RECEIVED MORE EXPLOSIVES AND TROOPS IN SURROUNDING AREAS ARE DIGGING IN ON MAIN ROADS. MORE TROOPS SENT EAST. TO FALAISE? SOME NON-FIGHTING TROOPS AND CLERKS HAVE BEGUN TO MOVE WEST.

HIGH VALUE TARGET READY TO MOVE ON INSTRUCTEONS.

Eve's deliberate spelling mistake was there, fourth to last letter of the final word, same every time.

Lemke stood over Bohler's shoulder. 'Was that Eve broadcasting?'

The legs of his chair scraped noisily over the floor as Bohler stood up. 'No doubt about it.'

'Over here.' Lemke nodded his head towards the corner of the room where no one could overhear. Lemke took the message from Bohler and read it.

'The 'high value target' is being dangled once again, isn't it?'

'So it would seem.' Bohler was smiling appreciatively.

'What do you think is going on here, *Scharführer* Bohler?'

'I am not aware of extra explosives arriving in Paris but I think it's perfectly plausible that if that had happened, the Resistance would have seen it being delivered. So the first part of the message is not saying anything the British would not be capable of working out for themselves.'

'And the high value target?'

'One could only assume London is yet to take Berner's bait. Berner had once told me patience was one of the finest attributes of an intelligence officer, and Berner was one of the most patient men I have ever met. So, to me, this is classic Berner, if I may say so. He's playing it *very* patiently.'

'Thank you, Bohler. I am very glad we have a talent like you working for the SS now.' Lemke looked around the rest of the watchmen contemptuously. 'Right, I want you to record this message and get it filed.'

'Of course, Sir,' said Bohler taking back the sheet of paper with Eve's message on it.

Lemke turned to leave and then stopped himself. 'And Bohler,' he said loudly, 'that is an excellent piece of work, well done.'

'Thank you, Sir,' said Bohler. If the *Funkmessstelle* staff hated him when he had arrived, they really hated him now.

Bohler set to filing his report, banging away at the keys of the typewriter. As be prepared to write another line, he heard a faint crackle come from his earphones on the other desk. He leapt to his feet, grabbed the headphones and forced them onto his ears and caught only the last two letters of a word: O and W but he had heard enough to know that it had been Eve, not London, sending that message.

'Did anyone else hear that?' he shouted.

'What do you want now, golden boy?' replied a sarcastic voice.

'There was a transmission, just then! A very short one. Did anyone hear it? It's *very* important!'

'Sorry, we were told not to listen to the same frequencies as you. Secrecy and all that.'

Bohler very rarely swore but he did just then.

Friday

Sauer walked into Lemke's office in somewhat of a hurry.

Lemke looked up from reading a file, irritated at interruption. Irritated at Sauer in general, actually.

'Berner's just got back from the Hospital Du Vésinet. He's been to see Rommel.'

Lemke nodded his head slowly at the news. 'So what?'

Sauer looked puzzled. 'The high value target, it has to be Rommel. It all checks out, his driver – who's SS by the way – has it all detailed in his log and Berner was recorded by the hospital staff as having spent over an hour with the Field Marshal.' Sauer smiled desperately, seeking approval.

'You're not sure what this means, are you?' asked Sauer after a moment of pensive silence from Lemke.

'Well, it was hardly a secret visit, was it? What did they talk about whilst Berner was there? Don't tell me, you don't know that bit and didn't think to ask?'

Sauer bit his lip.

'I thought as much.' Lemke whispered something sharp and monosyllabic under his breath as he got to his feet and walked to the window. 'Berner goes in broad daylight, in full view of everyone, and you think Berner's up to no good.'

'I didn't say that, actually. You could be right,

maybe Berner has told his injured old friend that he's part of a clever ruse to draw British agents out from cover. But what if it's not? What if Rommel genuinely does want out and he's using Berner to book his ticket across the Channel for him? The attempt on the *Führer's* life has got a lot of our senior Generals on alert and maybe he's on the run.'

Lemke paused to think. Sauer was making very relevant points.

'Do you want me to bring Berner in for questioning?' asked Sauer.

Ah, thought Lemke to himself again, that flash of inspiration was short lived: Sauer was back to his usual self again, a blunt instrument in search of a bludgeoning.

'Sauer, think back to what Professor bloody Bohler said about Berner the other day. "*You have to admire his mind,*" is what he said. So you have to assume, Sauer that he's a damn sight cleverer than you. What are the options,' Lemke cogitated out loud. 'One, Berner's just gone to see an old mate in hospital. Just happens to be a Field Marshal but both Berner and Rommel are still very much on our side.'

Sauer nodded slowly.

'Two, Berner's telling his old mate he's being used to lure out British agents, in which case they're still both on our side; three, Berner is *actually* dangling Rommel out for the Brits because Berner's a double agent; four, Rommel has given up on fighting and wants the British to get him out of a suicide, in which case Berner and Rommel are for the firing squad; or five, Sauer - five is he's laying a very obvious smoke screen to protect someone else, like Von Kettler, in which case it's Berner and Von Kettler the firing squad's taking aim at, not Rommel.'

Sauer was impressed. 'That pretty much covers it.'

'The trouble, Sauer,' continued Lemke rocking on his toes again, 'is knowing which one of those options happens to be the truth.'

'That depends on whether you actually want to get to the truth or just declare your version of it. If you want rid of Von Kettler, Rommel, Berner or the whole lot, now's your chance. It doesn't take much to accuse someone of conspiracy around here right now, does it? An accusation is as good as saying guilty in the kind of show trial they'll get. Instead of proving your options, just eradicate them one at a time. It'll save having to investigate it.'

Lemke rocked gently, thinking. 'I'm not so sure killing everyone is what I want to do right now. So, for argument's sake, let's assume Berner happens to be one of the brightest officers the *Abwehr* ever had. In which case, whatever it is he's up to, he's got a plan and he's thought it through in minute detail.

'If he's got every move on the chessboard already worked out for himself, that means he's probably got his reaction to anything we are likely to do in reply worked out as well. If it's one of the other two, it may be a little easier to weed them out. Berner's probably the most difficult one of the lot because he's trained in subterfuge, pretty much wrote the textbook back in the twenties.

'We need to get the initiative back. Give them a bit of a shock. Whoever's up to no good, under the extra pressure, they might just do something they didn't think they'd have to and start making mistakes.'

'Assume someone's bluffing and call it, you mean?'

'Exactly.'

Invigorated, Lemke picked up the phone and asked to be connected to the RHSA in Berlin.

He covered the mouthpiece. 'You know what, Sauer? I think you've cracked it; I think calling everyone's bluff is what is needed here. Give the hornet's nest a good kicking. Watch this.'

Lemke's voice was steady and pure malice.

He navigated his way patiently through a long series of minions before being directly addressing the Chief of the Reich Main Security Office, the man second only to Heinrich Himmler. Lemke cleared his throat.

Sauer watched, spellbound.

'Sir, good afternoon. I need to speak to you about something important and highly sensitive. I assume this is a secure line and you have no one else with you?'

Lemke waited; clearly staff were in need of dismissing at the other end.

Prompted, Lemke made a start: 'I have good grounds for General Von Kettler and Field Marshal Rommel to be recalled to Berlin for questioning.'

The phone went quiet for a while. Sauer breathed out heavily, not really believing what he was hearing.

Eventually, Lemke replied: 'I want to see if they are in on the conspiracy to murder our *Führer*, Adolf

Hitler.'

A short pause.

'I cannot say for certain, Sir, but there is enough evidence to justify a recall now and perhaps enough for a trial later. If we surprise them, they may panic, make a mistake, and that could lead us to a conviction. If we leave them as they are, we may never know their true loyalties until it is too late.'

The voice at the other end asked questions.

'Are they really traitors?' replied Lemke. 'At the moment I do not know - but I have my doubts and in this game, that's often enough. However, my reason for my recall request, if I'm honest with you, Sir, is to attempt to trigger a panic amongst other conspirators. We could get a good deal more.'

Another longer pause.

'You have my full attention, Sir, what do you want me to do?'

Lemke uttered a few ah-huhs and mm-hmms to the instructions being given to him.

'Of course, Sir, I will comply as soon as I have word from you to proceed. One question, Sir, if I may. Will my instructions come from you or a deputy? ... Direct from you in person, Sir, of course.' Lemke stared in astonishment at Sauer. 'I understand, Sir. Thank you. *Heil Hitler.*' The phone went down.

'My God, Lemke, did you really just do that?'

Lemke looked at the phone, not really believing what had just happened.

'It so happens Rommel and Von Kettler were being considered for recall anyway. The RHSA don't care if they're guilty or not. Both have been observed voicing doubts about the Führer's conduct of the war. My call provides the pretext Berlin required for their ... disposal. Apparently, another Field Marshal has committed suicide today also. It appears, Sauer, that the Army is full of Generals focussed on saving their own skin rather than fighting the Allies, or taking the quick way out. He said it's no wonder the Allies are as close to Paris as they are.

'We are to wait for our orders but Von Kettler is to be recalled first, as soon as Berlin has had enough time to appoint his replacement. Rommel ... is more tricky: he's a household name across the world, not just Germany. A little more time is required to devise something for the Field Marshal to succumb to.'

'Like a fractured skull?'

'He already has one of those, Sauer. But don't worry, Berlin will come up with something very good, I'm sure. So for now, Sauer, you and I should leave those two to their fate and focus on the activities of Walter Berner. Get me his file and let's see how he reacts to the news when it gets out.'

'Do you really think he's up to no good?'

'No. But rule number one in this game is assume everyone's up to something all the time.'

'I'm not,' said Sauer.

Lemke smiled patiently. 'I know.'

Saturday

The sun rose over the Pantin marshalling yards to the now familiar murmur of people, hundreds of people, waiting for a train. But this was no ordinary train. The passengers had guessed their fate already and yet they stood, waiting. Sometimes a nose would be wiped, a sneeze, or a futile attempt made to stop a neighbour weeping.

The guards stood also, impassive and keeping their distance. They knew only too well, just like everyone else in Paris that morning, the war here would soon be over and the guards were keen to protect their identity. They wanted to enjoy the post-war peace and try to forget scenes such as this. Those in the queues were unlikely to get such an opportunity.

The railway track sang and the prisoners jolted as the train approached. As it got closer, the guards started herding the crowd towards an open area near the track. The prisoners were going to have to climb up into the trucks from the ground, not from a platform.

The prisoners were separated into groups, one for each truck. There seemed to be way too many people for the size of the train. All protests fell on distant, deaf ears. Passively, the prisoners waited. The train gently came to a halt, with the driver carefully avoiding eye contact with today's cargo.

Soldiers opened the truck doors and, shouted at

by the guards, the people began to help each other up and in. Standing room only. The people craned for a last look at Paris before the doors shut with a bang.

Then there was another bang, followed by another. Everyone seemed to stop, not quite comprehending. The guards looked around, confused.

Then someone from behind barked orders in German. Other voices could be heard coming from inside the trucks, pleading, moaning.

The guards began to shoot at something. The prisoners in the trucks began to scream, thinking it was them. A siren began to wail. Then all hell broke loose.

The air filled with the sound of automatic fire. Rounds ricocheted off the rails, the trucks, the air was suddenly full of sharp splinters.

Still the firing continued, getting closer to the train. The guards turned a machine gun on one of the trucks and began to fire indiscriminately into it.

Then a gang of Resistance fighters ran out into the open to shoot at the guards. The machine gunners, when the ammunition ran out, sprinted for their lives.

Then French voices began to scream. 'We are the Resistance! We are your rescuers! As soon as you can, run!'

The door of one of the trucks sprung open. The crowds lurched forward and people spilled out, landing on the stones. Arms and legs snapped in the confusion.

The people needed no encouragement. Those

who could, ran. Some turned to look for family members and friends, but the majority ran headlong towards Resistance fighters who were waving them through holes that had just been cut in the fence.

The guards put up a fight but as they'd only been given enough ammunition to herd prisoners, they soon ran out.

The resistance fighters, after years of occupation, were in no mood to accept surrenders.

Before long, only the dead and the dying remained.

* * *

Lemke was all smiles as he walked in.

'General Von Kettler, thank you for agreeing to see me. May I?'

Von Kettler gestured Lemke to a seat. Lemke was now in the habit of seeing him every morning, to vet the General's diary and check his orders. What was unusual was to have Lemke come in so early.

'You've heard about the incident at the marshalling yards, then?' asked the General.

'I have. I understand our troops are trying to round up as many prisoners as possible?'

'They have their work cut out, Lemke, to be honest. The French took two of our soldiers hostage. I've got the only reserve companies I have left going house to house to find them. Based on the reports coming in, the Resistance were uncommonly organized and were fully ready. They've shepherded prisoners into houses and warehouses all over the place. This was very well organised. To us, this marks a significant change in tactics, scale and audacity.'

Lemke nodded his agreement but Von Kettler noticed how he had a strange smile on his face.

The General continued a little hesitantly. 'Maybe we now have British and American agents in the city co-ordinating the attacks, that would explain it, or, perhaps worse, the Resistance have been planning this for a long time and this is how they start the uprising. The police are on strike, as is the Metro, I think Paris is about to turn on us.'

Von Kettler threw a pencil onto his desk. 'It could take days to get my men back but I don't think time is on our side any longer, do you?'

Lemke responded quite cheerily. 'Then we too will take hostages. Shall we say one thousand for every one of our soldiers taken?'

'Not again.'

'I'm sorry, General?'

'I have had to take hostages before and the soldiers, frankly, botched it. It was a slaughter.'

'So?'

'Taking and killing hostages doesn't instil fear, it instils *hate*. I don't want to give the locals more reason to rise up. More practically, perhaps, I need my soldiers to defend the city, not chase the dregs of your political prisoner list.'

'You're saying it's not a good time to take hostages when French terrorists are holding our soldiers at gunpoint?'

'What I'm saying is I need to get my soldiers back and get down to defending this city. Dealing with the locals will have to come second, unless of course you have some troops you could throw at this?'

'Of course! The *Milice*. Send Frenchmen to kill Frenchmen, leaving the Germans to defend what's left of their city. It has a poetic irony to it, don't you think? The *Milice* are desperate now. They all know the moment the Resistance get their hands on any of them, they're strung up. Their desperation makes the *Milice* even more dangerous than usual. Anyway,' continued Lemke, 'perhaps your lack of enthusiasm for teaching French terrorists a lesson is an indicator as to why it is time for you to go.'

Von Kettler's face drained of all colour instantly. 'I beg your pardon?'

'You must be for greater things, General, as you are being recalled to Berlin. With all possible speed.'

'Are you ordering me?' Von Kettler's voice trembled.

'The higher echelons of the Army are in some state of confusion at the moment, shall we say. Lots of senior people being arrested. I can only assume that means there's a space for you in Berlin. I thought you'd be pleased.'

'I will serve my country as best I can, of course, but these sort of orders normally come from the Army's headquarters direct. Not via, well, you.'

'As I say, the Army is in a state of disarray and so the SS take the steps necessary to maintain order.'

'When do I go?' asked the General.

'Your replacement has an appointment with the Führer this afternoon and will then be on the next train here. So I suppose you should get packed and be ready to go at about lunchtime tomorrow.'

'Where or to whom should I report when I get

there?'

'I expect you will be collected from the station, don't you?'

'And my family?' asked Von Kettler weakly.

'Will no doubt be pleased to see you,' lied Lemke.

'Who will replace me?'

'Möller. A good SS man. Now, if you'll excuse me, I will get the *Milice* ready for what might be their last hurrah.'

The huge doors were familiar to him but General Möller had never been inside before. Two guards in black uniforms stood at each side of a doorframe which must have been 4 or 5 metres high with a shield emblazoned with the initials AH on it.

Möller waited nervously outside for twenty minutes before being ushered closer to the massive doors. He tugged his jacket down, squared his tunic collar and wiped the toes of his boots down the back of his shins.

The doors swung open grandly. Some distance away, Hitler sat behind his desk. The room was mostly brown in colour; a couple of big oil paintings hung on the walls but otherwise, it was sparsely furnished. It was a room that ensured your attention was on the man at that desk, not the surroundings.

Möller's escort marched forward and Möller had to pace quickly to keep up. When his escorts halted smartly, Möller halted as smartly as he could.

Hitler scratched his handwriting across a document. Möller felt his pulse racing as he waited.

'Möller, you are to go to Paris and take over from that traitor Von Kettler,' the *Führer* said quietly without looking up.

'Von Kettler-' Möller stopped himself quickly. 'It is my pleasure to serve you, my *Führer*.'

Still looking down, Hitler went on: 'I went there once, Paris. I don't know what the big fuss was about, personally. It is nothing compared to Berlin.' Hitler looked up and locked eyes. 'Mark my words, Möller, when I have rebuilt Berlin, it will make Paris look like a backwater.'

Hitler's voice was calm but quick.

'But there is an allure about Paris, is there not?' Hitler clasped his hands together neatly. 'It's drawing the Americans nicely into my trap. They can't help themselves: like a moth to a lamp. It's all part of a much bigger plan of mine, Möller. They won't know what's hit them.' Hitler gave a slightly lopsided smile, his voice picking up speed and volume. 'They'll need those little boats to get back across the Channel where they belong soon enough, mark my words. And with them gone, I shall turn east again and destroy the Bolsheviks finally.'

His fists thumped into the desk.

Möller jumped.

At full pace, he thumped the table repeatedly to emphasise his words. 'You see, we are actually winning this war, it's playing out exactly as I want it. I just need some competent Generals to carry out my plans, that is all!'

'Möller,' Hitler continued, 'you will defend Paris. You will make the Americans pay a very heavy price for every metre they wish to take forwards.

And you mark my words: that city will not fall into the enemy's hands unless it is lying in complete rubble. You understand?'

'Complete rubble, my Führer, I understand.'

'COMPLETE RUBBLE, YOU HEAR ME!' Hitler was on his feet, both fists crashed into the desk.

Möller gulped weakly before replying: 'Yes, my Führer.'

In an instant, Hitler was calm again, clasping his hands in front of him. He nodded crisply.

Möller's escort turned to leave and Möller realised his interview was over. He quickly caught up with his escort and before he knew it, the doors were closed behind him.

Möller kept himself to himself all the way through the Chancellery building and out to the car waiting for him.

'To the station as planned, General?' asked the driver.

'Please,' replied Möller. *And get me as far away from that madman as you can*, he thought.

* * *

In black tie, Berner stood at the door waiting for Eve and Lotti to arrive. They were already late and Berner was getting concerned.

Eventually, arm in arm and laughing merrily, Eve and Lotti walked up the entrance steps. Every soldier stopped to watch them breeze by. *Not your average secret agent, is she*, thought Berner.

'Unfashionably late, ladies?' he asked, giving them

both each a kiss on the cheek to welcome them.

'The Metro's on strike, would you believe it?' replied Lotti, handing her cape to a doorman. 'They're all out on strike now, apparently. What's a girl to do, eh?'

Quietly, Eve added: 'See, I told you this was a leaving do.'

'Ladies, do you need to powder noses before we go in?' asked Berner. Eve widened her eyes at Lotti to say *go, please.*

'I have a better idea,' smiled Lotti taking a glass of champagne from a tray. She spun around to one of the officers standing nearby, who took no time to be convinced to offer Lotti his arm and escort her to the party. Lotti cast a triumphant look over her shoulder.

'All set for tonight?' asked Berner quietly.

'Oh yes,' replied Eve enthusiastically, knowing he was not talking about the party.

'Good, because he's been told he's off to Berlin tomorrow morning, so we proceed as planned. Ten o'clock. Just as we arranged. OK with that?'

'I certainly am, Walter. I'm quite looking forward to this, if I'm honest.' Another waiter walked past with a tray of drinks. Eve stepped forward, took two glasses, passed one to Walter, and chinked her glass against his. : 'Shall we?'

'It would be my absolute pleasure, Eve, to escort you.' And with that, they linked arms and walked in step up the stairs towards the ballroom.

Despite the Allies getting closer and closer to Paris and an insurrection about to start anytime soon, the room was surprisingly light and joyous. Lotti, in her element, held court with a few old flames. Eve and Berner watched on, impressed as she radiated and chatted, quick witted enough to keep people engaged but at arm's length as she sought out her prey for the night.

'She's quite a sight, isn't she?' said a voice from behind that Berner recognised instantly. Eve and Berner turned.

'Horst Lemke, at your service, madam … oiselle,' he said, checking Eve's finger for a ring.

Eve offered her hand for Lemke to kiss, feigning a smile. She could smell the alcohol on him. 'How do you do.' Eve looked warily at Berner.

'Forgive me, yes. Lemke, meet Eve who … works for me.'

'Ah!' said Lemke slowly. 'At last I have the opportunity to meet Eve. The photograph in your file does you no justice may I say.'

'Thank you, Herr Lemke.'

'Call me Horst.'

Berner felt his stomach twist as Lemke held Eve's hand for a second too long.

Eve retracted her hand without snatching it away and stepped to one side slightly to place her empty glass on a waiter's tray. It seemed Eve and Lotti were never far from a waiter at events like this.

'I can see why Colonel Berner likes to spend so much time working with you. You must be the most closely supervised agent in the city, no?' Lemke had a little laugh.

Eve maintained her grimace of a smile and looked around quickly. 'I don't think we should be discussing my work here, do you? These are still very dangerous times, especially for a girl like me, working for Germany.'

'I agree, I really shouldn't have. It's just that I rarely get the chance to chat to such a beautiful, confident woman.'

'So, if we're talking about what we all do for a living, Horst, may I ask you what you do?'

Lemke's smile was lewd . 'I'm in the same line of work as Walter here. In fact, he works for me. So I suppose that means you work for me too.' He'd returned to rocking on his toes again.

Berner felt his stomach contract a little further and started to look around for an escape - but Eve had other ideas, it seemed.

'Well,' she said, 'I'm a great believer in getting to know your colleagues as best you can in the circumstances. So ...' a waiter appeared with more champagne, 'I reckon we have a glass or two and a chat but don't let me hog you, Horst. How's that for a plan?'

Lemke looked a little more than happy with her suggestion and so Eve led him along, learning things about him that even Berner did not know. Berner helped Eve in making sure Lemke's glass was never empty as he regaled stories of his successes since the war began. It was the war that was making him, he said, devouring her body with his eyes.

After a while, Eve gently led a drunken Lemke into a group of other guests who looked less than pleased to see him. Eve wasted no time in making her escape, past a group of inquisitive, youthful and uniformed admirers, and back to Berner.

They talked and talked, pretty much ignoring

everyone else. It was good to spend time talking about anything but their work and the task ahead. Berner would make a quip, Eve would throw her head back in laughter and the evening passed quickly. Eve looked to be genuinely enjoying herself.

Franck tiptoed along an alleyway that led past un-emptied bins and out onto Rue de Belloy. The streets were already dark but if stopped by a patrol now, Franck would have had a lot of trouble explaining away the large tube he carried over his shoulder, draped in a tarpaulin. Not that it really mattered anymore, thought Franck as he and twenty of his men, every one of them armed with a rifle or a machine gun, moved silently towards the Hotel Majestic. For years, this would have been impossible in Paris but now, with so many German eyes looking west, it was possible for an armed platoon of Resistance fighters to walk the streets of Paris unhindered.

Lotti glanced at her watch and was eventually able to make eye contact with Eve and give her one of those wide-eyed looks that told Eve now was the time.

Eve looked at her watch, 'Ah, of course, it's time. Is he where we think he should be?'

'Yes, in his office.'

Eve unclipped the fastener and had a peek into

her handbag. 'I'm all set. I'll see you a little later,' and with that, she leaned forward and gave Berner a little kiss on his cheek.

'Be careful. Please,' he said, but Eve didn't hear him. She was already making her way out into the crowd. Berner knew he'd remember that kiss for a very long time.

'Here, help me with this,' said Franck as he started to remove the tarpaulin cover from a pristine bazooka. Franck gave his men a small, nervous, smile before shouldering the weapon. It felt good at last to be going fully onto the offensive. To be the man to trigger a rocket and a revolt.

Obersoldat Hans Seidel handed his new colleague Gunter Brandt his cigarette. 'There, this should help you get that going.' He put a finger into the collar of his tunic. 'It's warm, even for this time of night.'

Brandt got his cigarette underway. 'Not long now though, it's nearly ten.'

'Hhmm, I wonder how the party's going back there.' Seidel nodded towards the Majestic. 'Crazy. Here we are getting told to be ready to fight to the death in this city - which we're all looking forward to, I know - and that lot back there are busy using up all the champagne before the Yankies arrive. Well, I suppose guarding a party is better than going house to house out in Pantin. They've got-'

Seidel saw something move on the street corner.

'What is it?' asked Brandt.

Seidel did not answer, but stepped out from behind the sandbag wall that had been his and Brandt's station for the last few hours to get a better view. He unslung his rifle slowly.

Brandt put his cigarette to his lips and reached for his rifle.

Seidel pointed. 'There!'

Brandt saw a handful of men run out from the shadows and out onto the street, lifting their guns, ready to fire.

Brandt and Seidel raised their Gewehr 43's to take aim, but they did not quite see the sudden flash of light come from the far corner.

Officers hurriedly put down glasses and ran to their stations, leaving the few women to crouch into the corners of the room as the air outside seemed to fill with the noise of a street battle.

Everyone, that is, except Lotti, who picked up an abandoned glass and bottle and sidled up to Berner.

'You and I seem to be the only ones not panicking around here, Walter. Now, I wonder why that would be,' she said with a mischievous smile on her face. 'Want some?' she gestured with the bottle.

'Thanks, Lotti but no. I've-'

'Gotta go,' the both said together.

'Story of my life,' Lotti went on to say. 'Well, don't let me stop you, Walter,' she said, gesturing towards the door with a champagne glass. 'You've clearly got other things to do.'

'If you'll excuse me,' said Berner as he stood up and set off.

'Just one thing,' said Lotti, forcing Berner to stop and turn round.

'Yes?'

'Bring her back in one piece will you, for both our sakes?'

Berner smiled before turning away. Lotti found a chair, lit a cigarette, perched her feet on the chair opposite, blew a puff of smoke elegantly into the air and began finishing off the bottle.

* * *

More Resistance fighters emerged from cover and advanced towards the Hotel Majestic's main entrance. Franck handed the now empty bazooka tube to an underling and gleefully started to fire his MP-40 from the hip.

This is more like it, thought Franck, emerging from the shadows. He ran past Hans Seidel and Gunter Brandt who, having lost their fight, lay amongst the ruins of the sentry post, collapsing in a burning heap. With a little pride, Franck watched his men and how the training was paying off; they were taking aimed shots despite the excitement of attacking the main German headquarters in the heart of the city. They all alternated between firing shots and sprinting forward from cover to cover. The overall effect was a steady advance and the Germans didn't seem to have anything right now that could stop it.

* * *

With the noise of gunfire outside getting louder, Von Kettler's door swung open. He raised his head from his hands to see a woman in a dress at the door, holding a pistol.

'My name is Eve. I'm a British agent and I'm getting you out of here. You will do everything I say, understand?'

Open-mouthed the General nodded.

'Good, now on your feet and follow me.'

The General smiled as he left his office for the final time, not bothering to look back.

She sped off. Von Kettler thought he was fit but had to work hard to keep up with this woman, whoever she was. And Eve was in no mind to hang around. With a map of the building long committed to memory, she took long strides along the corridors, counting doors as she went. Third left, second right. With all the panic at the front of the building, the way through the centre of the building was for now thankfully quiet.

Eve led Von Kettler off towards the north side of the building, away from the shooting. They sped up a set of stairs and along further corridors.

They turned a corner and Von Kettler could see two soldiers up ahead. The soldiers stiffened a little as their General appeared.

Eve was not for slowing down. In French, she shouted back to him: 'Tell them you're being chased or something!'

Short of breath, Von Kettler shouted ahead: 'Don't stand there! Take cover on the corner behind us. You're doing no good there!'

One of the soldiers lowered the barrel of his Mauser and started to move towards them, with the clear intention of carrying out his General's orders. The other hesitated – something was wrong. The soldier moved slightly to his left, blocking the corridor.

'Out of the-'

Von Kettler didn't get the chance to finish his sentence. Eve shot the soldier; suddenly stopping, she used her left arm to shove Von Kettler against the wall to give herself a clear shot at the other soldier, who was dead before he realised what was happening. She then grabbed Von Kettler's arm and dragged him on.

'Come on!'

The first soldier was still squirming on the floor and Eve saw a twinge of guilt in Von Kettler's eyes.

Around another corner, Eve slowed down, counting doors out loud to herself. 'This one,' she said putting a hand firmly on Von Kettler's chest to stop him. 'Wait there and don't loiter in the doorway when we go in,' she said.

Eve silently turned the door handle and then threw the door open. Before Von Kettler knew it, she was in and crouching down to the side of the door.

'The room is empty, get in!'

Von Kettler did as he was told, and Eve closed the door behind him.

Von Kettler reached for the light switch.

'Don't touch that!' said Eve forcefully. She put her own hand on the light switch and turned the lights on twice for two seconds each.

Then, with the lights still off, she walked to the window, stopping short to allow her to look outside without been seen. Satisfied, she opened both windows and checked the street below. Von Kettler heard a car engine approach at speed.

Eve looked Von Kettler straight in the eyes, and whilst her eyes burned with a fierce intensity, her voice was completely calm. 'When I say so, you climb over and let yourself down. There will be someone there to help catch you. Understand?'

Von Kettler indicated he did. Eve turned to look out onto the street again. The car pulled up below.

'OK, over you go.'

Von Kettler needed no encouragement and threw a leg over the window still and lowered himself down until his arms hung straight. He felt someone's hand brush his boot.

'Go on, let go!' ordered Eve and the General released his grip and landed with a crump onto the pavement. He nodded thanks to the gruff-looking man in a flat cap who had helped him down. Composing himself, he glanced up just as Eve prepared to climb over the ledge.

'Do you mind?' she asked, and both men quickly looked away and moved aside. Eve landed and stood up.

'Haven't done that in heels before,' said Eve cheerfully. 'Now, get in the car, please, General.'

The man in the flat cap got into the driver's seat. Von Kettler jumped into the back. Just before getting into the passenger seat, Eve picked out a second-floor window where she saw Berner smiling from the shadows.

The car was already moving as Eve shut the car door.

Von Kettler sat up and looked around behind him as what had been his office and his prison disappeared into the distance. Eve told him politely but firmly to keep down and out of sight. Laying on his side, he looked up through the windows and watched Paris speed by. The car swung around corner after corner, presumably avoiding any roadblocks, and every now and then, a truck full of soldiers would pass in the opposite direction.

* * *

Franck was in amongst the thin trees outside the hotel as the battle grew in intensity. The Frenchmen approached the front doors. He looked over his shoulder and with him squatted one of his best and most trusted men, Georges.

'Still got it?' asked Franck over the noise of gunfire.

'Yes, you want it now?'

Franck looked over towards the hotel and made a decision.

'Yes, but I'm going to try and get it a bit closer once it's been initiated.'

Georges, by the look of him, was not sure if that was such a good idea.

'Don't worry, Georges,' said Franck, 'it won't take long and it's not far. Just there, see, by that stone pillar.'

George shrugged the small canvas rucksack from his back, undid one of the straps and passed it to Franck.

Franck dipped his head, reacting to a grenade going off nearby before flipping over the lid of the rucksack and feeling about inside. There it was, the Number 4 switch. He pulled it forward a little so he could see what he was doing, removed the safety pin and then pulled the circular ring at the end out a bit before letting it go. The ring snapped back, starting the timer, and the 60-second count to when the bomb would explode had begun.

'Shouldn't you have done that when the bomb was in position, Franck?'

'Shut up, Georges, it means we need to move. Now, cover me!'

And without waiting, Franck was sprinting forward. Georges started to put down covering fire. The other fighters who could see what was happening increased their rate of fire. Stone and wooden chips flew from walls and window frames. Glass smashed.

Franck, thankfully, did not have far to go. He slung the rucksack with the bomb in it down at the foot of a stone pillar. It landed perfectly but the Germans must have spotted him – suddenly the air around Franck was like it was alive with wasps. The noise was unbearable.

Franck ran back to Georges, keeping very low and sheltering the sides of his head with his hands, his machine gun swaying below his body on its sling.

Franck didn't wait. He ran straight past Georges

and kept going, urging Georges to get moving. Georges needed no such encouragement and beat his boss back to the next piece of available cover, a car filled with bullet holes.

Franck fumbled into his jacket and pulled out a small flare gun, cocked it, pointed it straight down the road towards the Germans and pulled the trigger. Soon enough, the Germans in the area were blinded by the light of the flare, giving Franck's men the time they needed to withdraw. Knowing the bomb had been laid, the avenue soon filled with French fighters sprinting for the next street corner.

Hobnail boots scratched at the paving stones as the men ran for cover. German voices could be heard shouting – seeing the Frenchmen break and run so suddenly meant only one thing.

From behind a corner, Franck's hair suddenly swished across his head and he was pushed bodily away from where the bomb had gone off. His ears rang and he sucked air back into his lungs. Already, the air was burnt and dusty. His cheek stung. It stung even more when he put his hand up to it, grazing a sharp piece of glass and pushing it further into his flesh. He swore.

Looking around, Franck knew he needed to get his men out of here quickly before reinforcements arrived. He was about to give orders but the men were already on their way, shattered glass crunching beneath their running feet.

'Time to go, Georges,' he said but Georges couldn't hear him: the explosion had muffled his hearing.

They jogged away, turning every now and then to

see if they were being followed. The men were separating out, some running faster than others, heeding Franck's advice not to bunch together on the escape.

Franck was starting to feel better; his lungs did not have to work so hard to support his running, but his hearing was nowhere near back to normal.

And then Franck noticed Georges pull up and stop.

Franck turned his head whilst still running and there lay Georges, hit, sprawling on the pavement. Franck turned round and ran to Georges. Whatever Georges was saying, Franck could barely hear him, but Georges was in quite a panic and pointing down the road. Franck soon saw blood spreading across Georges' shoulder from an entry wound; he must have been shot from the front.

Realising what this meant, Franck glanced over his shoulder and froze. There stood four or five German soldiers, pointing their guns straight at him. Franck put his hands up and stood up slowly, stooping in submission. Before they turned him to face the wall, he got a quick look at these Germans. They were not the usual bunch of low-life who guarded the HQ, these were tough-looking regulars.

Franck heard a shot and was expecting to have been hit himself but wasn't. He seemed intact. Either way, it didn't stop him pissing down his own trouser leg in fear. Franck glanced down onto the pavement and there lay Georges with a hole clean through his forehead. Franck began to weep. Now surely, they would kill him.

But no. With his hands on his head, his fingers

interlaced, Franck was marched harshly back and into the smouldering Hotel. His bomb had blown in every window, doors hung off but as he was bundled downstairs into the basement and into a room for interrogation, Franck realised his bomb had done very little damage.

Franck was pushed down into a chair; his hands roughly tied behind his back and then he was left alone to await his fate. He probably only had minutes or hours left to live and, in the crushing solitude of the cell, Franck broke down and cried. Unable to wipe his eyes, his tears dripped on the stains left of his own urine and Georges' blood.

There is little a counterintelligence officer can do in the middle of an attack but once the shooting had started, Lemke got to work. He gave orders for an elaborate set of roadblocks all around Paris and he ordered the railway shut, even though reports were coming in that the railways workers had just gone on strike.

Berner looked busy too, checking up on all his contacts. If Berner was here, then he probably wasn't part of the plan to get Von Kettler out of Paris, thought Lemke to himself. Either that or Berner was unbelievably cool under this kind of pressure.

'Where do you think he is, Walter?' Lemke asked for probably the fifth time.

'I have broken protocol and contacted all my agents. Nothing. No one seems to know anything. I will need to see them face to face tomorrow to check they're not lying to me, Lemke, but for now, I'm none the wiser. Sorry.'

Berner's answers were consistent and whilst different every time, the details were always the same.

But on this occasion, Berner went on to say a little more. 'Maybe Von Kettler was your man after all. I mean, why escape, except to run from what might have been an attempt to kidnap him?'

Lemke laughed. 'The French are getting brave, Berner, but I don't think they're good enough to capture a General from within his own headquarters do you? And get out in one piece?'

'The General has lots of loyal staff,' mused Berner. 'They're the sort who would happily have smuggled him out. There are reports of vehicles leaving from the other side of the hotel as the attack started and quite a few legged it in all directions. That bit is understandable: it's people running for their lives. It would have been easy to slip him out in amongst all that. Maybe giving the guards the slip by saying he was escaping a kidnap attempt.'

'No, Berner, he was escaping us, not the French.'

'How can you be so sure?'

'Because his wife and kids have disappeared as well.'

But of course, Berner already knew that.

'You're smiling, Berner, why's that?'

'You won't like me saying this but a bit of me is always impressed at times like this. You and I are counterintelligence professionals. Stopping this sort of thing is what we do for a living and yet, we couldn't stop this from happening. He's done it right from under our noses and I just didn't think he had it in him.'

'Well I'm not at all impressed and the CSSD won't be impressed either when he finds out.' Lemke meant the Nazi head of the SS and SD in Berlin.

'We'll find him.'

'How?' asked Lemke.

'Simple. Where's he going to go? It's got to be west to the Allies, that's the shortest distance to safety from Paris. The only other possibilities would be, what, Spain or Switzerland? That's a lot of German-occupied territory to cover. Although, going west might be such an obvious thing to do, he's headed elsewhere. I mean, how's he going to sneak through the front line when practically every German soldier in France will recognise him?'

Lemke wiped his face with his hands, tired.

'Lemke, you've done everything you can. We both have. Go and get some rest. Take your mind off this for a while. You'll be better when you have had a rest.'

Lemke looked up. *Berner seemed so genuine.* 'You're right. If you hear anything, let me know.'

'Of course,' said Berner, 'I'll stay up and monitor things. You take over when you're fresher, all right?'

'Thanks, Berner. Oh, while you're at it, how's your friend Rommel getting on?'

Berner looked surprised. 'He was in good spirits, thanks for asking. He is going to recover and the sooner the better for all our sakes, don't you think?'

'Very much so, Berner, very much so.'

Berner could not help but think that was an odd question to ask at a time like this but let it pass for now. 'Look, Lemke, while you're at it, why don't you go and see if the bar in the ballroom is back open. You look like you could do with a drink.'

For once, Lemke was in complete agreement with Berner. Yes, he needed a drink.

The bar was closed but sat on her own in the ballroom was Lotti, sat at a table with a bottle of champagne open in front of her, smoking her cigarette and bobbing her foot up and down elegantly.

Lemke walked down the few steps to the main floor and approached her.

'Where's your friend?'

'She's long gone. She must have legged it once the firing started.'

'Why didn't you go with her?' asked Lemke gesturing to a chair. Lotti nodded her consent.

'I was attending the call of nature when all the noise began, so we were separated. When I got back here, she was gone. So was everyone else for that matter. And I can tell you,' she said with a grin on her face, 'I didn't fancy the prospect of walking out of here and facing getting shot by the French or your guards. I thought that I would keep this bottle and its empty friend there company, until things got a little safer.'

'May I?' Lemke gestured again, this time to an empty glass. Lotti poured it for him. They chinked glasses.

'Are you leaving any time soon, *mademoiselle*?' he asked, looking at her across the rim of his glass.

Lotti gave one of those smiles. 'Wasn't planning on it...'

* * *

As the lead counterintelligence officer on duty in the building, Berner made it his business to check the cells. Apparently a new prisoner had been taken during the attack. Berner checked his watch; the timing had to be perfect.

Down in the basement, checking the log, Berner recognised Franck's name immediately. So it was true. *Of all the people to be taken in tonight, it had to be him, didn't it?*

'Give me the keys to Cell Twelve, will you?' Berner asked the Sergeant.

'I'll get one of the boys to open it up for you, one moment, Sir.'

'No need. It's the cell I've used many times, in fact I was a prisoner there myself only a few days ago. Just give me the keys.'

'Not sure about this,' said the Sergeant hesitantly.

'Come on, it's me. You've been signing the key out to me since, what, December?'

The Sergeant relented and handed Berner the keys with a weak smile. Berner was down the corridor before the Sergeant could get him to sign the log for them.

Berner unlocked the door and making sure no one else was walking down the corridor he walked in. Franck's voice caught in his throat. 'Thank God it's you.'

Berner winced. No resistance fighter in his right

mind would ever be pleased to see a member of the SS's own counterintelligence unit unless he knew something about Berner the rest of the SS did not.

'I'm sorry it's come to this, Franck. Your men did a good job last night. How did you get captured?'

Franck told him.

'You have to get me out of here,' Franck then pleaded.

'I'm very sorry to say Franck but I'm not going to be able to do that. This place has been sealed, no one in or out. Every vehicle and person is being searched and checked. You're not getting out of here today.'

Franck looked down.

'Are you going to interrogate me?'

'I haven't time. I need to be back upstairs.'

'Then what are you doing here?' asked Franck, making eye contact.

Berner reached into a pocket and lay a small white tablet on the table in front of Franck.

Franck started to weep.

'It's not like that, Franck. At least I hope it isn't. I will ask to come and interrogate you later today but if someone else comes before then, think about using this if you need to. If Sauer comes in, just bluff away as best you can and don't mention me or Eve. You'll survive that even if he beats you up.'

Franck groaned.

Berner pointed behind himself, 'But if Lemke walks through that door. Get that tablet between your back teeth and bite. Lemke's the dangerous one and he will kill you - but he's the sort who will take a long time doing it and you will talk because of the pain.'

'Will it hurt?'

'The tablet? No. Almost instantaneous.'

'I see.' Franck fixed his eyes on the tablet.

Berner looked at his watch. 'I have to go. Good luck.'

The guard shift had changed over and still settling into their routine. No one thought to check the cell keys in, as Berner slung them onto the desk on his way out.

Sunday

They didn't like him, but all the staff at the *Funkmessstelle* knew Bohler had been drafted in for a reason and was working for Lemke, the other newcomer. But Lemke was SS from head to toe and was the boss; they all knew who was telling Sauer what to do these days. So instead of telling Bohler about the hurried and unscheduled message they intercepted in the early hours of the morning, they sent it straight to Lemke. All the duty staff smiled proudly, confident this would get them back in Lemke's good books.

But in their hurry, they had applied no analysis and provided little detail about the message, such as duration and whether the Radio Direction Finding teams had located where the message had been broadcast from.

Having started the day with a spring in his step, with the message in his hand, Lemke felt a weariness come over him again. 'Get me Bohler,' was all he could say,

To make a bad situation worse, it took ages to track the Professor down.

'Where were you? Why are you so damned difficult to find?'

'I go looking for ancient sites in the city, Sir. I like to scratch around looking for artefacts before I go to work. You'd be surprised what comes up.'

'I'm sure but from now on, you are confined to

barracks until this operation is over, do you understand? In fact, I'm going to have you move into the *Funkmessstelle* block so we can have you in the room when surprise broadcasts like this happen, you understand? You will eat and sleep there and your blessed artefacts will have to wait. This is important.'

'I see, Sir. In which case, I agree.'

Lemke was not the sort of officer used to having to agree with soldiers.

'Take a look at this,' said Lemke abruptly as he handed Bohler the message. 'Look at it, anyone could have sent that. It was sent at an irregular time, just after one this morning, and on an emergency channel. What I need to know, Bohler, is this: was it Eve who sent this message or not?'

Bohler smiled as he studied the sheet of paper with Eve's message on. 'The log doesn't state when the message started and ended. That's unfortunate.'

'Because?'

'Well, firstly,' said Bohler, unable to resist a little dig, 'it's normal procedure. It's such a shame my colleagues in the *Funkmessstelle* didn't record the exact timings of the message. That way, I would have been able to take a more educated guess on whether this was Eve signalling or not. You see, I could have timed myself sending the message at the rate Eve would normally broadcast at: I play their messages in their head like a tune, keeping the right time. If my timing matches the timing of the message then there's a better than average chance we can identify the signaller. It's rudimentary and approximate, I know, but that's the best I can do without hearing a recording.'

Lemke let his impatience show and Bohler was getting better at spotting it.

'However, on a more positive note,' Bohler continued, 'the deliberate spelling mistake is there, so this *could* be Eve but without hearing the message, I really have no way of telling. You see a lot of Allied agents put their spelling mistake in that place, but the combination of their timing *and* the deliberate mistake are the fingerprints I'm looking for.'

'So you don't know?' asked Lemke tired.

'Not for definite. The best I can do, Sir, is say that I'm fifty per cent confident it's Eve.'

Bohler handed the message back to a silent Lemke. It simply said: MOBILE. REPEAT. MOPILE. Lemke let Bohler go and pack. Getting to his feet, Lemke kicked his wastepaper basket across the room and swore bitterly. There was a knock at the door and in walked a very nervous-looking Scholz.

'This doesn't look like you are bringing me good news.'

'Er, no, Sir. It's just that the CSSD has heard of how Von Kettler has, er, disappeared, and wants to talk to you at ten this morning sharp. I have been told to tell you he is not a happy man.'

The wastepaper bin got another kick.

'Anything else, like a sighting, a clue, a tip-off? Anything?'

'No. Only-'

'Yes, Scholz, spit it out.'

'A fair few of the *Milice* were strung up last night

whilst they were out looking for the captured soldiers. And there's no sign of them either.'

'Get out.'

Scholz knew better than to prolong this conversation and was almost out the door when Lemke called him back.

'Is Rommel still tucked up in bed safely?'

'Is … I'm sorry, Sir, I don't understand.'

'Go and check for me. I want to know if Rommel is still in his bed. He was when I checked last night, I want to know he's still there, understand?'

Scholz said yes and got out of the office as quickly as he could.

Agent Saxon had lain in the treeline, surveying the village ahead, for some time now. He had watched the horizon turn from black to green and now a faint blue. There were no signs of life up ahead, just houses and a few farm outbuildings on top of a valley to his left. All was peaceful. *For now,* thought Saxon with a small smile.

Clement lay next to him now, studying the village ahead. 'The Germans are there, no doubt about it,' he said, gripping his unlit pipe between his teeth.

'How can you possibly tell that?' asked Saxon, astounded at how Clement could draw such a conclusion when not a soul had been seen so far.

'Easy. Flags. That village is not flying the *tricolor.* Trust me, the moment villages are liberated, those flags are up in a heartbeat. No flags, no liberation, and no liberation means the Germans are still in town and that gives us a problem, doesn't it?' Clement shook his head.

'We go for days without seeing one and just when we are in a hurry to make an RV, the Germans miraculously appear.' He turned to Saxon. 'You may well have a battle on your hands today, my friend. That means we need breakfast.'

Saxon gave a short and silent laugh before staring back at the village perched on the hilltop, looking for flags. It appeared Clement was right. 'Do you ever stop thinking about food?'

Clement feigned hurt and placed a hand defensively on his own chest. 'Me? What if I didn't think about food, huh? You think always of the enemy, I think about making sure my men are fuelled for the fight. Trust me, in the last war, I watched too many men go hungry in the mountains; hunger drains you, Saxon. From that moment on, I said to myself, Napoleon – another great Frenchman - had it right, an Army marches on its stomach. That goes for my lot, too.' Clement gestured to the gathering band of resistance fighters further back in the woods.

'Anyway,' continued Clement with a sniff, 'I'm a Frenchman and even though my country may have been occupied by *Bosche* for all these years, I have the reputation of my country to uphold.' The defensive hand on the chest curled into a fist of pride.

'I don't want a battle today, Clement, if I'm honest. I just want to meet up with whoever's coming down that road at us and get them safely back to the American lines. Then we can go looking for trouble again.'

'I just don't think it's safe to assume the Germans are not there,' said Clement slowly.

'All right, in which case I propose we get in and around that village quickly to check it's clear. That way, if there are any Germans around, we'll be there waiting for them as they start to get up. We know their routine this far back behind the fighting, they won't be expecting anything. If indeed, they are even there.'

'I agree. Let's get the men to eat enough to keep them going for a couple more hours, then eat properly when in the village with nothing more to do than talk to the locals and wait for your agent to arrive. I bet you wish Slater and his boys were here right now, don't you?'

'I do. Fifty SAS soldiers to help us out right now would do me just fine but he's still busy back west. OK, let's get back and brief the boys.'

Agreed, both men got up and walked back to the fighters who were beginning to crowd together, sensing something was up. Jim Jackson was amongst them, drawing air through a cigarette, the tip glowing brightly in the gloom. Jim offered it to Saxon to light up with.

'Thanks, Jim. You can't see it from here but there's a village up ahead and Clement says Jerry might still be hanging around. So Clement's going to make sure his men get a quick bite and then we're off to occupy it before the Germans get out of bed.'

Jim smiled. 'OK, what's the plan, just drive in and wait for the Krauts to come out in their nightwear?'

'Pretty much.'

Saxon swept away the leaves and twigs on the forest floor and began to draw in the dirt with the toe of his boot.

'So we are in the forest here and there's the tree-line behind me ... there. There's a shallow valley running parallel with the forest here, and the village is on top of the other side of the valley – it's quite a shallow valley really, as you'll see – and the village is about here. It's like nearly all the others around here: one long street with houses on both sides quite spaced out. There's a church in the middle, about here,' He drew out a rectangle in the centre of the village, 'That's where the Marie is almost certainly going to be. There're also some outbuildings on the left, here. The valley sweeps round, so the left side of it looks down into the valley like so. No idea what's on the right but the map – for what it's worth – says it's open fields and a wood.'

Saxon stopped to look across to Maurice. 'Anything on the radio?'

Maurice looked up and shook his head. 'Nothing. All is quiet.'

Saxon stubbed out what was left of his cigarette. 'Do you want to go and take a quick look, Jim?'

'Sure.'

'You might as well come along too then, Maurice, so we're all in the picture.'

Saxon led them forward as the Resistance men around them hurried away some bread and sausage. Everyone could tell the possibility of action was in the air: Clement was buoyant and perky.

Jim, trained to be covert and silent, was still

getting used to just how casual the Frenchmen men could be, living in the woods as they did. They would happily light fires and cook, fix cars and trucks without much of a care for the noise. Jim sometimes wondered if they were goading any local Germans into a fight.

Saxon looked across as Clement held court, sat against a tree with a metal mug of coffee parked beside him, his pipe lit.

'The village ahead is not yet flying the tricolor, and we need to be on the other side of that to make a *rendezvous*. We can't have any German interference in this, boys. Don't ask me why because I don't know but London asked us to be careful, which normally means we have to be *very careful*. If there are any Germans there, I want to take them prisoner rather than start a fight, understand?'

The men nodded grimly.

'Then we raid any stores they have, it's gasoline I'm after the most if you find any.' Clement spoke as he watched Saxon approach. 'Now Saxon will tell us how it is to be done.'

Clement looked at Saxon, amused at Saxon's reaction to being given no notice to start his briefing.

Saxon drew another dirt map on the floor and the men gathered around to get a view.

'We need the far end of that village secure, so we will do this in three moves. I will take the Jeep around the village to the left, through that valley and end up about here, covering the other entrance and exit to the village. Hopefully, there will be some cover for us in some bushes or something.

Meanwhile, Clement, I think you take all the other vehicles but two straight up the road, drive through slowly and see what pops out at you. Meanwhile, the other two vehicles sweep out to the right, keeping an eye on the woods beyond the village. If the Germans are there, they are probably parked up in the middle where the church is. Pretty straight forward. Any questions?'

There were none; they had done this twice before and it was becoming a drill. Clement nodded in agreement and gave more detailed instructions to his men to divide up who was going to be doing what. In very little time, the men were packed up and ready to go.

Fixing his goggles onto his head, Saxon walked up to Clement's Citroen truck. 'I'm all set, the others all look ready too. Happy enough?'

'I am. We're getting good at this.'

'Good. Any problems, I'll be at the end of the village or stuck in that valley having a fight, all right with that?'

'Sure. Happy hunting! If I think you're getting slowed down too much, I may come left and help you out. It depends on what I find in the middle.'

'Thanks. Right, I'll see you later.'

And with that, Saxon climbed into the passenger seat of the Jeep. He cocked the two Vickers guns mounted in front of him, pulled his goggles down over his eyes and nodded to Maurice to get going.

Maurice switched the ignition and the Jeep burst into life. He threw it into gear and sped off down the valley with Jim in the back manning the rear machine guns. Clement watched them go for a while, giving them a lead to cover the greater distance and get around the village. Having checked there was plenty of tobacco in his pipe, Clement gave the word to get going and his convoy started to roll forward.

As if the noise was not enough, the dust rose and drifted from the tyres, hiding all his other vehicles as if in a smoke screen. 'With all this dust, if there are any Germans in this village, they'll only have us to shoot at!'

The driver gave Clement a sideways glance, not sure if he was joking before returning his eyes to the village ahead. There was still no one to be seen.

Clement watched two cars veer off to the right as planned, moving quickly over the baked earth and throwing up still more dust.

They got closer. Clement waved slowly with his hand and the driver reduced to a crawl as they approached the first house. He pushed his window open and tried to listen for anything above the whine of the gearbox. Still not sure, he banged on the back of the cab and his men started to clamber out, form two lines and walk forward cautiously, weapons at the ready.

Gradually they crept forward. Clement's eyes scanned every window, every door. With all his vehicles now in the village, they kicked up no more dust, but the rumble of the engines and the grinding of gears echoed off every wall.

Further they went, past the church and the Mairie.

Onward and still nothing.

And then gunfire.

Not from inside the village but off to the right. The boys in the two cars must have found something. There were just a couple of shots at first but the number of rounds being fired was increasing.

'Looks like we've got a battle on our hands, boys!' Clement wasn't sure if he should be glad of a fight right now. What he wanted was the village to be quiet so they could make their rendezvous with the agent coming in the other direction.

Clement's men in the village stopped walking and made their way forward, slowly and at a crouch. Clement got out of the cab, slung his rifle and urged them forward, walking down the middle of the road, in front of the truck, and pushing a faster pace.

He could hear nothing from over on his left, Clement assumed Saxon was making good progress at least.

Then, back on the right, he heard two machine guns open up. MG 42s. They had to be: the rate of fire was so quick they sounded like someone ripping bedsheets in two.

Clement waved forward. 'Right, boys, let's get going, the others sound like they'll need a hand. Get up to the other end as quick as you can.'

And with that the men broke into a jog for a while. Then, over the noise of gunfire came a deep rumble.

Everyone stopped. It was a tank.

The rumble got louder suddenly. It was more than one tank. That probably meant a platoon of them, which meant three. And usually, with a platoon of tanks, comes a company of infantry.

Fearful eyes shot back at Clement.

'Well, we're here now, let's get to the end of the village before they do!'

Clement was breezy on the outside but on the inside he could feel the apprehension kicking in. There could be up to 100 German soldiers up ahead, which meant the Resistance fighters were outnumbered more than two to one. His men were good, but this was different. They hadn't fought against Germans in tanks before.

They might just have walked into a fight too big for them.

Up ahead, at the far end of the village, they saw a German soldier, running while crouching low. He carried a rifle but wore a camouflage smock.

'Waffen SS!' shouted Clement as he raised his rifle to his shoulder. The German had vanished before he had time to get a round off.

A tank gun boomed somewhere out of site. The power of the explosion shook dust from the roof tiles.

Another German soldier appeared at the far end of the village, running from right to left. Clement and a few others of his men fired. The German was hit but instead of flying forward onto the ground, which was how most running men died when shot, this one was flung backwards. Saxon must already be in place and engaged.

'OK, leave the vehicles here. The rest of you come with me,' shouted Clement.

Clement heard a car speeding up from behind. He swung around. It was one of theirs. The driver yelled out of the open window:

'Tiger tanks! I could see two, not sure where the third is right now. Infantry is with them, at least a platoon. Three machine guns. Pierre is dead.'

'Right.'

Clement thought for a moment. 'Go back and tell the boys to just give covering fire until we're ready to attack. Then I need maximum covering fire from you lot, you understand? And, if the tanks look like they're going to do us some real harm, go for a drive and lure them off us.'

'Thanks a lot, Clement,' said the driver sarcastically.

Clement turned back. 'I will take Claude and Andre's men to the end of the village and make an attack from there. Gerard, you take your lot down and then right and give covering fire from there, understand? Good. And don't any of you stray too far out the other side of the vill-' Another tank round boomed out, '- village. Saxon's out there and I don't want any of you lot startling him and getting shot. Right, let's go.'

There was no stress in Clement's voice. He sounded as matter of fact as ever, giving his men that little extra bit of confidence he felt they needed right now. They stood up and followed him forward.

***

Eve heard it first. That was a heavy gun, a tank or an artillery piece going off up ahead.

'It can't be, the Allies are nowhere near here yet,' replied Von Kettler, as confused as she was. He shifted in his seat to look forward, past Eve and the driver.

'Hang on, slow down a little,' Von Kettler said after a little while. The driver pulled over onto the verge. In the distance, they could make out the unmistakable rasp of an MG42.

'Eve, what have you arranged?'

'I didn't arrange a firefight, if that's what you're asking me. No. All I'm expecting is for the Resistance to meet us near the next village as they will be able to get us past the Germans and on to the Allied front line. Drive on a bit,' she ordered.

The car continued on at a slower pace and with the windows open, they could soon hear the noise of a pitched battle further up the road.

'This is a village I think we could do with avoiding, Eve,' offered Von Kettler. The driver nodded his quick agreement.

Another tank round rattled the air.

'All right, let's get around the next corner so we can see the village. Then we'll look for a way around it. Trouble is, I'm expecting us to meet our escort near here.'

Eve began to wonder, correctly as it turned out, if it was her escort that was engaged in the battle raging before her. Eve's throat went dry.

***

Clement's men moved into the buildings that formed the far edge of the village. Clement entered the furthest building, said something reassuring to the family cowed in a corner and climbed some stairs to look out from a window, standing well back so as not to be seen from the shadows.

Clement swore. Across the field, the treeline opposite was alive with muzzle flashes. He knew he was outnumbered. The floor beneath his feet rumbled. Clement shifted a little to his left and there, halfway between the woods and him, was the first of the Tiger tanks. It looked huge, boxy and impregnable. Both its 7.92mm machine guns were hard at work. Clement knew he was out-gunned as well.

'Conserve your ammunition, just enough fire to keep them interested, you understand? If the number of gun flashes out there suddenly decreases, you come and tell me, all right?' he shouted. With their eyes still on the enemy ahead, the men nodded.

Clement bounded back downstairs, out the door and across the road. He could see Saxon parked up in a few bushes about fifty yards away. It was too risky to run over, so Clement waved to attract Saxon's attention and got shouting.

'It doesn't look like they're readying for an attack. My guess is that if we can get the tanks out of action, they might not bother attacking at all.'

Saxon agreed.

'Or, I keep them busy here and you press on to make the meeting. What do you want to do?'

'I can't get much further forward,' shouted Saxon.

'They've got at least one machine gun covering the road. It's too risky going back down the valley, there's no cover.'

Clement sighed.

'OK, in that case, we need to get the tanks. Can you see the third?'

'No. Maybe it isn't here, maybe it isn't working.'

'We haven't done this before, Saxon,' said Clement with, for the first time, a hint of doubt in his mind.

'I have,' shouted Jim, having paused firing to listen to the conversation. 'Back in Africa.'

Saxon looked across at Jim. 'Go on.'

'Clement, could you lure the tanks a little further towards you?'

'It would be a pleasure.'

'I'm not sure I believe you there, but I need to be able to get them close enough to run out to. Could you do that? What the hell am I doing? To save me shouting, I'll reverse up and come across.'

Saxon gave a burst from the twin Vickers guns mounted in front of him as Jim steered the Jeep back and over the rough ground and into the village.

Jim leapt out and grabbed the bazooka.

'That should do the trick!' said Clement.

'This ain't the half of it, Clement. Here, hold these,' he said passing Clement a couple of metal tubes containing bazooka rounds.

Jim rummaged to the bottom of the well behind the driver's seat and pulled out two circular, heavy-looking landmines. 'And this, my friend, is the other half. Oh wait.'

Jim placed the landmines down and opened his rucksack. He smiled indulgingly at Clement as he reached down deep to pull out some socks.

Stuffing the socks into his jacket pockets, Jim slung

his M1 Carbine and the Bazooka, picked the mines up and lumbered forward under the weight of it all. 'The socks are for the gun sights if this goes wrong.'

That, Clement was to admit later, did not fill him with confidence.

Jim and Clement walked back through the house, the family now sheltering under the staircase and up to a window, pushing a Resistance fighter aside for a moment so they could both see. Jim studied the terrain.

There was the tank, a couple of hundred yards away, limiting itself to moving slowly parallel with the village and firing its machine gun. Clearly, the commander had not yet selected a target worthy of the 8.8cm gun.

'Clement, I need your guys to give the impression they're grouped over to our right somewhere. I need 'em to draw that tank a little further away from the trees.'

'Give the German something to shoot at?'

'Sorry, Clement, but yeah.'

Saxon approached. 'Good,' said Jim, 'I'm going to need a hand.'

After a few short minutes, a burst of rifle and machine gun fire erupted from one of the houses further down. Bullets pinged off the tank's armour, with little splashes of dirt flying into the air.

A gear shifted and the tank lurched forward.

'They've taken the bait!' shouted Jim, 'It works every time! Off you go, Saxon.'

And with that, Saxon ran out the back of the house and into the field, carrying the mines. Rifle fire from the trees started to creep in on Saxon as he sprinted forward, running low, his ankles rolling over the shallow furrows.

The tank stopped and a whine could be heard as the turret started to traverse the gun onto Clement's men.

'The far track, Saxon, now!' shouted Jim. 'We've only got a few seconds!'

Saxon sprinted forward, the air around him alive with bullets, zipping past like hornets. Brushing up against the side of the tank with his sleeve, he ran around to the front of the tank, crouching down so the crew inside could not see him. Ducking under the moving barrel, he placed a mine just in front of the track. Bullets from the Germans in the woods pinged off the tank whenever Saxon came into view.

With one mine down, Saxon ran as fast as he could back around the tank to place the second just behind the same track. Job done, he needed no encouragement to sprint back to the house where Jim was watching, zigzagging to spoil the German's aim, his lungs bursting with effort and dust.

Clement's men ran for it. The gun was now aiming straight at them.

'Thanks, buddy,' said Jim as he ran out into the field and knelt down. It felt to him like every German was now aiming at him. The noise all around him made it feel personal: *they weren't aiming at anyone but him*. He brought the Bazooka to his shoulder took a quick aim and 'pop'; the bazooka fired. The rocket went low and hit the tank's wheels. Happy, Jim turned and ran.

The Tiger Tank seemed to freeze in time – nothing about it moved. The crew inside must have known something had happened but were still trying to work out what.

The engine revved a little as the driver tried to move the tank forward, but its right track snapped just where Jim had hit it. The track split and fell out sideways like a dead snake. The engine revved again as the driver put more engine power into a move. The tank lunged forward on its remaining track and Saxon's mine exploded. Saxon and Jim both shielded their eyes from the fine particles of dust flying towards them.

'Go get it back Saxon, I'll help cover you!'

Saxon, less than amused, ran back to the tank and grabbed the untouched mine and sprinted back like mad. Eventually, he noticed Jim who had moved back out in the open to draw German fire. Both men dived back into the house with bullets banging against the wall behind them.

The driver's hatch sprung open and out of it appeared a man in black overalls. Clement's men needed no encouragement and the German fell back dead into the tank. The same happened with the radio operator's hatch, resulting in one more dead German.

The commander's hatch on top of the turret flew open but no one appeared. The gun was still pointed at the village, but the tank's occupants must now have other things on their mind.

Saxon helped Jim reload the bazooka.

From the treeline, another tank jerked forward and made straight for the other tank.

'You got that other mine?' asked Jim.

'Sure have. Same again?'

'Maybe. Here he comes.'

The tank went straight to the other tank and fired into the house which many of Clement's men had occupied earlier. Bricks and dust flew in all directions. Jim could just make out the survivors of the first tank getting out and taking shelter on the far side of their dead tank.

'Change of plan, come on!' shouted Jim and he was gone, out onto the street and running down to the square, where a few of Clement's men were waiting.

'Get in that car, drive up there and get that tank's attention. Then lure him down here!'

The ground rumbled and then another building further up erupted in dust.

Two of Clement's men jumped straight into the car and sped off down a lane to the end of the village, where they both quickly emptied a magazine of ammunition on the tank before driving back.

The tank changed direction slightly to follow them.

'Woohoo!' shouted Jim excitedly, pushing Saxon into a doorway to take shelter. 'We're gonna get this one as well! Come on, let's move up.' Saxon nodded calmly and they made their way forward.

The two men walked calmly through the house, using their ears to track the slow progress of the tank as it advanced. Saxon, Jim and the tank crossed: they were now behind it.

Saxon sucked the sweat from his lips, it tasted of brick dust.

Saxon and Jim quickly looked out towards the

woods.

'See any foot soldiers?' asked Jim.

'No but there's fewer men firing from over there, so they've probably just realised their mistake and are getting ready to come across.'

'Let's see about that.' Jim checked the bazooka and held it out in front of him.

Casually, he stepped out into the road and took aim. Saxon watched the rocket land right between the exhaust covers and explode.

'Jackpot!' shouted Jim, ducking back into the house.

The two men stood still in the house.

'Hear that?' asked Jim.

'Hear what?' replied Saxon.

'Nothing! Sweet nothing. The engine's stopped. That's our second dead tank of the day.'

Saxon and Jim could hear German voices from inside the tank as they ran back through the house. The traverse engine whined and Jim and Saxon stopped briefly when the gun banged against the building with a loud bang, dislodging some bricks. They heard the barrel swing and hit the next building. It couldn't move and it couldn't shoot at anything. This Tiger was trapped.

A German swore loudly from inside.

A few of Clement's men crowded at the corner where Saxon and Jim now stood watching and panting. The commander's hatch opened up slowly, then, hands first, came an officer wearing a field cap and earphones.

'*Nicht Schiessen! Nicht Schiessen! Wir geben auf!*'

Slowly, the remaining hatches opened, and Jim

counted the crew as they clambered out to stand on the tank with their hands in the air.

'One, two, three, four, five,' counted Jim. 'Yep, they're all out, we can approach the tank.'

Clement appeared. 'Very well done!'

'Let's kill them all,' said one of the men.

'I have a better idea,' said Clement.

A moment later, a white flag appeared from the corner of a house. Clement's men had stopped firing a little earlier and at the sight of the white flag, a small, ironic, cheer could be heard from the Germans in the woods.

The cheers turned immediately to silence when the man holding the white flag emerged from cover, carried by one of the tank crew. The rest of the crew then joined him out in the open. The tank commander looked back and saw Clement flick his gun barrel up: *go on.*

Pushed by the officer, the Germans edged forward, further out into the field.

The village and the woods, only a moment ago filled with a frenzied firefight, became eerily silent.

Nervously, the Germans moved forward, the men's eyes constantly checking back at the village to see if the French would begin shooting again.

The crew walked out as far as the first tank. The crew of that tank joined them, walking slowly, nervously, apprehensively, back to the woods. With only a few metres left to go, they dropped the white flag and ran for cover.

'Good,' beamed Clement, lighting his pipe. 'They won't attack again without their tanks, well, not until dark and I hope you agree with me, Saxon,' he took a few puffs from the pipe, 'that the likes of us should be far, far away from here by then, no?'

'Agreed,' said Saxon in between draining a water bottle. 'But we still haven't achieved what we set out to do.'

'Maybe. But you, Jim, get to keep your socks for another day!'

'I do indeed, Clement, I do indeed.'

'Come,' said Clement, 'let's head back up to the far end of the village and see what we can see.'

'Where is your commander, Lieutenant?' asked Von Kettler, getting out the car.

'About ten kilometres south. We are quite spread out here at the moment, Sir.'

'I meant your company commander.'

The Lieutenant hesitated. 'I'm the company commander, Sir. All the Captains except one are dead, and he's commanding the Regiment right now.'

The General looked down. This is how it got on the Eastern Front when the Russians started winning there too.

The Lieutenant took off his helmet and wiped his face. 'I've lost two tanks and a few other men. I will have to wait for reinforcements before I attack again.'

'Of course.'

'Forgive me, General, but what are you doing here?'

'I'm the military head of the German Army in

France, Lieutenant. Every now and then I get out and about so I can see for myself what's going on.'

'But you have no escort, no protection, just this man and a woman. You can see for yourself, it's not safe even this far back any longer.'

'Oh, I get your point, don't worry. It's the same in a few other places. Tell me, why are your men hiding in that wood, Lieutenant?'

The officer looked surprised. 'Because the Allies command the air and I can't afford to get shot up.'

'Precisely,' replied Von Kettler. 'Field Marshal Rommel was injured only the other day, being driven in his big, black and all too obvious Mercedes staff car. I cannot afford the same fate, so I drive in a civilian car with people in civilian clothes. I don't wear my hat so as not to draw attention.'

Von Kettler went on, 'So while this may not be the front line, Lieutenant, the front line is my destination. How can I get around?'

'You're not going that way, General,' the Lieutenant gestured with his chin to where Clement and Saxon now stood, hidden.

Von Kettler could sense Eve's impatience from where she stood just off to one side, staring at the village with her arms folded, one knee bent.

'Lieutenant, I need to get forward.'

The Lieutenant hesitated again.

'What about down there,' pointed Eve, 'down through that valley?'

'That makes no sense; the Resistance will cut you off in no time. No. You need to head back and then try a road to the north or south that runs parallel with this one and trust the partisans are not there as well. I'll radio my headquarters to see if we can plot you a route, if you would like.'

'That will not be necessary, Lieutenant,' said Von Kettler a little too quickly.

'But I thought you said you wanted to get ahead?'

'I do, but I don't want the entire German Army to know I'm here. It never works, everyone tries to be helpful and protect me and only end up advertising my presence to the Allies.'

Eve looked back towards the village. *It was so close.* She stood as far into the middle of the road as she could, hoping she would be seen by the men in the village.

She was. Saxon, Jim and Clement, looking through binoculars, could see Eve clearly and watched Von Kettler talking.

'It that them?' asked Jim.

'I recognise her,' said Clement.

'You do?' asked Saxon.

'Yes, she was at the far side of the airfield the day you were flown out back in January. She was standing beside a German then as well.'

Saxon was convinced Eve was looking straight at him and even though he knew that was very unlikely, hidden in the shadows as they were, Saxon could not help but wonder if she was imploring them to come to the rescue. But to cross that no-man's-land between the village and the woods would be suicide.

'What if we go further around, staying away from the woods but get close enough if they want to make a run for it?' asked Clement.

'It might start another battle.'

'So what if it does? We just won the last one, didn't we? Well, drew it anyway.'

Clement went on: 'Those Germans won't leave that tree line unless they absolutely have to. They clearly don't feel up to it. They'd be attacking by now if they did. You know what those German officers are like, especially when there's a General around, any chance to get swords on the Knight's Cross! Come on, let's create another distraction. You could lay some covering fire with the Vickers guns on your Jeep, and maybe you could direct your tall agent in the skirt over there to drive down into the valley you were in earlier. The Germans would not be able to shoot at them in there once they're past that clump of bushes. And if the Germans decide to attack, I can hold them off and then get the men out of here in no time.'

'I wish I could read her mind,' said Saxon slowly, wondering how best to help Eve away from the Germans.

'Come on, Saxon,' said Clement, 'you go up there all guns blazing and go and get her and the General. I'll cover you from here.'

Saxon stared out across the field. Whatever the Germans were talking about, they appeared more animated to Saxon. One of them, probably the local commander, had just been handed a piece of paper by one of his men.

'OK, we'll just have to risk it. It looks like time is

running out.'

And with that, Saxon was striding off to the Jeep.

'General, have you made your exchange?'

'I'm sorry, Lieutenant?'

'This message here says I'm to ensure you make your exchange and then wait for someone to escort you straight back to Paris.'

Eve and Von Kettler shared a quick but wary glance.

'Let me see that,' Von Kettler took the slip with the message on it and read it. 'May I confer privately with my staff?' he asked.

The Lieutenant gestured and Von Kettler took Eve over to the other side of the road.

'What's this about an exchange?' he asked.

'Search me. I don't know.'

Eve looked once more towards the village. She had no plans for an exchange of Von Kettler. Had Berner's reach come as far as this Lieutenant?

Eve looked at the message in the General's hand and sighed as she thought.

'Tell him you need to go to the village. They have something highly secret and you are not to divulge what it is. Tell the Lieutenant here he needs to let you go on, maybe under a flag of truce. Tell him he is only to open fire if it looks like things are going wrong.'

The General's eyebrows dropped uncomprehendingly.

'I think this is Berner's work,' Eve went on. 'Just

tell the officer in charge over there to tell his men not to shoot and let's get driving. You are still a General, remember?'

Von Kettler turned to speak to the Germans again. 'Lieutenant, I cannot give you the details of my work here today and I must say I'm surprised at the content of this message. Usually, work of this nature is not so explicitly referred to in messages.' The General feigned concern. 'So you need to let me drive over to that village over there-'

'But the French!' gestured the Lieutenant wildly.

'They are here to meet me. They are going to hand me something very important, but I can't tell you about it. You were not supposed to be here, Lieutenant, but that's not your fault. The battle you were in - that wasn't supposed to happen either.'

'I've lost good men here, General.'

'I don't doubt it. But let me go forward and their lives would not have been forfeited for nothing,' lied Von Kettler.

The Lieutenant clearly wasn't happy but the gruffest of the NCOs standing behind him smiled at the intrigue. Or maybe, thought Von Kettler, the NCO thought his company should not be here either.

'I need you to let me drive over there very slowly. You will provide me with cover, but you are not to shoot unless I'm fired upon or I fire my pistol. That will be the signal. Otherwise, it's fingers off triggers. Understand?'

'And then?'

'And then, we come back and I won't want to be hanging around, so I will need you and your men to let me go straight through, please, so I can get back to Paris,' he lied again.

'Yes sir.'

'And it goes without saying, Lieutenant, you and your men have not seen me at all today.'

'Seen what, Sir?' said the Lieutenant conspiratorially.

'That's the spirit, Lieutenant.'

Eve walked to the car.

Unexpectedly, the Lieutenant seemed to cough and reached for his throat.

Everyone looked at him, not understanding. Eve paused to look with one foot already in the car.

Then blood started to gush through the gaps in the Lieutenant's fingers. Pale faced, gasping and gurgling, the Lieutenant sank to his knees.

'Get in the car!' screamed Eve and Von Kettler made a run for it but one of the German NCOs, diving forward, reached out and grabbed Von Kettler's ankle.

'Come on!' screamed Eve as the air began to crackle. They were under attack.

Von Kettler kicked at the NCO's hands and wrists and tried to roll away but the NCO was not for letting go.

'Roll away, now!' shouted Eve and Von Kettler gave an almighty shove.

The NCOs chest erupted. Von Kettler looked up and there was Eve, pistol still smoking. 'Come on!'

He reached up a hand and Eve helped him up.

The remaining Germans did not understand what was going on but were not reacting well to the murder of one of their Corporals.

The driver released the clutch and the car started forward as Eve and the General dived in. Eve pulled her door shut as she spotted a Jeep driving full speed towards them, the muzzles of its machine guns ablaze in flickering, yellow light.

Eve's driver propelled them on, and the Jeep moved off the road to let them pass. The soldier in the front of the Jeep was pointing them off to the right and down into the valley. Eve's driver understood immediately and veered off into the cover of the valley.

The car bumped over the rough ground with the rear doors open, flailing and banging as the car sped on. The Jeep turned and pulled up alongside without stopping, the driver gesturing 'follow me'.

They hurtled on.

Eve turned around to check on Von Kettler.

He wasn't there.

The door continued to swing on its hinges and Von Kettler was nowhere to be seen.

Eve was not to know but Von Kettler was already in the back of a German truck. 'Let me go! Let me go! It's of vital importance I get into that village,' he shouted but his orders were getting him nowhere.

Facing him was a Warrant Officer, pointing his Mauser rifle straight at Von Kettler's chest.

'I don't know what's going on here but with my Lieutenant dead, I'm in charge now and I'm moving you away for your own safety.'

'I don't need that!' yelled Von Kettler, desperate. 'I have a secret mission! I have to go, now!'

'Not today, you don't, General. Sorry. Not today.'

The truck started up and began to trundle

eastwards.

***

Eve sat on some rubble with her face in her hands.

'What happened to him?' asked Saxon, his face dusty from the drive.

'I don't know. One minute we were getting in the car. I saw him get in. Trust me, I saw him get in and yet when I turn around, he was gone. He must have fallen out.'

'I didn't see him once,' said Maurice, Saxon's driver.

'There were two men at the back of your car when I looked,' said Clement.

Eve's eyes blazed. 'I saw him get in. He was just there as we set off.'

'So you weren't expecting two men in German uniforms in the back?' asked Clement.

'No!' replied Eve.

'Then I think a German reached in the car and pulled him out thinking he was saving a friend from our attack.'

Eve, Saxon, Clement and Maurice stood silent. The firing between the two sides had dropped off.

'But I haven't failed a mission yet,' said Eve, 'and I'm not starting now.'

'Sorry Eve, but we wouldn't have got all the way across without being hit. I can't break through an infantry company. I can't give it another go,' said Saxon, clearly agonizing over another way.

'So we've lost him?' asked Eve, devastated.

'Sorry, mademoiselle but I have to agree with

Saxon here,' said Clement. 'I think he's back with the Germans. I also think we should go; there's nothing in this village for us. Not even gasoline. And the Germans will probably want this village back sometime soon.'

As they drove off, Eve did not take her eyes off where she last saw Von Kettler until it was completely hidden from view.

Oberst-Gruppenführer Möller pulled his gloves from his hands and stepped over some rubble into his new headquarters. Möller resisted the temptation to flinch as a rifle shot echoed through the air from somewhere else in the city.

Knowing Lemke was away somewhere, Walter Berner waited inside the Hotel Majestic and offered Möller a small bow as they shook hands. Berner dispensed with the *Heil Hitler* and simply welcomed Möller to Paris.

'Thank you. So here it is at last, the Hotel Majestic. I must say, Berner, I thought it would look a little more … pristine than this?'

'The Resistance are getting braver every day. Their courage is directly proportional to their distance to the invading American army.'

'And what do you do here, Berner?'

'I'm SD and will be one of your counterintelligence officers and security adviser.'

Möller looked at Berner in a way that suggested how the current security situation in the city may be a reflection on Berner's competence.

'And where is *Standartenführer* Lemke?'

'He's out, cleaning up after last night's entertainment.' Berner gestured down the corridor to lead the General to his new office. 'He does know you are coming, and he'll be here soon.'

Berner thought it wise to not let the newly arrived General know the *Milice* were being strung up across the city and Lemke was hurriedly putting SS and SD men into jobs previously done by Frenchmen.

They turned a corner, sentries flung open high double doors and Möller entered his new office for the first time. Berner stepped short to let Möller take in the view and soak up the opulence.

'Your predecessor loved this office,' said Berner truthfully.

'But he was in no mood to hang around, was he?'

Berner hesitated. 'He decided to make his escape when the attack started; perhaps he assumed the Resistance were after him.'

'Or was it that Von Kettler knew he was a suspect in the *putsch*?'

Berner hedged his bets. 'We are not sure.'

'Where is he now then?'

'Can we get on to that a little later? I'd rather bring you up to speed on the bigger picture before we get into the details.'

Möller placed his cap upside down on his new desk and sat down.

'OK, Berner, as you wish. So, what's the situation?'

Berner closed the doors and asked the sentries to ensure they were not overheard.

After some minutes, Möller pushed his fingertips together thoughtfully.

'Not good. How are our preparations to destroy this city if needed?'

Berner paused. 'Strictly speaking, that's an Army matter and you'll get them to update you shortly.'

'Of course.'

'But what I will venture,' Berner went on, cautiously, 'is should we?'

'What?'

'Yes. I mean look at it,' gestured Berner out the window. 'How many soldiers will it take to fight here? Thousands. We've already had one Stalingrad, I'm not entirely sure the Army would appreciate another. Anyway, are we really contemplating flattening *this?*'

'The *Führer* certainly is.'

'And tell the world we don't think we'll ever be back?'

Möller studied Berner. After a short pause, looking out of the window, he replied thoughtfully: 'We can say whatever we like, Berner. If we flatten the place, the *Führer* can later say he will rebuild it in twentieth century National Socialist splendour.'

'And if not?'

'I doubt anyone in Berlin will care.'

'Are they your instructions, though? To raze Paris to the ground?'

Möller looked down a little. 'Yes. The *Führer* wants me to be the man who destroyed Paris. I wouldn't get the glory for it, of course. Doctor Goebbels will no doubt make sure that glory would be reserved for the *Führer* alone, with me reduced to being merely a functionary.'

The room went quiet. Berner made his mind up about Möller that instant: here was a man caught between his orders and his post-war reputation.

Möller's head turned towards the door. 'Can you hear someone?'

Berner listened. 'That's probably Lemke. Shall I invite him in?'

Once in, Lemke effused charm to his new boss.

'General, General, welcome, it's so good to see you again. How do you like your new quarters?'

'We were just saying,' said Möller with a glance towards Berner, 'how grand it is.'

'I'm so sorry I was not here to greet you in person but once I heard you were here, I changed my plans. The terrorists will have to wait a bit longer.'

'Berner here has updated me on the growing confidence of the Resistance. Do you think the Allies are leading them?'

'By radio, probably. We haven't picked up any new agents on the streets, so I don't think the city's deemed safe enough for the Allies to land more people here yet.' Lemke raised himself onto his toes a little. 'Mind you, Berner here has the inside track on all that, don't you?'

Berner was not expecting that. 'Well, I, er…'

Lemke pressed ahead: 'I have instructed Berner here to use the contacts he has built up with London to listen out for any future plans they may have.'

'You haven't mentioned Von Kettler once yet, Lemke,' challenged Möller.

'Ah, well, Berner wouldn't know the latest news,' beamed Lemke. 'We've got him.'

Berner tried his absolute hardest not to show any reaction. 'I beg your pardon, Lemke?' he asked.

Lemke stared straight into Berner's eyes, looking for any form of reaction, any admission of guilt. Berner's face froze like a seasoned poker player.

'He seemed to be heading west,' Lemke went on, 'to make contact with the Allies but was intercepted. He's on his way back here. I can't wait to hear what he has to say.' Lemke licked his lips greedily, not taking his eyes off Berner.

Berner felt that awful coldness return and creep through his body and down his legs. He felt queasy, his knees wanting to flex.

'You look shocked, Berner,' asked Möller.

Berner fought to keep his composure. 'I am, General. I had no idea Von Kettler was making a run for it.' Then to Lemke, Berner asked: 'Is he alone?'

'Yes. His driver seems to have escaped.'

'I see,' Berner struggled to control every millimetre of his body. *Eve was safe.*

The room went silent again.

'Lemke,' said Möller, forcing Lemke to break eye contact with Berner.

'Yes, sir?'

'Whilst I'm glad we have Von Kettler under arrest, I would be interested in what I consider to be slightly more pressing matters, the security of Paris, for instance?'

'Why of course,' said Lemke, distractedly.

'Although, I have already had a good situation brief from Colonel Berner.'

Lemke's eyes flicked back to Berner. 'Have you,

indeed?'

Berner saw it in Lemke's eyes: the tell-tale look of suspicion.

Lemke turned back to Möller and went on to give an update that matched Berner's almost exactly. But things began to change when they started to discuss the future of the city.

'General, you cannot be serious: you want to ignore the *Führer's* orders? You haven't even been here an hour and you're contemplating the same fate as your predecessor?'

'You would do that to me too, Lemke? Shoot me like you will Von Kettler?'

'Sir, you're SS. You're here precisely because you're SS. It is our job to lead the Army at times like this. Our loyalty to the *Führer* is total. Don't let the Army get to you about this.'

If Möller needed a reminder of his predicament, here it was. Möller decided to retreat a little. 'It's not that. I just want to buy some time, Lemke. If we are going to make the Allies pay for entering the city, then we need to be ready for them and Berner here tells me we are not as prepared as we might be.

'So order the Pioneers to rig all the key bridges for demolition and continue with the building of strong-points. But no demolition is to be fired without my permission, do you understand?'

'But we have no time, Sir! We need to get underway if we are to make sure this city is demolished *before* the Allies arrive. We can't just blow the whole place up in one go!'

'Nevertheless, Lemke, I will be the sole authority for demolitions within the city.'

'But-'

'Sorry, Lemke, no ifs, no buts. Understood?'

Lemke's lips went white as he forced them together. Berner watched Lemke's hands form fists. Berner was pretty sure that hadn't escaped Möller either.

'Ask the Army in, will you?' asked Möller, looking like it was time to get off the subject.

Berner needed no encouragement and was gone. Lemke rushed past him, turned and stopped to confront Berner at the top of the staircase.

'Does Von Kettler's capture concern you, Berner?'

'Only in as much as I'm shocked to have our worst fears confirmed. I didn't think he was a conspirator.'

Lemke continued to scan Berner's face for the slightest indication of guilt. Berner was set to not give him the satisfaction.

'Well he was - a conspirator, that is. I knew it all along. I wonder who it was who helped him out of here the night of the attack? Any ideas?' Lemke's face was centimetres away from Berner's.

'I can interrogate him when he arrives if you like.'

'Oh no, Berner, that job is for me now, not you.' Something seemed to occur to Lemke. 'Which reminds me, I still have a prisoner in the cells. I think I will get some practice on him before Von Kettler arrives.'

Berner knew what that meant for Franck. Berner wondered if Franck would have the courage to bite down on that tablet. Subconsciously, Berner checked his jacket pocket to make sure his own suicide capsule was where it should be. He wondered if he would have the courage to take his own if it came to that now the likelihood of detection seemed to be increasing by the minute.

* * *

The soldier put the key in the door and looked at Lemke, waiting.

Lemke swayed his head from side to side, like a boxer preparing for a bout, and then nodded to the soldier who turned the key and opened the door.

Lemke walked in slowly, rolling up his sleeves.

* * *

General der Infanterie Von Kettler sat in the back of an Army truck, his head swaying with the movement. It appeared, thought Von Kettler, no Allied aircraft would come to *his* rescue, forcing a stop amongst the trees.

Von Kettler counted the hours down to his return to Paris. He wondered, oddly calm, how many hours and days he had left to live. Inwardly, he prayed his wife and children were still safely on their way to Switzerland. To have been so close to escape! He even got to see the Allied soldiers sent to meet with him. He just hoped he had it in him to keep his dignity knowing what was coming. The beatings, the torture, the hangman's rope.

Eventually, owing more to the needs of the driver's bladder than his own, the truck pulled over, stopping under the cover of some trees. Once the driver had urinated against the tyres, being a General, Von Kettler suggested he should be owed a little more privacy and strode off deeper in amongst the trees.

Von Kettler paused for a moment and smiled at the wind whistling gently through the trees. The beautiful birdsong.

The Warrant Officer swore as the report of the pistol rang through the woods. He threw down his water bottle and ran. There lay Von Kettler, the right side of his head a bloody mess. The air smelt of singed hair. The Warrant Officer kicked Von Kettler's small pistol away and dived down to help. He withdrew a little, recoiling at all the blood but soon composed himself and got to work. The General had lost an eye somewhere but was still alive.

'Over here!' he shouted. 'Help me get him on that truck, we need to get him to a hospital!'

'How did he die?' asked Lemke, already having a good idea what the answer was. Franck's body lay lifeless next to the chair.

'Cyanide poisoning,' said the doctor putting away his stethoscope.

Lemke swore.

'No doubt about it.' The doctor grunted as he got to his feet. 'You didn't see him take it?'

'I saw him with his hand by his mouth. I then started speaking to him, you know, let him know in advance what I was about to do to him unless he talked. That's when he started convulsing.

Lemke took a look at Franck's face. There was still some foam around his mouth and his nose was blue.

'If you look closely, although I don't advise that you do,' said the doctor looking down at Franck, 'you will see bits of powder on his lips. There's more in the back of his mouth. That means he crushed the tablet between his teeth and my guess is he did it as soon as you walked in.'

Lemke swore again.

'That doesn't,' the doctor coughed delicately, 'explain all the bruising, though, does it?'

'You don't have to worry about that, Doctor,' hissed Lemke. He must have been dead when that all happened.

The doctor looked down on the dead Franck.

'How did he get that tablet in here?' Lemke asked. 'What are his shoes like?'

'There are no signs of any hiding places in the soles, if that's what you mean,' said the Guard Sergeant, appearing from behind.

'OK. Let me take a look at the log. In the meantime, Sergeant, get the body out of here.'

Lemke instinctively dusted off his hands, looking around the cell. This was turning into another really bad day.

The Guard Sergeant returned. 'Here's the log, Sir. No visitors.'

'Oh no, that's not everyone,' interrupted the sentry at the cell door, with his rifle slung over his shoulder.

'Colonel Berner was here as well. I'm doing a double shift because of the attack, so I was here when he popped by.'

* * *

Some way back from the scene of the morning's battle, Clement's men cooked lunch. Their mood was sombre. Although they had fought off a German company and two Tiger tanks, the sense of having collectively failed to bring Von Kettler back hung over them all.

Maurice, with his beret on the back of his head, held on by his headphones, listened intently to a message coming in. He took notes and deciphered it using the code words printed on the silk sheet he had brought with him from Britain. As a result, Maurice was quicker at getting messages out and back than Saxon had ever been.

Maurice read it and started to smile. He handed his notebook to Saxon.

'Well I never.'

'What?' asked Clement.

'Fancy a trip to Paris, Clement?'

'You what?' asked Eve reaching across to take the notebook and see for herself.

Saxon continued: 'We're to wait for an airdrop of weapons just down the road and then take them to Paris.'

'To the Prefecture,' said Eve slowly.

'The Prefecture?' asked Clement. 'Why there?'

'It's where the revolution will begin,' said Eve.

Seeing the confused faces looking at her, she continued, 'we've been planning this for months. When the Parisian Resistance is ready to topple the

Germans, they are to attack and hold the Prefecture. And hold out until the Allies arrive. The resupply of arms and ammunition was a pre-condition for helping out with the release of Von Kettler. It looks like they're going to get their side of the bargain at least.'

There was a moment of silence. 'So we are to help liberate Paris?' asked Clement, lighting his pipe.

'We are,' stated Eve.

'That makes up for this morning,' he said tamping down the tobacco lightly. 'Where's the airdrop?'

Saxon studied his map. 'Here.'

Clement took a look. 'Are they landing or dropping by parachute?'

Maurice replied, 'They will be landing.'

'We can get going in what, just over an hour. If we see any Germans, we just keep out of their way. Agreed?'

Everyone nodded.

'What about you? You coming with us?' Clement asked Eve.

'I know all the main Resistance leaders in Paris and I've been working there since Christmas. I can make sure you deal with all the right people and I know where I'm going. I'll get you to the Prefecture and then head off to check up on my own contacts. I want to make sure they are all right.'

'Then that is agreed,' stated Clement. 'I can't wait to tell the boys this one.'

Monday

Back in his office, Lemke had some thinking to do. The problem was that Sauer was here to help him and that was the last thing Lemke wanted right now.

'Berner saw the prisoner but it wasn't logged in the occurrence book? The next thing, the prisoner's dead.'

Sauer looked proud of himself. Lemke despised Sauer when he was in this frame of mind. Sauer would convince himself he was a spy-catcher extraordinaire, when he wasn't.

'But it's not that simple though, Sauer, is it?' Lemke said, wearily, 'Yes, Berner goes to see the prisoner. Yes, the prisoner dies but did Berner kill him? No, he couldn't have done. Berner sees him in the morning and the prisoner is alive and well when his evening meal is served.'

Sauer looked momentarily crestfallen until his face beamed in pleasure yet again: 'So Berner gave him the tablet?'

'Lemke thought about that. 'It's possible, yes. But why?'

'Maybe Berner told him what an interrogator you are. We all know Berner doesn't like violence, but you? We all know you're not scared of the sight of terrorist blood, don't we?'

Lemke could feel his frustration building.

'So what?'

'So Berner takes pity on him and asks the soon-to-be-dead prisoner if he wanted a tablet so he could take his own life and spare himself a torturing?'

Lemke studied the top of his desk. 'Possibly.'

'I mean, why else would Berner want someone from the Resistance dead?'

Lemke's head shot up, like he'd been electrocuted. 'Go on.'

'Well we know Berner's got all sorts of shady links with the Resistance. What if this guy knew more than Berner wanted him to?'

'Like what?'

'Like who told him to attack the Hotel Majestic just as the leaving party was about to start!'

'So the General can take the slip out the back door, aided by a British agent.'

Sauer, so shocked by his own apparent brilliance, stared in wide open-eyed silence at the wall.

Lemke knew he needed more time to think. He also knew he needed to be rid of Sauer.

'Sauer, you may well be onto something. It's fanciful but go get yourself a drink at the bar. You've earned it. I'll be down in a moment.'

Sauer was gone in an instant.

Lemke opened his draw slowly and pulled out a sheet of paper and a pencil. He started to draw up the options of why Berner might have wanted Franck dead. The scribbles of the pencil grew faster and faster.

Moments later, Lemke was up and out the door, leaving Sauer to fend for himself at the bar, where the staff were trying to avoid eye contact.

* * *

The Dakota aircraft turned and, in broad daylight, revved its engines to take off. Saxon and Clement braced themselves against the backwash of the aircraft as it bounced off the field and into the air. They watched the aircraft circle and then fly direct over their heads, giving the wings a wiggle in salute as it set off back to Britain.

'They sure are more confident than they used to be,' observed Clement.

'Yeah?' asked Jim Jackson.

'Oh yes. Many a night we had to lie out for hours waiting for a parachutist to be dropped in, maybe with a canister or two of ammunition for us. All done in the dark, not broad daylight like this. We had to post sentries for miles in case the Germans were out on patrol. If the pilot wasn't happy, then they would not come and not bother to tell us. And now? Look at it. They land where they like, with us many miles behind the German lines, and even give us a little flying display on their way home. Jim, this is a very different war to what it used to be. It must be: I lead a Resistance unit from Rouen but here we are, this afternoon, about to set off to Paris!'

Jim gestured towards the stack of rifle and ammunition containers. 'I think you might need some bigger trucks, Clement. That's a lotta guns to shift.'

Clement looked across at the stash quietly. Jim might have had a point.

'Yes, although all that gasoline they dropped off will come in handy.'

* * *

Lemke's tyres screeched to a halt on the gravel drive at Le Vésinet. His pass was checked on a number of occasions, but no one wanted to be in the way of this SS man.

Once inside, Lemke made his way from corridor to corridor, room to room and eventually found a number of Army doctors in a state of commotion. *This must be it*, thought Lemke.

'Is he in there?' Lemke asked a doctor.

'Who are you?'

Lemke showed his pass once again.

The doctor showed genuine nervousness. 'You lot don't take long, do you?'

'How do you mean?'

'He only died a few moments ago.'

'Von Kettler?'

'Yes. I'm sorry.'

'Me too,' replied Lemke, as he barged his way through to the room the doctors had been looking towards.

'Hey!' cried one, 'you can't go in there!'

'Watch me,' said Lemke, without even turning.

Lemke pushed forward and ordered some fussing nurses out of the way. Lemke recognised Von Kettler's features between all the bandages wrapped around the head.

The General's boots and trousers were stowed neatly to one side, but his tunic was all ruffled with a pocket button undone.

Lemke blew out his cheeks in disappointment. He

studied the face a little longer. A doctor approached hastily.

'Excuse me, Doctor. The General here, he died of his wounds?'

'Not quite. He had a seizure and his wounds probably brought that on.'

'A seizure?'

'Yes, you know, jerky movements, confusion…'

Lemke stepped forward to take a much closer look at the General's face and swore viciously.

'Cyanide poisoning!'

'Very likely, I'm sorry,' said the doctor quietly.

'Do you know that for certain?'

'No, but I can test if you want.'

Lemke stepped up to the doctor and, up on his toes, bore down on the doctor.

'You do that, understand, and I need that result now.'

The doctor squirmed. 'That will take a little time, if you don't mind me saying, but I will get you the result as quickly as possible.'

Lemke changed suddenly and was all charm and lightness. 'Not at all doctor, I will happily wait. In the meantime, could you tell me where the Field Marshall is?'

'Rommel?'

'Yes. He is being treated here too, isn't he?'

'He is but access is strictly controlled.'

'I'm not surprised, looking at what just happened to this General.'

'It's not just that, it's that his medical condition is severe. We want him back to normal as quickly as we can, any interruptions could disrupt things.'

'You're quite right, Doctor but access is strictly controlled by the SS, is it not?'

The doctor smiled. Lemke needed to press his point no further.

'This nurse will show you to the Field Marshal's room. I should be ready to tell you for certain about the General's death in about an hour.'

Lemke thanked the doctor and willingly followed behind the swaying hips of a nurse who led him to Rommel.

Rommel sat upright in bed, not too happy about the SS to visit unannounced. But the Field Marshal relaxed a little when Lemke said he was here simply check up on security.

Rommel said he was happy with the arrangements. 'I'm still fighting this war, *Standartenführer*. So visits by security staff are welcome. Your boys out there seem to be doing a good job. I do not want some Commandos coming to take me away!'

'Certainly not. I will make sure you are well attended to.'

'Thank you. Believe it or not, Lemke, I may not look it, but I'm still at work.' Rommel gestured to his notebook. 'I'm due a visit anytime now, I was wondering if you would not think me rude if perhaps…?'

Rommel left the sentence hanging, waiting for Lemke to get the hint.

'Of course, Sir. I shall not disturb you any further. You will get an occasional visit from some of my officers, but I will ask them to cause the least amount of disruption as possible, with your permission?'

'Of course,' smiled the Desert Fox.

Lemke's moment had arrived. 'I will put one of my best men onto the job. Do you know Colonel Berner, onetime of the *Abwehr* and now working for the SS?'

'He works for you now?'

'Now the *Abwehr* has been subsumed, yes.' Lemke was up on his tiptoes.

'Well, of course I know Berner! We were in the Württemberg infantry together. In fact, he was here just a moment ago, you have just missed him.'

Lemke's heels struck the floor heavily. Rommel had just told Lemke what he needed to hear. It was time to get the results about Von Kettler, though he was pretty certain what the answer was going to be. Then it was going to be time to get back to Paris. Fast.

Between them, Clement and Eve were able to talk their way past the number of barricades set up on the roads to Paris by the braver locals and resistance fighters.

'Where are the Germans?' Clement asked one man.

'They're all gone! All gone. Back to Paris.

'Ah,' said Clement slowly. 'We may have a fight on our hands sometime soon.'

'Not on this stretch we won't,' said Eve, 'just look at all that.'

Looking down the road, they could both see

people thronging out onto the streets. Flags were making an appearance. Conversation was alive with news of the general strike in Paris and the approach of the Allies. Rumours abounded that it was to be French soldiers who be the first to liberate the city and De Gaulle was to be with them. Clement rather fancied some French resistance fighters led by him would beat them all to it.

The scene was one of pure elation. Confidence rose in the air.

Loyalties were shifting fast.

Before long, they approached the city limits. They made a short pause at a crossroads, to make certain they were on the right road.

The excitement was palpable and a few of Clement's men sipped the celebratory wine, making eyes at the girls. The inevitable jokes of how liberated the girls were feeling today were made.

Turning her back on the crowd, Eve said dryly, 'Saxon, we can't stay here. Clement's men will all be in bed with someone if we don't get a move on.'

'Good point.'

The crowd suddenly surged. 'They're here! They're here!' some started to shout, looking westward.

Every neck craned. Saxon climbed up the side of Clements truck.

'A convoy! The Yanks are coming!' he shouted, climbing down wearing a huge grin.

Eve grinned uncontrollably.

'Right, I'll nip on ahead with Jim and make contact with them. They could come in very handy getting us into Paris.'

'Good thinking. I'll stay here and pretend to be Mother Superior with some of these girls,' smiled Eve.

Jim sounded the horn and slowly the crowd parted. Being in uniform, everyone wanted to reach out and touch them, kiss them, give them a drink or all three. Ahead they could see a convoy of Allied half-tracks and trucks heading towards the same crossroads ahead. They all had the white star painted on their doors.

Saxon brought the Jeep to a halt and stepped out, putting his beret on to help him stand out as a soldier. Jim, tall and in his American uniform, politely pushed a handsome girl aside and walked out into the middle of the road. Saxon raised a hand to signal 'halt'.

Behind them, Eve walked forward holding Clement's hand.

The convoy approached, the vehicles all brimmed with soldiers in American uniforms, smiling and waving. The cheering from the crowd grew louder.

The convoy slowed down and pulled up next to Saxon and Jim. The soldier in the driver seat leaned out to shout:

'*Hola! Es bueno verte, pero tenemos órdenes de no parar, tenemos que entrar en la ciudad!*'

Saxon froze. 'I'm, I'm sorry, what did you say?' asked Saxon, nonplussed.

'*Dije, tenemos que irnos. ¡Tenemos que llegar a la ciudad!*'

'Well, I'll be…' said Jim, laughing to himself.

'That's not French, Jim, is it?'

'You bet it isn't French, my friend. That language they're speaking? It's Spanish.'

'Spanish?!'

Jim looked at Saxon with the biggest smile possible on his face. 'They're speaking Spanish.'

Saxon had been through some unexpected things in his time but this one took first place.

'What do you mean, Spanish? What are they doing here? You speak Spanish?'

'I'll find out and yes, when you come from California like I do, you pick up Spanish pretty quick.'

Saxon was lost for words. Jim walked forward casually and started a conversation. The soldiers on the trucks looked down, seemingly surprised to come across another Spanish speaker here of all places. Soon enough, noticed Saxon, they were all chatting away, and Saxon had not the faintest idea what they were on about. But whatever it was, there was plenty of pointing in the direction of Paris and then pointing at a map of the city centre.

All around them, the locals celebrated joyously.

Jim leaned back, still smiling.

'OK. They are heading to the same place as us, so they say we should slot into their convoy at the half-way point and all we have to do is keep up.'

'I don't believe it,' said Eve to Saxon, struggling to be heard above the celebrating.

'Me neither,' said Jim, swinging a leg into the Jeep.

Someone from the convoy shouted *'¡Venga! ¡Vamonos!'* and the lead half-track started to move off.

It took a while for Clement to prize his men off the local girls and into the trucks but, as if by magic, a gap appeared between the Spanish vehicles. Saxon led their supply convoy into that and then they were underway. Next stop, Paris.

'Spaniards!' laughed Clement, 'I don't believe my eyes! Think about it, Eve, I'm fighting a war with British and Americans by my side, off to liberate Paris, with a load of Spanish soldiers wearing American uniforms who somehow are in the French Army!'

'This is a day we won't forget in a hurry, Clement,' said Eve, raising her voice over the hum of the tyres on the tarmac and the sound of *La Marseillaise*.

* * *

Möller listened at the open window and all he could hear was gunfire.

'They're in open revolt, now, General,' said Berner. 'Barricades across all the main roads, all the transport staff are on strike, as are the police. They seem well organised; they're even using children to run messages and small supply runs.'

Möller listened and nodded his acceptance.

Berner continued: 'They seem most focused on the Grand Palais, Chamber of Deputies, and the Prefecture. I suppose we shouldn't be surprised.'

'But they're not here?'

'Not yet, General, no,' said Berner hesitatingly.

'Hmm, I doubt it will be long.'

'There are also reports of Allied convoys starting to probe their way towards the city centre.'

'I'd heard.'

'General, you've got a decision to make and you'll need to make it soon.'

'I've thought about nothing else since I arrived, Walter.'

Berner was certain where Lemke was right now and that his days or hours may be numbered, so he felt he could afford to be a little less cautious now. 'You can't destroy the city.'

'I'm sorry, Berner? What did you just say?'

Berner corrected himself. 'Surely, you don't think we can destroy this city and hope to get out alive. You don't have the troops to quell this uprising. They'll be spilling over the walls for us soon.'

'If I let the Allies in, Walter, I shall be a traitor to Germany, which gets me shot. Or, if I chose to fight and destroy the city, I'm still likely to be lined up against a wall but will feel the sharp point of a French bullet rather than a good old German one.'

Möller looked back out the window with his hands behind his back. Berner could feel his indecision.

'But knowing my luck, Walter, the French would shoot me with German bullets.'

Möller smiled, despite himself.

'Maybe you're not as damned as you think you are, General,' said Berner.

Möller turned from watching the number of clouds of smoke over the rooftops increase to stare Berner straight in the eye. 'How do you mean?'

Berner took a sharp breath in. *Here goes.* 'I'm a counterintelligence officer. I have more contacts with the French and Allies than you would be comfortable knowing. But the thing is, I know if you were to give the order to withdraw without destroying the city, the French would let you drive out and not rip you or what's left of the Army here to shreds. You'd survive to fight another day.'

'Are you crazy, Berner? Did you not hear Lemke and what he had to say about loyalty!' Möller looked down at the carpet for a moment. 'Have you been negotiating with the Resistance?'

How little you know, thought Berner.

'The French have used their contacts to speak to mine. They said they had a message to get to me. I'm not surprised they used the agents to get the conversation with us started. They're hardly going to just walk up to the front door and ask to come in for a drink and a chat, are they? But I believe them when they say we can walk out of here if we want to.'

'And then what, Walter? Straight back to the patient and ever-forgiving arms of the *Führer*? He told me, Berner, in no uncertain terms, he wanted this place *destroyed*!'

'Did you agree with him?'

'What?' said Möller, astonished.

'When Hitler said he wanted Paris destroyed, did you think that was the right thing to do? What did your instinct tell you?'

Möller froze and that gave Berner the answer he had expected, confirming his opinion of Möller since the moment he had arrived.

Möller turned to face out the window again.

'I can't believe it's come to this. I mean,' he gestured forward with his hand, 'I'm given the greatest command of my entire career and in no time, it soon becomes clear it will be my last.'

'You can't fight your way out and it's too late to start blowing everything up. We've only got a few hours left. But I think you have a choice in how this ends, General. Few in your rank do, so this is a moment of some importance.'

Möller contemplated for a few seconds. Quietly and with his head bowed, Möller asked: 'What do I have to do, Walter?'

* * *

'I have never seen so many flags!' Clement had to shout above the noise of the crowd, singing at the top of their voices.

The crowd danced along with the convoy went past Place d'Italie, not stopping to celebrate.

'It's getting dark,' said Clement to Eve, 'and the crowd is slowing us right down.'

'Don't worry,' she replied. 'I know where we are and we'll get to the Prefecture in daylight, even at this rate.'

Clement, with his arm out the cab, reached out with his fingers to greet people, smiling.

Suddenly, the crowd seemed to collectively duck their heads and then look about curiously, hesitantly. Then there was another crack in the air.

'Look out! Sniper!' shouted Clement.

Whether they heard Clement or not, the crowd ran first to the walls and back, disappearing into side roads.

Slowly, the convoy moved forward, every pair of eyes straining for the first sight of the enemy.

After a few hundred metres, they saw a German

soldier round a corner. Seemingly stunned at recognising the convoy facing him, he fired his sub-machine gun in their direction. Resistance fighters and Spanish soldiers alike fired back and in a heartbeat, the German was lost in a cloud of brick dust and stone chips. The man raised an arm to protect his face before his legs abruptly collapsed beneath him.

Heads turned to watch the man die as the convoy raced by.

'Did you see that?' asked Jim over the sound of the Jeep's tyres on the road. 'the epaulets on that dead Kraut's tunic? Blue, he was a signaller. So, if he's a signaller, where are the infantry?'

'Don't know,' replied Saxon. 'Maybe we are closer to the centre than the Germans think we could be. Maybe we're taking them by surprise but if we're up against the chefs, bottle-washers and the headquarters' staff, I'm not complaining.'

For no reason, the convoy slowed a little, wary of what was around every next corner. It was not lost on any of them how there were no more crowds. This part of Paris was still a battlefield.

The convoy came to a halt. 'What's the matter?' asked Clement impatiently. A voice from the back of the truck said around the next corner was the Île de la Cité, and the Prefecture.

Clement got out of the cab and climbed down onto the empty street. He could hear gunfire everywhere, but it was sporadic. Nowhere, it seemed to him, were there any running battles. It seemed like the fight for Paris was hundreds of little, independent and very personal battles all happening at the same time.

He trotted along to walk alongside Saxon, still sat in the back of the Jeep.

'We're nearly there, aren't we?' asked Clement. Saxon could hear the excitement in Clement's voice.

'Apparently, so. I don't know much about Paris, but guess what, Jim here knows all about it. He's proving rather useful.'

As they continued to edge forward, Saxon clambered out and having picked up his Carbine, walked forward with Clement. Ahead, peering around a corner was the Captain commanding the 9th. He spoke very quietly.

'The Prefecture is over the bridge and straight up that road there.'

'Great,' said Clement, 'let's make a dash for it.'

'Not so fast,' came a whispered reply. 'There are Germans on the bridge. My guess is,' he continued, 'I don't know if that bridge is rigged for demolition or not and I don't fancy finding out just as we drive across.'

Saxon agreed. 'Got any Sappers?'

'No.'

'Well,' replied Saxon, 'I'm known for blowing *up* bridges but if I can get up close, I might be able to find a way to cut the firing circuit. I'd need some help, though.'

The Captain nodded his agreement. 'Take Sergeant Alamilla and his squad with you. He has passable French and he's a good man.'

'Thanks, I'll head up the road going parallel to this one if that's OK with you?' asked Saxon.

'Of course. Good luck. I'll be watching and the moment you signal me on, we'll be driving by as fast as we can!'

'OK.'

Saxon walked back down the convoy to where the Captain had pointed out the gruffest-looking Spanish soldier Saxon had ever laid eyes on. This man was massive, his rifle looked small in his hands.

'Alamilla?' asked Saxon.

'Yes.'

'Good stuff. You and your men are to come with me. We are to make sure the bridge is not rigged for demolition. All I need you to do is buy me time to get up close and take a look. Kill any Germans you like but keep them off of me, understand?'

'Of course!' With that, Sergeant Alamilla shouted orders Saxon had no hope of understanding and in a minute, Alamilla's men were briefed and ready. Saxon liked the look of them, they appeared experienced and totally reliable. Clement, spoiling for a fight, brought along a few of his own men without asking for permission.

Jim appeared with them. Cocking his Carbine, he explained how someone else was driving the Jeep right now. 'The guy looked pretty keen, so I let him take over.'

* * *

Lemke smashed his hand against the steering wheel in frustration. He was getting nowhere fast. Every bend he drove around seemed to have a barricade up or being built further ahead. He was not able to make any progress forward, into the city. Instead, he seemed to be moving right all the time, trying to find a way through.

The Metro and the railways were now shut, he had no other choice but to drive.

He knew it all now. The doctor had said Von Kettler had a seizure, *a cyanide-induced seizure.* Just the sort of seizure the prisoner Franck had had in the cells on Avenue Foch - and the connection between the death of both men was one Walter Berner. Berner would have wanted a resistance fighter and a suspected traitor dead for one reason: to cover Berner's tracks. To protect a big secret for or about Berner himself. *It could be the only explanation.* With Berner's links to London being what they were, Lemke had a good idea what that big secret was.

Lemke turned a corner and the road looked clear. He shifted through the gears quickly and propelled his car forward. 50, 60, 70 kilometres an hour. Lemke left his frustrations behind him, the engine revving hard.

Then his windscreen smashed and all of a sudden, Lemke could hear a plinking noise against the side of his car. Bullets cracked overhead and buzzed close by. Lemke leaned down to his side to take cover behind the dashboard, popping his head up every now and then to see where he was going. The car lurched from side to side with every correction. Lemke felt he had got past the ambush as the rounds landed now on the back of his car rather than the front. The claps of sound seemed to be reducing. Lemke dared to look behind; what looked like kids and a girl in a beret and shorts were firing wildly after him.

Feeling safer, Lemke sat up a bit more and brushed chips of glass of his chest and lap, laughing nervously at his close escape. He drove on still more determined. It was time to take his revenge on Walter Berner and also on this traitorous city. He bowed his head forward, into the onrushing air and hurtled on.

Perched across some steps that rose up to street level, Saxon peered gingerly around the corner, with his head at pavement level, where no German would expect to see him. Saxon surveyed what was now his own battlefield.

Off to his right, unmistakably, was the Notre-Dame. Directly opposite, on the other side of the Seine, stood Government-looking buildings, every window of which would have a clear view, and shot, the moment he broke cover. He could also see a tall tower. The Germans simply *had* to have a sniper in there.

Saxon was surprised at how there was *so much space* to his front: the road alongside the river was wide, the river was wide – there was just nowhere to take cover out on the street: it would be like running across a billiard table.

Saxon looked behind himself, the men were busy pressing themselves into every available recess. Their faces dropped when they saw the apprehension in Saxon's face.

Saxon turned back and edged himself a tiny

amount further forward on his toes and elbows to look around the corner.

There was the Pont Saint-Michel, about a hundred yards away. It was made of stone and from the glance he'd had at the bridge when back conferring with the Captain, he knew the roadway was open. That meant only one thing to Saxon right now: if that bridge was set for demolition, then the charges would have to be *under* the bridge. This was not getting any easier.

Saxon studied again the wide expanse of space in front of him and all the windows staring back. Going out onto that street would be suicide, but they *had* to get across that bridge. Saxon's brain was racing but he had no workable answers.

He was just about to crawl back into cover, when at ground level, at the next corner down, something caught his eye. A movement, a tiny movement. Saxon looked again. There it was, right opposite the bridge. In the doorway of what looked like a restaurant, the toe of a German boot popped in and out of view. That was all he could make out, just the toe of a boot, but it was definitely German, and that's all Saxon needed to know. He smiled and crawled back, turned towards his men and stood up, his earlier apprehension gone.

'Right, I've got a plan. Come with me, we're going back that way,' he announced, and proceeded to walk away from the river and back past the men, who watched him uncertainly as he trotted by. Their footsteps echoed between the narrow, high buildings on both sides. Clement followed. He knew better than to pester Saxon at a time like this. He raised his eyebrows in an amused way at his men as he followed on.

Saxon slung his carbine over his shoulder, looking at the doors and windows of the buildings on the left side of the road.

After a short while, he stopped. 'In here,' he said, disappearing into a doorway.

The men followed him through a dark tunnel and out into courtyard. Saxon waited for everyone to catch up before turning to them to explain.

'There's no way we will get to the bridge alive if we go out onto the main road out there: it's too open. We'd be cut to shreds in no time. But I did spot a German soldier on the corner, he was right opposite the bridge itself. There were also some wires running from the bridge and along the road. That's where I think the firing point is. So what we're going to do is creep through these buildings here, staying parallel with the river, and attack the firing point from the rear. They won't be expecting that.'

Suddenly, everyone was smiling at Saxon.

'Whoever gets into the room first, and remember it could as much be on the first floor as ground level, as soon as you see the firing device, probably a heavy-looking metal box about this size,' Saxon held out his hands to something the size of a large binocular case, 'with a tee-shaped grip on top of it to one side.'

Heads nodded slowly in comprehension.

'It'll have some wires sticking out of it, as you would expect. All you have to do is rip the wires out. Understand?'

They did.

'They will also probably try and fire the demolition the old-fashioned way by lighting a fuse, so if you see a German with a box of matches, kill him. Understand that too?'

Saxon was greeted with enthusiastic, maybe nervous smiling.

'OK, let's go.'

Saxon set off through the courtyard, with the men's eyes all up to the windows above, scanning for danger from above. With surprising speed, they were all across the first courtyard, their boots echoing off all the walls.

Up against the far wall, Saxon stood on his tiptoes to peer over a window ledge.

'We need to get through here and I can see light coming through from the other side. I reckon there's another courtyard like this one through there. Once we're across that, I think we'll be onto 'em. Anyone see an open door or a window?'

There was a sudden smash of glass off to Saxon's right. Sergeant Alamilla was wasting no time in getting a window open. He clambered in and in no time, a door opened.

'*Por aqui por favor,*' said Alamilla, nonchalantly.

With that, Saxon and the men were rushing along a long corridor. Saxon slowed and put his hand in the air to stop those running behind him from charging too far ahead.

Saxon crept forward again, his rubber soled boots silent on the floorboards. Peeking through the windows, into another courtyard, smaller this time, looking for Germans.

He could hear his men shuffling impatiently behind him.

Saxon licked his lips, trying to remain calm despite his heart pounding in his chest.

And then there it was, in a window on the other side of the next courtyard: the top of a German soldier's helmet going from left to right on the ground floor and in a hurry.

'We're not going across the courtyard, this time. There's a building on the right that looks like it connects where we are to where the Germans are and I've seen one, so they are definitely there. We will cut through that building on the right and the Germans will be on the other side of that. Everyone understand? Be as silent as you can be until we're seen and then make as much noise as you want. We need to take this lot totally by surprise. That way, the firing circuit might still not be ready to fire. They need vital seconds to connect the wires and fire the thing. So we will need to be quick, understand?'

'We've got it,' said Clement.

'Sergeant Alamilla, lead the way.'

Alamilla took a couple of his own soldiers forward, opening doors, waiting to see if there were Germans in the room behind before moving on quickly to the next door, running at a low crouch.

Alamilla looked back, with his hand on a door handle, at Saxon.

'I can hear them, on the other side,' he whispered.

'Right. All of you,' said Saxon in a hushed tone, only just loud enough to be heard. 'Bunch up close to the door. As soon as the door opens, I want you all through as quickly as you can. Understand?'

Heads nodded but less enthusiastically than before.

'And Clement?'

'Yes?' replied Clement cautiously.

'Take four blokes and head straight upstairs, in case the firing point is there, OK?'

'Fine, let's get on with it.'

Saxon nodded and Alamilla pulled the door open.

In a second all the men were in, but the room was empty. Crouching and ready for a fight but with no fighting to be done, the tension got to them and a couple of the men began to laugh nervously at each other.

'Clement, that way. Alamilla, come with me,' hissed Saxon. The laughter ended.

Saxon approached the next door and tiptoed forward. He listened and could hear German voices. He pointed to the door and nodded. His men nodded back. This was it.

* * *

Through Nanterre, Lemke charged eastward over a crossroads, hurtling towards the centre. He allowed himself a small smile which was suddenly cut short.

Phut.

He listened to the engine and there is was again, *phut, phut.*

Lemke groaned as he looked at the petrol gauge. Empty.

There was a sudden loud bang from the engine, and then the car was just cruising along with the engine dead. Lemke allowed the car to roll to a halt and swore viciously.

He climbed out to see his car riddled with holes, one of which probably explained his empty fuel tank.

Lemke swore repeatedly. He pulled out his pistol and put a round straight through his German number plate, which could have been the only thing to betray him to that French ambush back there.

He wanted to empty his magazine into the car, but a child's laugh stopped him. Lemke looked up and there, in a doorway was a young girl, probably four or five years old, holding a doll and laughing at Lemke.

'This city...' spat Lemke. He raised his pistol at her. There was a sudden shout behind the door and two arms, probably a woman's, reached out and grabbed the girl. She was swiftly gone from view.

Lemke stood with sweat dripping from his eyebrows, his Walther pistol aimed at a closed door.

He came back to his senses and, lowering his pistol, turned to look back down the street in the direction of the city centre. He started to walk, then jog, abandoning his car where it was in the middle of the road.

He kept running but controlled his speed: if he had to run all the way back to the Hotel Majestic, he would need to conserve his energy.

The streets were empty. *Where is the Army?*

He could see faces watching him from behind the glass of the many buildings he jogged by and began to realise how vulnerable he now was. If a French band of partisans came out into the road now,

Lemke knew he would be a dead man - and Lemke was not ready to die yet.

After a short while, Lemke got to the river to have his papers checked by a sentry.

'Why is this bridge still up?!' shouted Lemke. 'Why hasn't the demolition been blown? This is crazy, the city could be taken any time?'

'The Pioneers say they are waiting for the General to give the order. So we wait.'

Lemke screamed in frustration, spraying the sentry with spittle. The sentry looked uncertain as to what to do next.

A Lieutenant walked up, the black piping on his uniform gave him away as the engineer in charge of blowing up the bridge.

'Can I help you, Sir?'

'Blow this bridge, now!'

'I can't do that, Sir, I'm very sorry. I have to wait for the General's specific orders.'

Lemke pulled out his pistol and pointed it straight at the Engineer.

Unperturbed, the officer said, 'I've had this a few times through the war and that doesn't change anything. All of my men are briefed, we don't care who shouts and screams at us, how many of us get killed, the demolition isn't fired until we get the codeword from the General.' Despite looking straight down the barrel of Lemke's pistol, he maintained a steady and deliberate delivery. 'I have the radio checked every five minutes, so I know we are able to receive the message, it's just that it hasn't arrived yet.'

With his teeth clenched, Lemke continued to

point his pistol.

'And finally, Sir, and I have said this a couple of times this afternoon, if you kill me, my men over there will probably not take too kindly to it.'

Lemke remained still. His pistol sights remaining firmly fixed on the space between the Lieutenant's eyes.

'What I mean, Sir, is that I don't fancy your chances if you kill me.'

Lemke lowered his pistol and Lemke's frustrations got the better of him for the second time in only ten minutes. He screamed again. 'THIS CITY!'

The Lieutenant waited until Lemke looked like he was starting to get a grip of himself again.

'You were running, Sir. Would you rather have a car to get where you were going?'

'Don't you … don't you dare get funny with me!'

'I'm not getting funny, Sir, I just wondered if you wanted a lift somewhere? We've got a car just over there.'

* * *

Knowing death might be waiting on the other side of the door, Saxon took in a deep breath, twisted the door handle and shoved it open. He strode forward, firing his Carbine from the hip, squinting against the dust and the noise in the room. He wasn't so much as aiming but more looking for the firing point whilst pulling the trigger at random intervals. His men piled in behind him, all guns blazing.

It took the German defenders a couple of precious

seconds to realise what was happening. In that time, three or four of them fell dead.

Ignoring the bullets, and using his speed as cover, Saxon barged forward, knocking an unsuspecting German out the way with his shoulder.

The room filled with the noise of gunfire and screaming as men faced each other, many frozen still with fear.

The air around Saxon erupted in splinters, bangs and the buzz of bullets passing very close to his head. He daren't look but could feel the number of men behind him seemed to be reducing.

'Come on!' he shouted, as men rose up from behind overturned tables and chairs, hunching their shoulders as if in a heavy rainstorm. Two of Saxon's men crumpled to the floor immediately, but Saxon stalked on.

Approaching the far window of the restaurant, Saxon was beginning to wonder if the firing point was here at all. Then he noticed two Germans dash for shelter into the far corner, one of them reaching for a metal box to his side.

'There it is!' shouted Saxon but no one could hear him. Knowing his magazine was about to empty, he threw his Carbine on its sling over his shoulder and burst forward.

Saxon leaped with both arms outstretched and grabbed the German closest to the exploder. Both men scrabbled for the box. Saxon head butted the man in the chest and tried to get a knee into the German's groin, but it wasn't working. Saxon could hear his adversary grunting as he tried to stop Saxon pulling his fingers off the firing control.

Saxon raised his head a little and could see the wires were attached.

Drips of sweat from the German soldier fell onto Saxon as the man in the field grey uniform started to push Saxon against the floor, propelling himself with sharp twists of his hips. Saxon pushed his head forward to try and bite at the German's fingers but couldn't quite get close enough.

With his shoulders now against the floor, the German thrust a knee into Saxon's side and for the briefest of moments, Saxon released his grip slightly. The German ripped the exploder away and turned his back on Saxon. Saxon sat up to try and reach for the exploder when a hand grabbed him from behind and pulled him out of the way. Saxon, confused, glimpsed over his shoulder to watch Alamilla pour machine gun fire into the German soldier. Saxon looked back and felt blood splatter over his face as bullets ripped into the Germans ribcage.

Alamilla leaned forward to grab the exploder but the German soldier, his body slumped forward, still seemed to be guarding it.

As Saxon reached across and yanked the German back; his helmet flew back into Saxon's face. The pain forced his eyes shut. He pushed them back open. Alamilla was hacking away at the cables, pulling them away from the skirting board. Still alive, the German reached for the tee-handle on the exploder. Saxon pulled the German back towards him and momentarily lifted his adversary off the floor. He felt the German soldier exhale suddenly.

Saxon strained to see over the chest of the dying

German. In what seemed like slow motion, Saxon watched the soldier's trembling hand reach up to the tee-shaped switch, grip it and give it one twist.

Saxon opened his eyes. The bridge had not exploded and the German holding the exploder was completely still. Dead still.

Alamilla was still pulling on any electrical cable he could find as one of his men pulled a bayonet from the German's side.

Saxon came to his senses, rolled out from under the German and pulled the firing cables from the exploder. He heaved a mighty sigh of relief. A couple of German soldiers lifted their hands into the air. Saxon assumed they were the only ones left alive.

Saxon saw someone run past the window outside. Eve. Behind her, a half-track pulled up parallel, the gunner pouring half-inch calibre machine guns into a building on the other side of the river.

Clement thudded down some stairs. 'All quiet upstairs, Saxon.' Clement took one look at his British friend, 'You all right?' he asked.

Saxon raised the tee switch of the exploder in his hands. 'I don't believe it. It didn't go off.'

'Come on then!' shouted Eve through the window, pointing her pistol to the bridge. 'Let's get going!'

Alamilla helped Saxon to his feet and they all ran out, crouching, to get back into their vehicles and set off across the Seine.

Everyone held their breath, waiting for the bridge to blow up, but it didn't.

As each vehicle crossed, the men aboard cheered

but the celebration was short-lived and gunfire from the windows of the buildings on both sides erupted in orange and yellow muzzle flashes.

Berner knew he was no longer the master of his own destiny. He guessed Eve and Lemke were on their way but there was no way of knowing who would get to him first. Time was short.

What Berner did know was that he was not ready to die yet. Looking at his watch, he decided he was going to try one more time to convince Möller not to destroy Paris and whether he was successful or not, he would leave after that and try to make contact with the Allies. Berner looked across the office. General Möller looked distinctly uneasy as he put down the phone.

'Was that who I thought it was?' asked Berner.

'Yes. That was my second discussion with the *Führer* in a week. Aren't I a lucky man?' Möller said unconvincingly.

'My instructions, Walter,' the General continued slowly and calmly, 'are to destroy the city and fight to the last man. He also and helpfully added I was to either die in the defence of Paris or commit suicide.'

'I see,' said Berner. 'Instructions you intend to carry out?'

Möller snorted out a disdainful laugh. 'I have about as much intention of dying today as you do. My problem is that I don't have enough soldiers to hold the city. He's leaving me little hope.'

'And Paris?' asked Berner, apprehensively.

Again, Möller chose silence over betrayal.

Berner did not have time to wait for the answer. 'General, as I've said before, you don't want to know about many of the contacts I have.'

Möller laughed lightly.

If only he knew, thought Berner to himself, *you wouldn't be laughing then*. Berner continued: 'There is one contact in particular I'm keen for you to meet. In fact, he's been very insistent and he's waiting downstairs.'

Möller looked understandably suspicious.

'I have a delegate from the Swedish embassy to see you.'

'He'd better not be here to negotiate a surrender, Berner. I'm not going to do that.'

'Quite. He's not here to talk of surrender. He does, though, want to talk to you about not destroying the city.'

'Berner, if word gets out-'

'It won't. I know the risks and it's my job to protect you from them. Leave that bit to me. I just think you need someone else to talk your thoughts through with.'

'You think talking to a Swedish delegate will change my mind?'

'I think you have already made your mind up but need something to make you outwardly commit. Decisions like this usually need a catalyst, a reason. I'm not surprised. Your predecessor is already dead and your orders from the *Führer* could not be clearer, but you're not convinced, are you? You're certain following them is not the right thing to do and you feel caught, don't you? And you can't talk to the SS about it, you can't talk to the Army about it either.'

'I'm talking to you though, aren't I, Berner? What does that make you?'

Good question, thought Berner, thinking the answer to that had better wait for another day.

Not caring about being heard by the microphones in the office any longer, Berner said, 'I see both sides,' realising that was the most truthful thing he had said for a long time.

'Both sides?'

'Destroy the city or don't destroy the city. Even now, Berner realised he was still masking his true self. 'As I said, I see both sides of the question you have to answer. Maybe the opinion of an outsider might help you clarify your own thoughts on all this.'

Möller looked back out of the window.

Berner let him think.

'Send him in, Berner. He's got ten minutes, no more. And not a word to another living soul about this, understand?'

* * *

'There it is! The Prefecture! It's just there on the right. Drive for those big wooden doors!' shouted Eve, pointing the way at her driver. She could see how the joints of her fingers were getting paler.

The convoy pulled up around the tall wooden doors, alongside the stone walls of the Prefecture. The Resistance fighters inside could be heard cheering as they poured fire into the windows of the buildings on the other side of the road, assisted with the convoy's 0.50 calibre machine guns. Chips of stone flew everywhere in the dust.

The battle seemed at fever pitch. Saxon, Eve, Jim and Clement sprinted through a smaller door to be met by men and women of the Paris Resistance cheering uncontrollably.

Propelled by pats on the back, into the courtyard they went, only to meet a scene of utter chaos. The dead lay lined up on one side, the wounded staring wild-eyed but silent on the other. Elsewhere, people hugged each other. Most of the men, noticed Eve, were crying.

Next through the doors came the men of the 9th. The cheering seemed to intensify despite a full battle taking place only metres away, outside across the pavement.

Frenchmen held the men of the 9th in both hands, kissed their cheeks, not hearing above the din that their liberators were mostly Spanish. Every now and then, Eve and Saxon would laugh as they watched the face of a celebrating Resistance fighter suddenly freeze in disbelief. *Espagnol?*

A gruff-looking man in a grey suit entered the courtyard from a wide door. One of the sleeves of his jacket was torn, his face stubbly and his eyes red with fatigue. He walked straight to Eve.

'Are you Eve?' he asked her.

'I am,' Eve replied, a little surprised to be picked out so quickly.

'You are to go upstairs, there is a message waiting for you.'

Upstairs, Eve and the others entered a grand and high-ceilinged room, evidently the headquarters of the Resistance's fight for Paris. In the corner, Eve noticed Oberon, his face in his arms on a desk in what looked like a catatonic stupor.

A deep, silky voice off to Eve's right got her attention. 'You must be Eve?'

A slender man in an immaculate chalk-stripe suit, crisp white shirt and tie held out his hand to greet her. His eyes were the only thing that gave away any hint of fatigue, otherwise he was alone in being cleanly shaven, his hair neatly swept back. Even his shoes had a shine to them.

'We haven't met, I'm Jean and I cannot begin to describe how happy I am to see you all.' He took it in turns to shake their hands. 'You are so very, very welcome. We have just about managed to hold on but the fighting here has been fierce, as you can imagine. Ammunition was our most limiting factor, and now, here you are. I trust you brought what we asked for?'

'Truckloads of it. Plenty to keep us all going until the rest of Leclerc's division gets here,' said Clement.

Jean looked quizzically back at Clement. 'Your accent: where have you come from to get here?'

'Rouen but originally, I'm from the Haut-Savoyard.'

'My, you have come a long way.'

'Haven't we all, my friend, haven't we all.'

The two men smiled at each other for a moment before, with a start, Jean seemed to remember something.

'Of course,' he said, 'the message. Forgive me. Come with me,' and he led Eve, Saxon, Jim and Clement off into the adjoining room. They could all hear the battle continuing outside.

Jean led them into an office where a haggard-looking radio operator was repeating the same message into a telephone.

Jean sidled up and began leafing through an untidy pile of messages on the table. He went all the way through but couldn't find it. The man at the telephone clamped the receiver to his ear with his shoulder and tapped Jean's hands away from the message pile. Quickly, the man got to the message and handed it to him with a withering look. Jean smiled politely, checked it was the right message and then handed it to Eve.

Eve read the message through. Her head tilted back a little in surprise before she read it again.

'We're going to the Majestic,' she said in a matter of fact way.

'The Hotel Majestic?' asked Clement. 'The Nazi headquarters?'

'Yes. And we have a German officer to meet.'

'We're going to take the surrender?' asked Clement incredulously, looking at Saxon in wonder.

'If not, we'll be in the right place to see it.'

Clement and Saxon smiled mischievously at each other.

'Who's this German?' asked Saxon.

'Don't you worry,' smiled Eve, 'he's one of ours and you've both seen him before,' she said looking at Saxon.

'My God, what have you been doing?' asked

Saxon, amazed, as it began to dawn on him just what Eve might have been up to as an agent here in Paris.

'It's been a busy time, that's for certain,' Eve replied, 'and we can't hang around. Says here we have to hurry. Come on, let's go. We can leave some of the trucks here to offload the weapons and ammunition. I'll go and speak to Captain Dronne, I think he and his men should come with us. Jean, if you can spare some men, they may come in handy.'

'Of course,' Jean replied. 'This is a task I don't think I will have a problem getting volunteers for.'

'It'll do the Parisians no end of good to see the French Army and the Resistance driving through the city in broad daylight,' said Jim.

Clement rubbed his hands together, the grin fixed on his face.

Jean led them all back into the hall and after a few steps, halted and raised a hand. 'Can you hear that?'

'No, what?' asked Saxon.

'The shooting outside, it's stopped.'

Jean changed direction slightly and walked to one of the large wooden shutters covering a window. Leaning back, Jean opened the shutter with his extended fingertips, before craning his neck to get a view of the street outside. He smiled. 'They've gone. It looks like the Germans have decided that it was time to go. It's probably something to do with your arrival.'

Jean turned to look at his liberators, his head silhouetted against the light. 'I cannot tell you how grateful I am that you came here. Today, Paris will be liberated. I only hope to God we will live long enough to see it.'

Eve could see a tear on Jean's cheek.

* * *

'Thank you for your time, Herr Olsson,' said Möller sincerely.

'The thanks are all mine, General,' said the Swedish consul, pumping the General's hand in thanks energetically. 'Thank you for taking the time to listen to me.'

Olsson turned to Berner. 'And thank you to you also, Herr Berner. We all owe you a great deal.'

For the second time that afternoon, Möller's eyes narrowed suspiciously at Berner.

'Mr Olsson, you are welcome. I'm only glad to have played my part. Now, I urge you to please be very careful on your way home, it's getting dangerous out there.'

'I will,' said Olsson, shaking Walter by the hand warmly. 'Stay safe.'

'I'll try.' Berner looked nervously at his watch.

Olsson left and once the door was closed, Möller began to speak slowly. 'You do realise, Berner, the orders I'm about to give will be considered by many as treasonous. And that meeting,' Möller gestured towards the door, 'condemns you as much as it does me.'

Berner looked down. 'History won't remember me, General, but you will be remembered for this and I doubt history will remember you as a traitor. Far from it.' Möller stood still, so Berner filled the vacuum. 'You have made your mind up and you probably can't believe what your about to do. I can see your discomfort all too plainly. Your predecessor was the same. He had to make the same decision: his conscience or his *Führer*.'

'So Von Kettler was a traitor after all?'

'No more than you will be soon. And like many, no doubt, whilst you're about to commit treason, you don't consider yourself a traitor.'

'Why are you here, Walter?' asked Möller slowly.

'To help you as best I can and then get out of here.'

'How long have you known about Von Kettler?'

'Since he told me, a few days ago.' Berner realised just how much had happened in such a short space of time.

'He told you?'

'Of course. He felt he could trust me. Just like you do.'

'If I change my mind about Paris, Berner, you're for the firing squad,' the General said, joking.

'This room is bugged, so it would be a case of *after you*, General.' Berner smiled back.

All of a sudden, the General's door burst open and in rushed Lemke holding a pistol, screaming 'Hold it right there, traitor!'

Berner dropped his head. Eve was too late. It was all too late. But then something Berner was not expecting happened. Möller pulled his Walther pistol from his belt and pointed it straight at Lemke's forehead.

Lemke hesitated: he wasn't expecting this either.

'I'm not going lightly, Lemke,' said Möller

determinedly.

'What?' asked Lemke, confused.

'Lemke, you're not going to get me for this.'

'But … I … I don't understand.'

Lemke licked his lips and very, very slowly rotated to turn his pistol on the General.

A German convoy, filled with pensive-looking soldiers, raced up an otherwise deserted Avenue des Champs-Élysées. Only a few moments behind it followed a French and Spanish one.

Clement clung to the passenger door of the lead vehicle, his pipe clenched between his teeth, his hair swept back in the breeze, soaking up every minute of it.

The air snapped every now and then with a rifle shot, or the rattle of a machine gun. But the firing seemed sporadic and too random to be aimed, to be dangerous.

Inside the cab, beside Clement, Eve was navigating. They quickly reached the Arc de Triomphe. Eve pointed out Avenue Kleber.

'It's down there?' shouted Clement through the window. Eve nodded.

'Well, don't go direct. Go on, drive around this.'

'Clement, we haven't time!'

'I don't care,' said Clement, ignoring Eve and talking direct to the driver. 'Come on, just one lap!'

Eve thrust herself back in her seat in frustration as the driver enthusiastically changed course to lap the monument.

'*Vive la France! Vive la France!*' shouted Clement, with his spare hand clenched in a fist above his head. 'My God, Eve, this is unbelievable! Amazing! *Vive la France!*'

Saxon, behind, laughed as they went round.

'Man, this is liberation business can be crazy,' yelled Jim above the noise of his tyres humming over the road.

'I've never seen anything like it, Jim. It's … incredible,' replied Saxon, still not believing what was happening.

Clement's plea for a second lap 'of honour' was refused and as the convoy approached the Hotel Majestic, the mood in the vehicles changed. The grim prospect of one last battle loomed and this close to the end, no one wanted to die.

'Slow down and get ready,' said Eve.

Clement repeated it to the men sat in the back of the truck. There was a click of rifles being cocked and made ready.

The Hotel Majestic came into view. A shot was fired from front left.

'Everyone off!' shouted Clement. He turned quickly back to Eve: 'We'll fight our way down.'

The Resistance fighters and soldiers spread out evenly onto each pavement to begin a cautious but brisk walk forward.

'Hey, Eve,' shouted Saxon, 'what do we do when we get there?'

'Ask for Colonel Berner, I suppose,' she shouted back from the cab. 'Sorry, but I really have no idea. I know where his office used to be; he might be there, or in the General's office.'

'You know where these offices are?'

'I do, I've been there a few times.'

'My God,' Clement said to himself. 'No wonder we're winning.'

What firing there had been seemed to tail off. Eve gave the driver one last set of instructions and then climbed down onto the avenue. She ran towards the stone gateway Berner had led her through having just arrested her back in January. The stonework was burnt now and splattered with shrapnel marks. How different things are now, she thought.

A single German guard popped his head out from the doorway. Eve watched him raise his rifle towards his shoulder before the stonework around him erupted in splinters and dust. He dropped his rifle and crouched down. He was still shielding his eyes as the Spaniards ran past.

'Up here!' shouted Eve, pointing the way up the main staircase. Without a moment's hesitation, the men all followed her.

They were halfway up the spiral staircase when Eve caught something out of the corner of her eye. She looked up and there stood a German with a machine gun – Sauer.

'*Brigadeführer* Sauer died fighting to the last!' he shouted and pulled the trigger. All the rounds went high, showering Eve and the men with dust and plaster.

As if an unspoken order had just been given, Eve and the men raised their guns as one and fired. Sauer stumbled. Blood leaked from the side of his mouth. He fell downwards, rolling down a few stairs before stopping, spread eagle across the staircase.

Eve was up and on her feet, charging upwards to the first floor, straining her next to see up and forwards for any more German defenders, stopping only briefly to step over Sauer's dead body.

'Was that the epitaph he wanted?' asked Saxon.

'It's not what he's going to get,' said Jim.

***

Lemke and Möller stood with their pistols pointing at each other.

'Berner is a British agent, General! He has been stringing us all along for ages now. Hidden in plain sight, pretending to be spying on London when he's been spying on us the whole time! *He* killed Von Kettler, you hear me? He killed Von Kettler to keep his true identity as a double agent hidden. He had a French prisoner killed as well. *You have to believe me!'*

Keeping his pistol pointing at Lemke's forehead, Möller looked across at Berner. 'Walter, is this true?'

'Don't listen to him!' hissed Lemke. 'Point that pistol at him, not me, he's the enemy, not me.'

Berner looked Möller straight in the eye.

'He would say that, wouldn't he?' was all that Berner could think of saying for the moment. 'He's got it all wrong,' Berner went on to say.

'You're playing for time, Berner but it's run out.' yelled Lemke, turning his pistol back towards Berner.

Ignoring him, Berner said directly but shakily to Möller: 'I have been in touch with London on and off since '42. That is true and well documented. No surprises there. I trade information – I send them lies mostly but every now and then, to keep my credibility, I send them facts. Small, insignificant little facts but factual enough to keep London hooked. In return, I get the details of when their agents are about to be landed here in France or clues as to where their next operations will be. I'm playing them, not you.'

'*Lies!*' spat Lemke. 'Berner, you're under arrest and you're coming with me,' he said, his voice getting hoarse.

Berner sighed. 'You can investigate me all you like but right now, I think we all have something more important at stake. Do we or don't we destroy Paris. General?'

Lemke lowered his pistol. 'What?' he Lemke incredulously. 'He's trying to talk you into disobeying the *Führer's* orders?'

'No, Lemke,' said Möller irritably. 'It's a decision I alone have been pondering.'

They all stopped. There was a burst of gunfire somewhere in the building, then many more before it went quiet again.

'It looks like I'm running out of time,' continued Möller.

Lemke turned his pistol back on the General. Speaking slowly, he said, 'General, you will obey your orders from Berlin. Anything else is treason.'

'Anything else is madness, Lemke. Don't be ridiculous,' replied Möller.

For effect, Lemke cocked his pistol.

'General, this is your last warning. Give the order to destroy this city or be shot where you stand.'

'Go to hell, Lemke, you can't bully me-'

The door flew open and in burst Eve and Saxon, closely followed by Jim and some of the 9th Company.

Berner saw his chance and launched himself at Lemke's wrist, pushing it so the pistol pointed off at the ceiling.

Lemke flinched and squeezed the trigger hard. Plaster fell down from the ceiling.

'Step aside, Berner, now!' shouted Möller.

Berner and Lemke wrestled and Berner realised that Lemke was taller and stronger than him. Berner was going to lose this fight.

'Step aside, Berner, NOW!' bellowed Möller.

Berner leaned out the way and Möller pulled the trigger three times.

Eve turned to face the men who had just entered the room with her and raised her hands. 'DON'T SHOOT!' she yelled.

Berner watched the puzzlement and outrage in Lemke's eyes slowly fade as Lemke collapsed to the floor.

Möller stood completely still, smoke drifting from the muzzle of his pistol, which still pointed to where Lemke had stood.

Lemke's eyes lost focus and then emptied of life.

Eve turned back and stepped boldly forward, ignoring the General's pistol.

'Are you all right, Walter?' she asked, gently.

'So it's true?' asked Möller, dumbfounded.

Ignoring the question, Berner simply said, 'Thank you for saving my life, General.'

Möller seemed to become aware of his wider

surroundings as more soldiers and Resistance fighters pushed into the office.

'What do we have here?' asked Möller.

'Well, General,' said Berner, looking around, 'you seem to have the Allied army and the Resistance in your office.'

Picking out Jim's American uniform, Möller spoke to him directly: 'You are an American?'

'Yes, General, I am,' replied Jim not without some swagger.

Moller lowered his pistol. 'Good. I figured this morning that it was to an American officer I would want to surrender to.' Möller took his pistol in his other hand by the barrel and held it out to Jim.

Holding himself upright, he said formally, 'I am *Oberst-Gruppenführer* Möller, Military Governor of Paris and General Officer Commanding the German High Military Command in France. Please accept my surrender and the surrender of all my units in Paris and the immediate environs.'

Jim looked around at the others. Eve flicked her eyes to urge Jim forward. He took the pistol by the handle.

'On behalf of the Allied Army and General Eisenhower, I accept your surrender, General.'

Clement swore heartily in celebration.

Eve laughed upwards, towards the ceiling. Berner placed his arms around her. 'Eve, thank you. Thank you so much.'

'My God, Walter,' she replied pulling away a little. 'We've done it. We've bloody done it!'

Möller looked down at Berner. 'It would seem I have been spared that big decision after all. Paris will not burn tonight.'

'*El general alemán acaba de rendirse!*' said Sergeant Alamilla loudly to his men. By the look of their faces, however, they knew only too well what they had just watch happen.

'*Spanisch?*' asked Möller.

* * *

Berner was glad to not have been in uniform that day, or else he would have looked very odd amongst a load of Allied soldiers and resistance fighters, propping the bar up and helping to drink as much of what was left of the Majestic's supply of Champagne as they could find.

They could hear shooting out in the streets but the German Army, or what was left of it, was long gone. The gunfire Berner could hear was the sound of retribution: old scores with collaborators being settled. It was a chilling sound.

Berner talked almost exclusively to Eve. No one was surprised, after all, they had worked as a pair since January in the most dangerous of circumstances. Berner took in every detail of Eve's exploits and what had happened to Von Kettler, but with his eyes, he took in every detail of Eve's face, neck and shoulders.

Behind her, Berner watched American military police walk Möller down the spiral staircase.

'Excuse me a moment,' said Berner to Eve, putting his glass down.

Möller smiled as Berner approached.

'They have made you a prisoner?' asked Berner.

'No. I'm being escorted to the Hotel Meurice, where I'm to surrender again. To a French General this time. Who knows, Walter, I may be surrendering many times today.'

Berner smiled, sharing the joke.

Möller paused for a moment before continuing. 'I see you, an officer of the SS, are *not* under arrest or being escorted anywhere. I must say, you look very comfortable amongst your American, Spanish, British and French friends over there. Lemke was right about you, wasn't he?'

Berner looked over his shoulder at the men celebrating at the bar, and Eve.

He turned back. 'They are our new friends now. They have been mine for a while, that much is true. So yes, Lemke was right about me. I happen to think he was wrong about a lot of other things, however.'

Möller nodded. 'Was Lemke also correct about you killing Von Kettler and that Frenchman?'

'No. They both took their own lives. Admittedly that was after I had told them what was coming next. It was their decision to die then, not mine.'

Möller looked down towards the ground, nodding his head slowly.

'Thank you for saving my life,' said Berner sincerely.

Möller snorted a small laugh. 'You're welcome.'

The General paused to think again and then said: 'So London had a spy in my office all the time?'

Berner nodded.

'No wonder we're losing this war, Walter.'

Möller began to put one of his gloves on.

'What a day I have had. I surrendered a city, disobeyed my *Führer*, and didn't shoot an enemy spy.'

Both men looked at each other and shared one final, short, ironic laugh.

Möller looked over, beyond Berner towards the bar. 'You seem to make a good team, you and that girl over there,' smiled Möller, putting his head to one side.

Berner turned to take another look at Eve. 'Yes, we do. I rather hope we will be spending much more time together in the future.'

With his ungloved hand, Möller took Berner's and shook it. 'You're a lucky man, Walter Berner. I hope we meet up again after all this is over?'

'Perhaps, General. That would be nice.'

'Yes.' With that, Möller walked out into the street, still every inch a German General.

Eve approached, carrying Berner's glass. 'This is yours, is it not?' she said with a warm smile.

'It is,' Berner beamed back.

'He's off to prison?' asked Eve, turning to watch Möller leave.

'Not yet, he's got to surrender to a French general first.'

'I see. Well, this champagne is great but it's going to run out soon and I'm very much in the mood for some celebrating.'

'Anywhere in mind, Eve?' asked Berner.

'Not yet,' Eve looked back towards the bar, where Jim and Saxon were busy chatting to one of the Spaniards.

'Feeling hungry?' asked Berner.

'Good point. I hadn't thought about it until now but now you come to mention it, I'm famished.'

'Well in that case,' said Berner, 'this place has a good restaurant. It'll be shut no doubt but I'm certain we could knock something up.'

Eve turned and picked up two Champagne bottles. 'That sounds just fine, come on.'

Eve trailed behind Berner as they passed through the ballroom and across into the kitchens.

After a lot of searching, between them they managed to locate some chicken that did not smell too bad and some vegetables and soon enough, a sizzling could be heard. They poured the wine and chatted endlessly, laughing lightly and Berner loved every minute of it.

Moving out into the dining room, one bottle of Champagne down already, they continued their conversation quite undisturbed.

'So what next for you, Eve?' Berner asked.

Eve thought for a moment. 'What, after the war? I'm out. It's been interesting, Walter, don't get me wrong but I can't see myself doing this for the rest of my life.'

'But you're good at it. The spying won't just stop, you know.'

'Is that your future, Walter? The war will end but you'll just keep on spying?'

'It's my profession. It's all I know.' Berner reached across and topped up their glasses.

'This is a long way from our first meeting, isn't it?' Eve laughed. Berner took a moment to study the curl of her lips.

'It is,' conceded Berner. 'I remember I was asking

you to spy with me then, as well.'

'You did. You had me frightened there, Walter, no doubt about it.'

'I'm glad. It was an interrogation, not a first date.'

'Well, Walter, during that interrogation, you managed to get me to agree to help you spy on people, I'll grant you that. And I was happy to do it, working for you helped me achieve my mission too.'

'I know.'

Eve took another sip. 'But you're not going to succeed this time. This time, my answer's a firm no.'

'I see, well I'm naturally disappointed, Eve, of course.' Berner looked at his glass as he turned it between his fingers. 'So we won't work together again, is that it?'

'That is it, Walter. Anyway I doubt we'll need many spies who speak French in the future. German yes, Russian probably, not French. No, it's time for me to get out while I can. Start a new life, do something more … *positive*.'

Berner hesitated and took a deep breath. 'What about us two not working together but being together?'

Eve froze.

'I *like* you, Eve, I really do. You have been such a great companion through all of this war and danger and, well, all of it. I realised recently what was helping me through it all was the thought of you and despite all the things we have been up to these last few months, I've found myself thinking about you all the time. That means only one thing to me.'

Eve remained still.

'Eve? Are you alright? You never froze on me in

interrogation!'

Eve looked down a little. 'I don't know what to say, I suppose. I had us down as colleagues, not anything else.'

'And now I've got you thinking about it?' Berner was apprehensive suddenly.

She looked him in the eyes, mind made up: 'Originally, I would have said we could be very good friends and that's where I would have drawn the line.'

'And...' Berner slumped.

'Let's play it by ear, Walter, shall we?' She reached for the bottle and filled both their glasses. 'I propose a toast: to us.'

Berner was ecstatic. 'To us.'

They chinked glasses. Berner reached across, took Eve's hand and kissed it gently.

A door swung open noisily. It was Clement holding a bottle.

'Ah! There you are! And what's this? A little *tête-à-tête*?'

Berner winced.

'We thought we'd have a little celebratory liberation dinner.' Eve beamed enthusiastically, her eyes sparkling.

Clement walked up to Berner. 'It looks like there's going to be a lot of liberating going on tonight in this city, wouldn't you say?' Clement winked at Berner and Berner smiled back. 'So let's enjoy the night because tomorrow is another day, agreed?'

'Agreed,' said Eve and Berner at the same time.

Eve grabbed a bottle and got to her feet. 'Come on Walter, you've earned this more than most.'

Berner got to his feet and allowed Eve to lead him out.

Tuesday

It had taken some time for Berner to convince someone to drive him to Lotti's. In the end, grudgingly and nursing one hell of a hangover, Clement relented.

Berner knew the way and gave the directions. Eve had already gone on ahead, leaving Berner to destroy all his old papers and the secrets they held. Berner had smiled as he fed papers into the fire, he was in love and he knew it.

As Berner and Clement sped along, the party continued in the streets. Drunk men and women stumbled arm in arm along the roads, with Clement swerving around them. The Tricolor, Stars and Stripes and Union Flag hung everywhere. The rumours De Gaulle was on his way were spreading fast.

The smoke of burning German cars and trucks and *La Marseillaise* filled the air.

'What about you, Clement,' asked Berner. 'Where will you go now?'

'All the way to Strasbourg if I can. See the Germans out of France for good.' Clement swerved the truck around another group of revellers. 'The Allies and De Gaulle are not too happy having people like me around any more. They think having bands of men roaming around with guns could be dangerous!' Clement chuckled. 'When actually, they just don't want us, the people who fought for

France, to be left running it. They will want all the power for themselves, just you wait and see.'

'You don't mind that?'

'I don't care. All I want is to see my country liberated. Then I will go home.' Clement's eyes seemed to glaze a little before returning to reality. 'As I said, I don't care. I have plenty of fighting to do before I get home. I'm a soldier of the last war, like you. I want this war done with no chance of another.'

They continued on in silence for a moment.

'Anyway,' continued Clement, 'what about you? I mean you are probably the only man in Paris today to be on the winning and the losing side all at the same time.' Clement wore his old soldier smile again.

Berner smiled back. 'In truth,' he said, 'I don't know. I can't go east, that's for certain. I'm blown, of that I'm certain. I won't be welcome by my old employers anymore.'

'So what, then?'

Berner blew outwards. 'That's my point, I suppose. I just don't know. I'm not even sure I will even be able to go home and if I do, there might be a Russian Army there to greet me and I don't fancy that much either.'

'But what about your family?' Clement squinted against the bighting smoke of another burning German truck.

Berner's eyes lowered. 'I don't have one,' he said, sadly.

'Ah. I see,' said Clement, not really seeing. 'So you can go anywhere you like?'

'I suppose so. Maybe I could make my way here in France, or in Britain.'

'I doubt that will ever be your best idea, Walter,' said Clement. 'A fine upstanding member of the SS coming to settle down in France or Britain? I don't fancy your chances.'

'That's the problem, Clement. Unlike you, I don't think I have anywhere to go.'

'Who cares, Berner, you'll have Eve with you, no doubt about that.'

Berner beamed and watched the streets go by. 'It's the next left.'

Having persevered through the wild celebrations, Eve turned the final corner into Lotti's road. Ahead of her was a large crowd, centered around someone or something.

Curious, she pushed her way through. This crowd was different to the partying ones she had spent the night with: this crowd was not jubilant, it was angry.

Eve pushed her way to the front and gasped. The group had formed a dense circle around a woman, tied to a chair. Eve did not recognise the woman at first. Her hair had been roughly cut off and a swastika painted on her forehead.

A woman elbowed Eve in the ribs and nodded smugly. '*Collaborateur horizontal.*'

'Lotti!' shouted Eve, striding out into the middle of the crowd.

Lotti looked up and recognised Eve through tearful, red eyes.

'Thank God,' mumbled Lotti weakly. 'Eve, help me out of here. Get me out, for God's sake. Tell them, tell them who I'm.'

Eve felt the glare of the crowd shift onto her.

'This woman is no collaborator,' announced Eve. 'Her name is Lotti and she has worked for the Resistance since 1940. She's been spying on the Germans all the way through. This woman is a patriot, let her go this instant!'

A short, young man in his shirtsleeves, holding a machine gun, stepped forward and said, sneeringly, 'And who the hell are you? Sleep with a few Germans yourself, did you?'

'I'm a British agent. And who the hell am I, you ask? *Well, who the hell are you?* I've worked with the Resistance in this city for months and I've never seen your face before. Where have you been hiding all these years? Oh, you're brave now, aren't you, toting that gun around now the Germans have all gone. That courage you've just plucked up is as new as that gun you just about have the strength to hold. And what do you do with this newfound courage, eh? Pick on a defenceless woman who was working to liberate this country whilst you were still a boy! I tell you; she's done more for this country than you ever have. Free her immediately.'

Some in the crowd sniggered and the young man bristled.

'Hah!' he spat out, 'You want to be a little more respectful. We'll soon see who gives the orders around here.'

Eve saw the flash but did not hear the gun go off. She came to her senses, knowing she was lying on her side on the street. She struggled for air, winded from an almighty blow. Her shoulder should have hurt, she thought, but it didn't. Confused, she looked down onto the road and she knew instantly it was her blood pooling around her.

Eve looked up. Her view of Lotti was in black and white. Eve blinked to try and restore her vision, but it wasn't working. Eve could see Lotti screaming at her but Eve couldn't hear the screams.

Eve felt the cold. She looked over a little, to see the young man with the gun being beaten by women. Eve saw everyone in the crowd suddenly flinch as the man shot the pavement in his panic. Then the crowd flinched again and some of the crowd were all of a sudden looking down the road. The crowd opposite was starting to divide.

Eve slowly returned her eyes to Lotti and the two childhood friends maintained eye contact to the end.

Lotti screamed and screamed with her wrists still tied to the chair.

'No!' shouted Berner, running forward through the gap in the crowd. 'No!' he said again, agonised.

Clement ran in behind, his rifle at the ready.

Berner knelt down and took Eve's limp body up in his arms. Her head slumped to one side. Her empty eyes stared straight through him. 'No!'

The crowd heard Berner's accent and became suspicious. Reading the crowd, Clement stomped forward, walked up to the young man with the gun. 'I have fought for years to preserve the honour of France and yet your cowardice brings back all the old shame of the past.'

The young man tried to laugh, so Clement knocked him unconscious with the butt of his rifle.

Clement looked across at Eve and Berner. 'Oh my God,' he said, gloomily.

Berner looked up at Clement, helpless. The tears welled in Berner's eyes. He looked back at Eve and smoothed her hair.

'This woman,' Clement said to the crowd, pointing at Eve, 'was present when the German General surrendered yesterday. This woman,' Clement could not take his eyes of the dead Eve, 'is an agent and braver than any of you stood here now. And you killed her. Hang your heads in shame. Is this the France we fought for?' Clement looked around the crowd but no one could bring themselves to look at him. Most stared at the floor; those who could stomach it, watched Berner and Eve.

Clement bent down towards Berner, 'I think we need to leave before this lot get nasty again.'

'Cut her free,' said Berner, pointing his head at Lotti, 'now.'

Once free, Lotti ran forward, took Eve's cold hand and held it to her cheek.

'It's all right,' Lotti said quietly to Eve, 'it's going to be all right.'

'If you say anything, Walter,' said Clement quietly, 'they'll know you're German and they'll hang you from a lamp-post.'

'But...'

'You go,' said Lotti. 'I will care for Eve. You have to leave her with me now. I will take care of her.' Lotti continued to stroke Eve's hand gently. Lotti looked Berner in the eye. 'You have to leave, now.'

Clement stooped down and grabbed Berner by the elbow.

'Come on, it's time you left,' ushering Berner away through the crowd and back to the truck.

As they pulled away, through his tears, Berner's eyes remained on Eve, his wonderful, beautiful Eve.

Epilogue

Brunswick, an *Abwehr* Sergeant, leant forward in his chair to chink glasses with his old boss. 'It's good to have you back, Colonel Berner,' he said.

'Thank you,' replied Berner with a smile. 'I must say, when I packed you off back to Britain, I never thought I would end up following you.'

Berner took a sip from his glass and looked around. The nightclub was full. Men in uniforms from all over the world swilled beer boisterously with each other or poured sweet lines into the ears of beautifully dressed women. Cigarette smoke swirled across the ceiling and the band played gentle music. It was Saint Valentine's Day, after all.

'I can't believe you're still dressing up as a Colonel,' said Berner reproachfully, keeping his voice down.

Brunswick rolled his eyes. 'I've told you many times before, no one cares about a Sergeant around here or anywhere for that matter. There's thousands of Sergeants but Colonels, well, Colonels get shown the better seats. Seats like these.'

Berner smiled again. 'That was never my experience and I actually was a Colonel!'

'You never acted like one. That's the difference. Watch and learn and I'll teach you a few things.'

'And what's with that uniform, I mean, Polish?'

Brunswick looked down at the badges on the top of his sleeve saying 'Poland'.

'It means I don't have to cover up my accent any more. Let's face it, walking up to a girl and saying "Good evening, I'm a sergeant in German military intelligence" is not going to get you a warm bed for the night here in west London, is it? Whereas when I wear this, everyone is very *polite*.' Brunswick took another sip but Berner could see the smile on his face.

'But really, Polish? You're not worried that it might be a little too, well, ironic?'

'Not in the slightest.' Brunswick let his eyes glance around the bar. 'The British all say they went to war because of people like me. That cheers me up: I doubt they know they are much closer to the truth than they realise!'

Brunswick's eyes suddenly shifted to something behind Berner. Berner twisted around to look and then stood up to welcome the man both he and Brunswick had arranged to meet.

The broad-shouldered Colonel Smithens was allowed to limp unhindered through the crowd and shook hands with the two Germans. Berner gestured him to one of the empty seats at the table.

Smithens took one look at Brunswick's uniform, his eyebrows dropping inquisitively.

'Still pushing your luck, then?'

'I was just explaining how it helps … open doors.'

'I'll bet. Mind you,' said Smithens turning to Berner, 'yours isn't much better, is it?'

Berner brushed his hands proudly down his new tunic. 'A Lieutenant Colonel in the Intelligence Corps. Well, it's sort of suits me, doesn't it?'

'I'm sure it does,' said Smithens, not convinced. A

waiter hovered and Smithens ordered a drink. 'Anyway,' he said leaning back, 'It's good to have you two out of interrogation.'

'You're telling me!' retorted Brunswick. 'It wasn't the warmest of welcomes to Britain, I can tell you.'

'It's not meant to be, is it?'

No one could argue with that.

'Anyway, it's better than the sort of interrogation either of you would have got on the other side of the Channel. I'm sure you'll both get around to thanking me for that one day.'

Smithens looked straight at Berner. 'How are you?'

'Better,' he replied, matter-of-factly.

Both men knew that was not the whole picture. Since being hurried out of Paris and across the Channel, Berner had been in deep mourning. He'd felt the loss of Eve as acutely as he had the loss of his own wife and daughter years before.

Berner had been surprised to say the least to have found Smithens waiting for him at the Hotel Majestic the day Eve was killed. Seeing the blood on Berner's suit, Smithens had guessed quickly what had happened. Smithens, having sneaked into Paris amongst De Gaulle's entourage, was keen to get both Eve and Berner out alive but that was not to be. Smithens hid Berner in Paris until Eve's very private funeral was held.

'Well, what have we got here?' Jim's broad Californian dialect was unmistakable. Everyone got to their feet and another round of hand shaking began. Saxon and Jim took their seats and ordered champagne. Jim took one look at Brunswick's' uniform and burst out laughing. 'We haven't met but already I know who you must be!'

Brunswick hid his indignation as best he could.

'Oh, wow, I had no idea you would be here too!' exclaimed Berner as Lotti appeared from behind Jim to extend a hand of welcome. Her hair was back to normal and she looked divine, thought Berner.

'Yes, Colonel Smithens told me to head back to Britain for a while.' She gripped Jim's arm and looked up into the American's eyes. 'The good Colonel gave me a *very good* reason to come back, didn't he?'

Jim placed a hand on her arm.

The six of them sat drinking and chatted like old friends, talking about their recent experiences without giving anything away to anyone who might be listening.

After a while, Smithens leaned back and blew out hard.

'Walter,' he said. 'Have you got a minute?'

'Of course,' said Berner. Both men got up.

Smithens reached into his greatcoat pocket, pulled out a newspaper and then led them both to a quiet corner. Berner knew that whatever was coming next was unlikely to be good. Smithens gave Berner a copy of the Evening Standard. In big letters, the headline said: 'The Blasting of Dresden.'

Berner was still smiling as he started to read but Smithens watched his expression change from incomprehension to fury. Smithens let Berner read his way to the end of the column.

'I wasn't sure how to break the news, but I wanted

to make sure someone told you directly,' said Smithens, with obvious concern.

'What is this?'

'The RAF bombed Dresden and I'm told it's been a big one. A lot of damage and a lot of casualties. They say there's not much of the old city left, I'm sorry to say.'

Berner stared open-mouthed at Smithens. 'But why? I mean, the Soviets will be there any time soon by the looks of it. What sort of spitefulness is this?'

'Keep your voice down, Walter, you're not a German here, remember.'

Berner lowered his voice but he could feel the anger burning inside him. 'What have you done?'

'Nothing to do with me personally, you understand, but the locals …' Smithens looked across the room. '… don't look too bothered right now, do they? I knew you wouldn't like the news, so I wanted to make sure you got it from me first.'

Berner stood for a moment, nodding his head slowly as the news sunk in.

'I don't know if you had any more family left there…'

Berner flung the words back at Smithens: 'No. They were all dead long before this happened.'

Smithens winced. 'Thought so. Look, I don't know what you want to do next but if you want to go somewhere else, chat this through, get it off your chest, just say.'

Berner turned inward for a moment. 'No, no thank you,' said Berner eventually. 'Let's face it, I won't be going back there anytime soon anyway, will I?'

Smithens looked shifty.

My God,' Berner stared back incredulously, 'is there something else you want to tell, Smithens?'

'Not right now, Walter, no. I think that is enough for now. But tomorrow morning, in the office, perhaps …'

The bus driver's leg was tiring from all the changes of gear. The bus had been winding its way up and around the narrow sharp bends of the mountain pass. To avoid looking at what, with only one momentary lapse of the driver's concentration could spell his doom, Clement gripped the handrail in front and kept his eyes on the mountaintops.

After a long and thankfully straight stretch, the driver slowed to a halt and rubbed his thigh as he grumbled: 'Saint Jean D'Aulps.'

Clement and his son Paul stepped down onto the wet grass of the verge. A spring breeze ruffled Paul's hair.

The bus pulled away and both Clement and Paul coughed against the fumes.

'What crisp mountain air, eh?' joked Clement. 'My God, it's good to be back,' he said a moment later, taking in the mountains that towered above him. 'Look, the snow is still on the caps.'

Paul slowly span around, admiring the view. He had been only sixteen when he left here to help fight a war. The Alps seemed all too alien, all too quiet, after all that.

'Come on,' said Clement, picking up his rucksack and swaggered uphill. 'Not long now.' He struck a match and lit his pipe, squinting against the brightness of the sun.

After a while, Clement looked up and could see a tall, slim woman in a garden ahead.

'There she is!' he said loudly, making sure the woman could hear. The lady visibly froze. Recognising Clement's laugh, she turned slowly around, carefully put down the basket she was carrying, wiped her hands on her apron and ran to meet them.

A double-agent no longer, Walter Berner found the road he was looking for. Just off Victoria Street stood a tall but otherwise anonymous building on Broadway. His pass was checked three times and his accent certainly attracted some suspicious glances but everyone seemed polite enough. Berner smiled as he heard one of the doormen whispering about him as he started to climb the stairs. He smiled even more as he thought about Admiral Schneider learning that right now Berner was climbing the main staircase of the Secret Intelligence Service, MI6.

Mrs Wilkinson looked up, glancing at the clock on the wall. 'Ah, Colonel Berner, you're on time. It's very good to meet you.' She beamed as she walked around her desk to shake hands confidently. 'The Chief is on time today for once so you should not have too long to wait. Would you like some tea?'

Berner laughed inwardly. 'I am very pleased to meet you too, Mrs Wilkinson. I am an *Abwehr* officer but I have heard of you. Please, take that as a compliment. Thank you for the offer of tea but you wouldn't happen to have some coffee instead, would you?'

Mrs Wilkinson's smile froze for a fraction of a second and Berner heard her breath sharply inwards through her nose. 'I will have one of the girls ask around and see what we can find for you. The war is still on, you know but I'll get it arranged whilst you're in with the Chief.'

Berner's English was not bad, she thought to herself. She looked down to her desk and picked up a file with 'TOP SECRET' stamped across it, she held it across her chest with her arms folding protectively around it.

There was a moment of silence.

'You were kept very busy in Paris, were you not?' she asked.

'I was,' replied Berner circumspectly.

'I have to say, I'm very sorry about what happened to Eve.'

Berner looked downwards quickly to hide the tears welling in his eyes. 'Ah, yes,' was all he could say.

'She was a lovely girl. We all loved her, didn't we?' Mrs Wilkinson said, knowingly.

Berner's eyes lifted and he found himself smiling quite uncontrollably. 'Yes, I did.' He corrected himself. 'We did.'

Berner felt the warmth of her comforting hand on his left arm. 'At least you had Paris, the two of you.'

The light above the door behind her changed from red to green. Mrs Wilkinson jumped a little.

'Well, if you'll please follow me, the Chief will see you now.'

Mrs Wilkinson opened one door and then another and entered the wood-panelled office. 'Colonel Berner to see you,' she said, stepping to one side to allow Berner in. She then continued on to place the file squarely onto C's desk.

Berner recognised 'C' immediately, he had seen his photograph in files many times before. The two men walked towards each other and shook hands as friends.

'Ah, Berner,' said C. 'We were just talking about you. Do take a seat. It's very good to meet you at last. No tea?' he glanced at Mrs Wilkinson.

'Coffee is on its way,' glared back Mrs Wilkinson.

'Jolly good,' said C a little awkwardly, retreating behind his desk.

Emerging gingerly from a large armchair to Berner's right was Smithens, his back evidently playing up again. He shook Berner's hand also. 'I bet you never thought you'd step foot in here, did you?'

'No but I'm sure I'm not the first German agent to be in this office.'

Smithens and C glanced at each other, showing a hint of alarm.

'It's alright, gentlemen, I am only joking with you.'

'You are? Good, very good.' C did not appear that comforted as he watched Mrs Wilkinson walk towards the door.

'Now Berner,' he said, taking a seat, 'Firstly, I can't thank you enough for the work you did for us in Paris. Sterling stuff. However, I'd like to get straight to business if you don't mind, time is short. Smithens and I have got something we would like you do for us…'

Mrs Wilkinson shut the doors behind her, went to her desk and got someone to hurry up with the coffee.

THE END

HISTORICAL NOTE

This story is of course fiction but there is a heavy thread of truth running through it.

I have compressed time for dramatic effect: the attempt on Hitler's life took place on 20th July, whereas Paris was liberated on the 24th/25th of August 1944.

The character Walter Berner is based on a real man: Hermann Giskes of the *Abwehr*. Giskes arrested over 40 British and Dutch agents in Holland through the Second World War and was able to convince them, without the use of violence, to 'play back' messages to London. When British Intelligence eventually worked out what had happened, they were shocked at the extent of Giskes's success. The real Giskes was never a double agent for Britain but it is said he went on to work for US Intelligence after the war. He died in 1977.

Eve is a fictional character completely but in many ways typical of many of the young women who volunteered to be sent behind enemy lines. Few ever returned. British agents did leave intentional spelling mistakes in their messages.

General Von Kettler is based on the true character of General Carl-Heinrich von Stülpnagel, the senior German commander in Paris from 1942 and a conspirator in the attempt on Adolf Hitler's life. Von Stülpnagel attempted to take his own life when he learned he was ordered back to Berlin but failed. Despite his injuries, he went on a show-trial in August 1944, found guilty of treason and hanged.

Von Stülpnagel was replaced in Paris by Dietrich von Choltitz, whose character is fictitiously portrayed by General Möller in this book. It is true that von Choltitz was interviewed by Hitler before taking up his appointment in Paris and Hitler did tell him to be prepared to blow up and bomb Paris if necessary. As the fight for the liberation of Paris raged on, von Choltitz talked with Pierre Taittinger, the Chairman of the Municipal Council, and Raoul Nordling the Swedish Consul in Paris, and von Choltitz eventually decided not to destroy the city. Von Choltitz surrendered to soldiers of the 9th Company initially and then to the French General, Leclerc.

It is completely true that General Leclerc's 2nd French Division was the first to enter Paris on 24 August 1944, with the soldiers of the 9th Company in the lead. The 9th Company was led by a Frenchman but almost all of the others in the 9th were Spanish veterans of the Spanish Civil War. They are credited as being the first uniformed liberators in Paris in August 1944, quite an accolade.

SOE deployed over 90 Jedburgh teams like Saxon's into France after the D-Day landings, with a mission to lead and coordinate the activities of the French Resistance deep behind German lines. The teams were made up of three people: the commander, a radio operator and one other. The teams usually comprised of one British, one French and one American. The Americans were all from the Special Operations Branch of the Office for Strategic Services, America's wartime intelligence agency and forerunner of the CIA. Many of the earliest CIA officers to work in Europe after the war had cut their teeth in the Jedburgh teams.

The Hotel Majestic was on Avenue Kleber and used as the headquarters of the military governor of France, having been converted to government offices before the war.

Field Marshal Erwin Rommel was opposed to the assassination of Hitler but did ask his Führer to 'draw the proper conclusions' that the war in the west was lost. Hitler and his entourage were never to really trust Rommel again. Wounded during the battle for Normandy, Rommel was briefly hospitalized in Le Vesinet near Paris before going home for some sick leave. Rommel was implicated in the coup attempt and, given the choice of a show trial or commit suicide, he opted for the latter in October 1944 and was then buried in Herrlingen with full military honours.

Whilst the idea of 'the good German' to some can be ironic, trite or a fig leaf for Nazi atrocities, we must remember there were plenty who risked - and lost - their lives in the German Resistance from 1933-1945. The German Resistance Memorial Center, established in what used to be the German Army's base in Berlin, is a fitting and moving tribute to them all.

My interpretation and characterisation of the real men and women represented in this book is purely my own.

I hope you enjoyed this book.
Walter Berner will return.

ABOUT THE AUTHOR

S C Brown is a graduate of the War Studies Department of King's College, London, and served 25 years in the British Army, including time as an Intelligence Officer, before taking up writing fiction. An avid reader, battlefield guide and amateur military and intelligence historian, he now lives in Kent, England. His debut novel, *Initiation: A Spy Story* was first published in 2017.

Printed in Great Britain
by Amazon